MIST ON THE RIVER

MIST ON THE RIVER

Hubert Evans

Introduction by William H. New
General Editor: Malcolm Ross
New Canadian Library No. 86

McCLELLAND AND STEWART LIMITED

The Canadian Publishers
McClelland and Stewart Limited
25 Hollinger Road, Toronto 374

Printed and bound in Canada by
T. H. Best Printing Company Limited

INTRODUCTION

Hubert Evans's *Mist on the River* is a straightforward, realistic, somewhat sentimental narrative about life in the Skeena Valley of northern British Columbia. What makes it a little unusual in Canadian literature is not only its regional setting, but also the fact that its central characters are all Indian and all delineated with liberal sympathy. Cy and June Pitt, Bert Silas, Dot, Old Paul, and the others all possess individual personalities, act in character (whether admirably or rashly), come into conflict with whites, and basically help direct their own destinies. Markedly absent from the book are the cardboard stereotypes of American Westerns and any overexaggeration of the romantic notion of the Noble Savage. Still, the authorial point-of-view remains that of an outsider to the culture, the attitudes expressed by it typifying a 1950's white liberal position rather than that of 1970's Red Power. And readers accustomed either to the end-of-the-century smoothness of Pauline Johnson's verse or the contemporary rhetoric of Duke Redbird and Harold Cardinal may find Evans's work alien and unsatisfactory. It belongs—by attitude, though not stylistically—very much to its time, and whatever merits it has as a simple story, the book must, like Mazo de la Roche's Whiteoaks saga, be seen as an historical document as much as a work of art, revealing a stage in both the development of Canadian fiction and the unravelling of the popular prejudices of Canadian society.

The parallel with de la Roche is more widespread than at first appears and provides one route into Evans's work. The writers were born within seven years of each other; both have biographical ties with the city of Galt, Ontario; both began publishing in the 1920's and established at that time a format from which they never radically departed; both wrote children's animal stories in addition to their regional narratives; and both, in their evocation of moral stances—as epitomized by de la Roche's *Growth of a Man* (1938) and Evans's *Forest Friends* (1926)—look back to the didactic methods and homespun virtues enunciated in the nineteenth century by Ralph Connor.

In such a world, work, faith, individualism, and the purity of nature seem absolute and unquestionable ideals; if in *Forest Friends* they are overlaid by empirical observations, "science"

v

is used only to prove these assumed virtues. Thus the life cycle of a salmon, made anecdotal and anthropomorphic for its child audience, becomes a lesson in fortitude and determination, and at the very end of the book an adult character says:

'In Nature's school you'll never get a diploma to say you know it all. Some folks won't study a thing if they can't get to the end of it soon. But you two won't let that stop you. Nature's just waiting for folks like you. And for all the time you spend with her, she'll repay you a hundred times over by making your days interesting and keeping your mind content and clean.'

An honest commitment to knowledge and social harmony lies behind such an utterance, but the ordered world it speaks of seems strangely isolated from the pressures of modern life. The rural setting, moreover, compounding the issue, largely reiterates a romantic distinction between country virtue and urban wicked-ness. While the book is wholly contemporary in its explicit warnings about the danger of ecological imbalance, the roman-ticizing of wilderness life too drastically simplifies human behaviour for it to be either wholly credible or metaphorically sharp.

Mazo de la Roche guarded against such over-simplified ideals by often employing a sardonic tone; the character she creates in Adeline Whiteoak, for example, pugnacious and uncontrollable, breaks through any suggestion of pastoral order, and, because of her, *Jalna* acquires a double edge. Thus, while the Whiteoaks saga speaks its imperial prejudices, at its best it also recognizes them as such and acknowledges itself as a last idiosyncratic bastion of unrelenting imperialism. Evans's route away from maudlin sentiment was quite different. He sought harmonious reality, and found social pressure; he sought opportunities for independence, and found hypocrisy and prejudice impeding them. Too earnest ever to be a witty writer, he responds to such discoveries by drawing more deeply troubled characters than de la Roche and planting them squarely in the confusion of the contemporary world. *The New Front Line* (1927) depicts the problems of adjustment experienced by a soldier returning from World War One; *Mist on the River* (1954), focusing on an Indian brother and sister seeking town employment, points out the threats to the Indian way of life and reveals the size and force of the adaptations that white society assumes Indians should make. Constantly his characters must choose their future. Yet Evans is anything but an angry reformer. He trusts implicitly in the natural virtue of man–unadmirable people misguided rather than wicked–and all his books have happy endings.

Something of the tension that informs Evans's views can be seen in these early paragraphs from *The New Front Line:*

> It was one of those April mornings in Vancouver when many young hearts—some of them in bodies upon which the jostling years have left their marks—feel a tugging desire to veer skittishly from the shafts of duty and with chins ridiculously high, march on to some outdoor place to help install the spring.

> The lengthening newspaper columns headed 'Help Wanted' and 'Situations Wanted' testified to the radical promptings of that British Columbia spring. Even Hugh's mother had not escaped. For the first time that year she had opened one of the dining-room windows before breakfast. But to conciliate the conservative side of her nature she had qualified the open window by a brisk blaze in the dining-room fireplace.

The division between the landscape and the people, between commitment and qualification, spells out an effort at sprightliness rather than any true gaiety, which reflects the central character's dubiety. Hugh Henderson is a returned soldier, whose businessman father has been trying to urge into a respectable job. To be an urban copy of his father does not appeal to him, however; he seeks a "creative," "pioneering," "worthy," "homemaking" task rather than a merely "respectable" one, one which will allow him self-respect rather than the superficial approval of a restricted community. Such 1920's generation conflict–uttered even more forcefully by Evans's contemporary in British Columbia, Frederick John Niven, who also was concerned that youth's escape "from the uncompromising discipline of a narrow religious belief"–carries interesting 1970's overtones, just as *Forest Friends* does. The idea of abjuring the established community in favour of pioneering continues to prove attractive. It continues also, as in Evans, to demonstrate the essential conservatism of the rebellious position. What Hugh Henderson seeks are such traditional virtues as love, freedom, peace, and communal solidarity, and he finds them by leaving Vancouver and building a homestead in the province's northern hinterland. The assumptions of the move neatly reverse the pattern of so many American novels of the same period. The martial metaphor of

Evans's title describes a commitment to "duty" in preference to hedonism, a duty transferred from World War One into a rural social activism that concurrently provides individual fulfillment. The sentiment of the American popular song "How You Gonna Keep 'Em Down on the Farm, After They've Seen Par-ee?" is referred to, but simply declined. In the morality of natural balance lies the frontier Hugh must settle.

Though Evans never demonstrates how individual freedom and communal solidarity interpenetrate, and thus leaves his underlying idea largely unexplored, he observes the details of everyday life vividly enough to pace his story quickly. *Forest Friends* had proved him a precise lover of nature; in *The New Front Line* we are introduced with the same exactness to inventive bush practicality. His characters make curtains from "the light factory cotton inside the burlap of sugar sacks" and shelves from butter boxes, wall panelling from "laths dipped in shingle stain" and flower gardens from the wild ferns of the Pacific Coast forest. Though such "pioneers" are scarcely cut off from civilization, the details of their existence are stamped with absolute authority and offer a direct glimpse of a life gone by.

What *The New Front Line* also broaches is the concern for Indian-white relations that *Mist on the River* was later to pursue, but in this area Evans's details are less sure. He seems a little uncertain of his vantage point, perhaps even unaware of the biases of his language. Although he is silently contemptuous of a minor character's assumption that Indians have "no stamina" and "give in easily," he allows Hugh to praise his father's growing liberality by using the phrase " 'He's white . . . . Yes,–he's as white as they make them.' " There appears to be no awareness of any contradiction between these two attitudes, nor any indication that one of them might be ironic. As a result, the characterization seems flawed, and the optimistic resolutions that grow from the characters' ostensibly open personalities seem ultimately impossible to accept on any but the most superficial level.

Mist on the River marks a distinct change. Evans's style is still interrupted by passages of awkward indirect reportage, and in his liberalism he sometimes falls prey to the temptation to caricature whites. But the naïveté about social attitudes in northern British Columbia has gone. In its place we find a three-layered social conflict involving culture, place, and time, which provides a background for the central character, Cy Pitt's dilemma and gives it depth and meaning. Indians and whites are opposed, as are Coast and Interior affiliations, and modern and traditional cultural assumptions. Cy finds himself embroiled in all these tensions and only when in each case he has opted for freedom can he find a kind of optimistic, although tenuous, peace.

The division between Coast and Hinterland on the Skeena—between the Tsimshian bands of the Coast and the bands north of Hazelton, for example—is revealed most clearly in an episode concerning a tubercular child. A white doctor wishes to take the boy to a hospital at Prince Rupert, but the band objects:

> 'Since this man does not choose to cure him here, what can we do but to take him home?' And again, with passionate determination: 'He is not going to the coast. He is *ours*.'

The people's sense of prideful independence and their complete misunderstanding of the nature of the boy's disease pull Cy in two directions: he is emotionally sympathetic to them, but intellectually alienated. Evans adumbrates this tension at the very beginning of his novel when Cy, aboard the CNR train to Prince Rupert to get a coast job, is shown to have left "the Junction" and to be between his own village and the city. Rooted in one, obscurely desiring the other, he is neither confident enough in his past to be secure in "alien" territory, nor certain enough of his direction to adapt easily to a new life.

Just as the rural-urban contrast intensifies Cy's uncertainty of himself (and is in turn intensified by the contrasts between Prince Rupert and Vancouver, the wholly alien, *white* city of the south), so the personality differences between himself and his sister June demonstrate variant approaches to the white world. Whereas Cy is broadly sympathetic, introspective, and basically conservative, June is boldly independent, outgoing, and so self-assured that she runs a risk of a different kind. Cy can be easily wounded emotionally; June can be misled by the appearance of success; and in the relation between them, Evans examines the difficult consequences of each attitude. June is attracted to the showy smoothness of Bert Silas, who seems successful in the white world, and, as she is committed to achieving similar success and living in Vancouver, she copies and follows him, spurning her brother in the process. Cy retreats from Prince Rupert and marries in his own band, hoping always to move again from the village to the coast. At once he has tried to restrain and to imitate his sister, and because neither response is a liberating one, the family goes initially awry. Only when Cy accepts his difference from June, acknowledging the merits of both city and village life, can either of them prove themselves. Unbadgered, June can judge situations maturely rather than act solely from a rebellious urge to demonstrate her independence. And free of the compulsion to measure "success" only in unfamiliar urban terms, Cy can at last accept his village and acknowledge his cultural traditions without finding himself confined by them.

Evans underlines the virtues of these choices by setting up characters and subplots to serve as contrasts. Bert Silas is one such figure; Dot, the Rupert prostitute who has failed to make a happy transition to city life, is another. Bert ends up in jail, June tells Cy, because for all his bravado he never really believed himself to be:

> 'as good as anybody else...as good as whites....Bert fooled you and he fooled me for quite a while; and worst of all he fooled himself. At least he tried to, and I guess that was his trouble.'

And Dot herself underlines the parallel with June:

> 'Stop acting like June was headed straight for hell. If you don't, she could end up where a cousin of hers by the name of Dot has ended up. June knows what she wants, and she has the brains to get it....Don't you ever so much as hint to the kid that because she's Indian she can't make the grade. That's the very worst thing you could do. Take it from me; I know.'

But to leave Cy as in his earlier novel Evans left Hugh Henderson, swiftly resolving his doubts and presumptively heralding social harmony, would make mockery of the actualities that lie behind the novel's story. Not all the characters applaud Cy and June. Melissa, their mother, broods differently:

> The life here had not changed, only her children had changed. The content remained, the strong, sure discipline of seasons, the authorities worn smooth by long obedience, the regulated comings and goings, but her children's heads were filled with all new things. They saw restrictions where she saw protection; they resisted where she complied, and felt the safer for it. Yet this was spoken of as education! It held up enticements beyond their grasp, offering them the moon but at the price of the authenticities which were before schools were.

Such a poetically modulated passage, designed by rhetorical

artifice yet free of the artificiality that mars so much of the direct speech in the book, returns the situation from the outer rim of melodrama. The uncertainties go unresolved.

Mixed up in Melissa's mind are the paternalism of the reservation system and the ritual pattern of the traditional culture; her children, reacting against one, find it hard to separate it from the other, and are in danger of losing their entire heritage in the course of seeking their identity. It is the radical difference between traditional and modern cultures–epitomized by Melissa's contrast between eternal verities and temporal changes–that pressures Cy most basically. The title metaphor describes the tension in a different way:

> In other places up and down the Skeena the channel changed with the years, but here it stayed the same. Things were slow in changing in this village and valley; perhaps it would be better if they did not change at all.

> The mist lay close on the water....

Immersed in scientific rationalism, the white man–particularly the white man on the North American "frontier"–interprets such reluctance to change as slowness of mind, dullness of wit, a failure to recognize progress, and a perverse pagan backwardness. He seldom recognizes the limitations of his own point-of-view nor appreciates the essential mystery, and the recurring need to re-enact that mystery and give it voice, which lies at the heart of the other. Something of the enormity of the imposition of the white man on West Coast Indian cultures can be gauged from the self-denigrating plaintiveness of an 1887 Cowichan appeal to Sir John A. MacDonald against the forbidding of the Potlach and Tamanawas Dances:

> When our children grow up and are educated they perhaps will not wish to dance.

> Some only of us dance now, and we do not wish to teach others, but when one is seized with the ("Quellish") dance he cannot help himself and we believe would die unless he danced. On Saturdays and Sundays we will not dance as this offends the Christian Indians.

> The lands of our fathers are occupied by white men and we say nothing.

> We have given up fighting with each other.

> We have given up stealing and many old habits, but we

xi

want to be allowed to continue the "Potlach" and the Dance. We know the hearts of most of the Coast Indians are with us in this. We therefore ask you to have the law amended, that we may not be breaking it when we follow customs that are dear to us.

The legislation was not revoked until 1951.

Evans indicts the bureaucracy of Indian-white relations most clearly in *The New Front Line*, when he shows education for Indians to be brimful of "careful" (though often incomprehensible) religious training and boy scout activities, but to offer no opportunities either for learning Western technology or for preserving Indian culture. In *Mist on the River* that outrage trembles beneath Evans's sympathetic portrait of Old Paul, the village leader who embodies all that Cy initially tries to escape, all that he does not really understand, all that he must ultimately come to embrace *along with* his modern education, if he is ever to take "his rightful place among his people." In a sense, what kills Old Paul is the knowledge that he cannot communicate the ancestral mysteries clearly to Cy's generation; " 'Look at my tongue, gone dead,' " he gasps, throwing "himself back against the cushions,...like an animal fighting a trap." By contrast, what would kill the soul of that younger generation is a refusal to respond at all to the poetic truths of the legends that for centuries have enlivened their culture.

Implicitly, in Evan's work, as Western technology enters the Indian way of life, so an appreciation of the indigenous cultures must invigorate, strengthen, and give metaphysical depth to the empirically-oriented white society. Evans makes little of the proposition, being in 1954 more inclined to offer his novel as an entertainment than an analysis of the Canadian psyche, but *Mist on the River* marks a definite step in the generation of such an attitude. Canadian literature waited almost another two decades to explore the theme further, but by then it had attracted authors working sensitively in all genres: John Newlove with "The Pride," Alan Fry with *How a People Die*, Herschel Hardin with *Esker Mike and His Wife Agiluk*, and Rudy Wiebe with "Where Is the Voice Coming From?" among others. Compared with them, Evans is a minor writer, technically less subtle and texturally less rich; within the literary conventions he adopted, however, he affirmed constantly the prospect of an enfranchising unity between man and nature, and he adhered faithfully to the realities of the region and life he observed.

William H. New
The University of British Columbia

TO

Ann Winter Evans

who made possible
this story of
our friends

1

THE GREY-GREEN COILS OF THE RIVER HAD THE SHEEN
of evening on them still. But in the day coach the lamps
were on and cast swaying shadows on the Indian people,
their many bundles, and the passive, up-turned faces
of their sleeping children.

Cy Pitt let his head rest against the train window. The
glass was cool and he pushed his straight, black hair from
his forehead to get more of the soothing, cool feel. It had
been a long day and it was not over yet. He and June
and their mother had had to leave the village early to
get down to the Junction. Now he wanted to sleep, but
that empty feeling was inside him again. It was not the
same as being hungry or needing a drink of water. There
was more to it than that. Earlier, the changing scenes of
the day had been sharp-edged, but now his mind shuffled
them like old cards. He tried to forget them but they
kept on coming. All right, he would get a drink. He
stretched, stuffed the bottom of his T-shirt inside his
belt, and went along the aisle. Since leaving the up-
river villages, the floor had become littered with orange
peels, empty popcorn boxes, and candy wrappers. The
car was lurching and Cy had to reach ahead for the backs
of the seats, right and left, with his long, brown arms.

This afternoon, the first time he had gone for a drink, the newsie had had to show him how to get out a paper cup. But now he knew. The ice-water tasted good. He crumpled the cup and dropped it in the basket.

The newsie was in his corner looking at a comic book. He was a fat man, white, with glasses. He reached over the boxes of pop and clipped the book on the string across the two windows. "All set for a big summer's fishing, I guess."

Cy gave his head a little shake.

"Sure you are. You Skeena natives are all the same. When them salmon are running you can't stay away. I bet you're out to make a killing."

"Not me," Cy said.

"How come?"

"No boat for me."

"You're big and husky. The cannery'll rent you a boat. How old are you anyway?"

Cy pushed his hands into the pockets of his denims. They were new, cowboy style, with metal studs around the pockets. "Eighteen."

"Eighteen's plenty old. Lots of Indians your age get boats. I know."

Cy knew it, too. But his family had not gone to a cannery since he was twelve, the year his father was killed. A cannery liked you to stay with them season after season. No cannery wanted just the woman, with kids. If the man and the woman both worked, they were sure of a good house, and if the man was a good fisherman he was given a better boat. Besides, being an up-river fellow, Cy could not expect the manager to put him ahead of coast fellows who knew all about boats. All this was hard to explain to the newsie. Caleb McBride, hiring man for our village, sent for us, he could have said. Caleb promised my mother a job working on the fish and he has a job for me in the can loft. My sister will get a job, too, he says.

But the trouble with white people was that as soon as you answered one of their questions they got after you with others. They would not take one answer and let it go at that. They talked fast and it confused you, thinking in your language and trying to find the right words in theirs. The easiest way, as the Indian people had long ago learned, was to say no more than you had to, or leave them thinking you did not know.

"Did you ask for a boat? No? Well, there you are. Now don't get me wrong. Here's one who wants to see you natives get ahead, but the trouble is you let people push you round. A man's got to stick up for himself. Root hog or die, like the fella says."

Cy did not know what that meant, so he took out his billfold and asked for oranges. It was the first billfold he had ever owned, a gift from June for his birthday. The zipper was stiff, and with the white man watching, he fumbled in opening it. He bought three oranges, one for each of them, and went back down the aisle.

Early in the afternoon when they got on, they all sat together in a double seat at the rear end of the car. But besides their bundles there were the two boxes of dried soap berries and these did not leave much room for anybody's feet. So, first chance they got, he and June moved ahead to this other seat. They had gone back to the double one to eat supper but afterward June went to the car behind to be with some of the fellows and girls they knew. His mother was asleep now, so he left her orange on her window-sill and went to his own place, a few seats along and on the opposite side of the aisle.

He peeled his orange and ate it, then rested his head against the cool glass again. The train was coming around a curve and the end cars seemed to be chasing the ones ahead, dragging the light from their windows over the ground and along the wall of trees. Back there were the cars in which, so June said, the white people could lie down and sleep in real beds, and another car where they ate off tables like in a café.

White people. White people. Why was it that all day, whenever he started to think, he ended up thinking about white people? At home, at the head of their valley, it was not this way. At home you did what you liked, talked your own language without feeling shy about it, had native food in front of anybody, and didn't feel you were different.

He turned from the window and folded his sweater over the arm of the seat for a pillow. Lying with his knees up and his head next to the aisle, he tried to sleep.

In that position he could see his mother. Her small, short-fingered hands were clasped across her middle, and her gold earrings jiggled to the swaying of the train. The knot of her head-shawl was tight against the fat under her chin and the shawl had slipped from her smooth, black hair.

The thing about his mother—and it was a thing which gave him pride—was that she did not let what other people thought change her in the least. Even with whites around, she did what she wanted to do, what she had always done.

Yesterday June wanted her not to bring those two boxes of native food to trade with the coast people for seaweed or grease.

"Aw! Mama, do we have to?" June had coaxed. "Those sloppy boxes. And when we eat the grease we have a kind of smell. Cy knows what I mean. One time at the Junction we heard some white girls behind us at the movies whispering."

"The *gum-see-wa* have their kind of smell, too," their mother answered in Gitkshan.

"Well, we don't want them laughing at us."

"We can laugh, too, you know. We see lots of their ways to laugh about. I could laugh and laugh at the funny ways of white people I have seen."

"But they will. You watch." Yet at the station it was June who looked after those two boxes. She let no one see she felt ashamed.

He was thinking of this when June came along the aisle, swaying from the hips to the motion of the car.

"I came to get you. We're having fun; come on," she said.

Cy sat up and stretched, letting on he had been sleeping. He dug his thumbnail into the remaining orange and offered her the peeled half.

"You have it," she said. "It makes my fingers sticky."

Cy's strong, broad jaw worked on the chunk of orange in his mouth. He saw her tilt her head, looking down at him from under her long, curved lashes and fingering the red clasp in her hair. Her skin was browner than his and her eyes wider apart, more like their mother's, and over her high, rounded cheek bones was that rosy flush which came when she was excited and having a good time. Sometimes he could not be sure if she was pretty or not, but at times like this she seemed to be over-flowing with life and to give out a sort of warmth, so that he thought she was a very pretty girl and that she was growing into an even prettier woman.

"If you like," he said. "I might as well." He dropped

the rest of the peel to the floor and followed her along the aisle. Between the cars they met the newsie. He let June pass and then he winked at Cy.

"Some sister you got there," he said as the door of the other car closed behind June. "I see a guy in there making passes at her, but she looks like she knew her way around. She older than you?"

"Pretty soon sixteen."

"I'd take her for older. But when they're big enough they're old enough, like the fella says." He gave Cy a slap on the back and went on.

Everybody liked June and it was easy to see the newsie liked her too. Cy pushed against the door and went down the aisle. The girls and fellows were from the Junction, not from the village, but their language was the same, and Cy and June had known them all their lives. Bert Silas was the only one who had grown up in the village, although he had not lived in it for several years. Sometimes he hung around the Junction, but mostly he lived in Prince Rupert.

One of the fellows moved over and made room for Cy. "Pretty soon Angus," he said. All of them except Bert and Cy and June were going to work at Angus cannery for the summer.

The boy at the end of the seat next the window told Cy he wished he was going to the coast cannery. He asked if the train would get to Rupert in time for a show, and if the stores would be open.

Cy said he did not know.

"If it's a cannery pay-night they will," Bert put in from across the aisle. "A few anyhow. We'll take in the sights before we have to get on the steamer. June and me, anyhow. I don't know about old Cy. I guess all he wants is to get to the cannery." Bert laughed. "How about that, Cy?"

Cy knew from this that June must have told Bert about Miriam and he wished he had asked her not to. "I'm in no hurry," he said, rubbing the flat of his hands slow and hard over his knees, not looking at Bert. The others were using English so Cy did, too. "Just the same I like to get to work."

Bert laughed again. "I'll say you'd like to get to work. Got to make up for lost time, haven't you Cy?"

Cy felt the palms of his hands go moist. "I don't know what you're talking about."

"Now, boys, don't fight," June said. She was sitting next to Bert and she leaned forward, wanting to make Cy look at her. Bert put his arm around her and drew her back. Where his hand came in front, her dress drew tight and you could see she was getting to be a woman. June slapped his hand and he sat up straight, folding his arms and pretending he was sorry.

"I'll be good," he said with a grin.

"You'd better! Here." June reached behind her and took the guitar belonging to one of the Junction fellows and held it out to Bert. "Let's sing some more."

"The lady says sing something." Bert struck a chord and looked around. "What'll it be? Name it."

Somebody suggested *Home on the Range*.

Bert said he had all he could take of *Home on the Range*.

"*Carolina Moon?*"

So they sang that, working in the harmony and not afraid to let themselves go because they were all together and because in this car too it was mostly native people. Native people sang on the train going down to the canneries, Cy remembered. And their mother said that before there was a train, in steamboat days, they sang, only then it was mostly the gospel

songs. Probably their people sang even in the times
before that, when they travelled in the big canoes, when
there were no canneries, and no whites, and the country
all belonged to native people.

Bert was standing in the aisle, playing chords until
somebody called the next song, when the conductor
came from the car behind. He tried to pass, but Bert
was slow in moving over.

"Good singing," the conductor said. "Good
harmony."

Bert glanced sideways at Cy. "Not bad for a bunch
of savages."

The conductor studied Bert over his glasses. "That's
no way to talk."

"Then skip it," Bert said, with a don't-care shrug.

"No," the conductor said, but in a kindly way. "Tell
me what you're getting at."

Bert's laugh was nervous, curt. "As if you didn't
know!" He pointed along the untidy aisle. "Good old
cannery special."

"So that's it?" the conductor said. "Well, there'll be
space in the next coach back after we leave Angus, and
any of you young folks are perfectly free to sit there if
you care to. It's certainly cleaner. With you it's
different, but by and large no sooner are the kids
aboard than they start eating. Eat? I never saw
such kids to eat; peels and trash all over the place.
We've got to draw the line some place."

Cy stared at his hands and thought of the peels he had
scattered in the car where their mother was, and felt
ashamed.

He gave Bert a jab with his elbow. "Play something!"
he urged. "Go ahead and play something!"

2

BERT KNEW ALL ABOUT PRINCE RUPERT, BUT NEITHER CY
nor June had seen the town since they were small. While
their father was alive, he used to bring them here for a
good time after he and their mother were paid off at the
cannery. There were many places for them to spend
their money: the picture shows, stores, eating places,
the fair, and all used to be crowded with Indians
enjoying themselves after a summer's fishing.

Cy's childhood memories of Rupert were exciting,
happy ones but tonight his anticipation was clouded
somewhat by the way Bert behaved in front of that
conductor. What had Bert against the conductor,
and supposing he behaved like that before other white
men they met up town?

While they were getting their bundles from the train
to the wharf, Cy let June know he would just as soon
not go.

However, she talked him out of that. Bert took her
arm and led them up some stairs and across a bridge
over the tracks to where there was a small park with
paths leading right and left up the slope. Some other
people from the train took the right-hand one but Bert
steered them up the left one. June told him he certainly
seemed to know his way around.

"You can say that again," Bert answered.

June tossed back her hair, glancing at his face and smiling, not so much because of what he said but because of an undefined expectancy. She felt a glowing beneath her skin, and a pleasurable readiness, diffused and without thought of fulfilment.

Cy had dropped a few steps behind and Bert called out for him to hurry.

The impatience in Bert's voice jarred on the soft, passive pleasure she was feeling. "Cy's only looking at those totem poles," she said. And she herself looked up at them, three tall shafts on the crest of a small, rocky hill. One had its thunderbird wings spread, and against the reflection of the lighted stores beyond, it and the poles on either side reminded Cy of the Bible picture in Caleb's house which showed the three crosses on Calvary.

Most of the stores along the street were closed, but some had stayed open. In the window of one of them June saw the very kind of shoes she intended to buy with her first pay at the cannery. They had very high heels and open toes, like those in the catalogue. Bert was holding her hand and she drew him to the window.

"I think they would be suited to my style, don't you?" she asked him. "The catalogue ones are cheaper though."

Cy came and stood behind her. The set of her head, and her voice, so alive and eager, stirred the deep feeling of protectiveness he so often felt for her. He took out the new billfold and handed her the money. "You can pay me back when you get it," he said.

"Oh, Cy, thanks!" June's eyes were shining.

Bert grinned. "That's the kind of brother to have."

He went into the store with her, but Cy waited. When

June came out she was wearing the shoes and Bert was carrying her old ones in a parcel.

The café Bert wanted them to go to was on another of the streets where there were stores with windows as big as rooms. They had dolls in them the size of women, showing off their dresses. There were dark doorways, too, with signs marked "Rooms", but June's attention was all on the many beautiful things in the windows and the colourful confusion of electric signs. A rapt, acquiescent excitement possessed her and she thought that, without Bert Silas, she would have missed all this. She felt grateful and shyly proud that a boy who had left their village was familiar and at ease here.

The café had a tile front. Still with June's arm through his, Bert walked straight in, leaving Cy to follow. Cy would have taken a stool at the counter but Bert steered them to a booth.

A woman took their orders; then Bert jumped up and went over to the juke-box beyond the door. He started to read the tunes, then beckoned June over. "How about this one? It's new."

"Whatever you like."

He put in the money and the music started, fast and loud. "Look at old Cy over there, scared as some stick Indian," he said to her.

Going back to their table, June could feel the sprightly click of her new heels on the tile floor and when Bert put his hand against the small of her back to show her where to sit, a sort of tingle went along her spine and she thought this was by far the nicest evening she had ever had.

After they had had pie, and a second cup of coffee all round, Cy said it was time they started back to the wharf.

Bert glanced at his watch. "No hurry. But you go if you want to. I'll look after June."

Cy hesitated. "I think we all better go."

June touched his arm. "I won't be late. I promise. All I want is to take a little walk and see what's in the windows."

As soon as Cy went out, Bert lit a cigarette and held it loosely between his lips. "Old Cy sure hands me a laugh. What's the matter with him? Talk about your stick Indian!"

"You said that before. What's it mean, stick Indian?"

"Straight out of the bush. Hillbilly. Get it?"

June fingered the handle of her cup. There was much about Bert Silas she did not understand. His unpredictable, darting thoughts and many of his words perplexed her. And yet, beside him on the train and walking through the park with their hands touching, and here among the glitter and the lights, being with him held out enticements she could not have named. It was not Bert himself so much as what he represented in the warm mists of her imaginings that drew her. Of recent months she had grown conscious of the limitations of village life. And although she felt no definite impatience with them even now, his assurance in surroundings which would have felt foreign to her by herself, stimulated her strangely. Because of him, the world suddenly seemed larger and freer, holding a promise for her far beyond her immediate reach, yet glimpsed sufficiently for her to be aware that it was there. But what Bert just said disturbed her.

"I don't think Cy's like that," she ventured to say.

Bert crumpled his cigarette. "All I meant was when you're in a swell place like this one, you've got to act like you belong."

"I didn't see anything wrong in what Cy did."

"He sure didn't act natural. Anybody could see he doesn't belong."

June looked down and her long, black lashes hid her eyes. How he answered her next question was important to her, of such great importance that she shrank from voicing it lest the quickening expectancy she felt be drained away. "Do I act natural," she murmured, "like I belong?"

Bert leaned back, his narrow face intense, his hands pushed against the edge of the table. The erect, pliant way she sat, her high, smooth forehead with the gleaming hair swept maturely up so that it revealed her small, flat ears, the moist demureness of her mouth, and her high, rounded cheek-bones filled him with desire.

He reached for her hands and held them. "You belong," he assured her, his voice excited and confiding. "Baby, do you ever!"

3

THE STEAMER WAS LATE. BY THE TIME IT TIED UP AT THE
wharf in front of the cannery office and store, the afternoon starting-whistle had set the echoes bouncing back
and forth across the rocky bay; the people were at
work; and only Victor Henderson was there to meet
them. Victor had a push truck and as soon as they had
their bundles and boxes on it they walked around the
head of the small bay at the far corner of which the
native quarters were.

Victor pulled the truck and Cy pushed. This cannery
was different from the cannery at Angus and the other
canneries at the mouth of the Skeena. It had no flat
ground behind it. The mountains went straight up
from the water so that almost all the buildings had to be
built on piles, with plank walks between. The bay was
a pocket between the mountains. The wind could not
blow through it and it gave a shut-in feeling which, as
an up-river person, Cy did not like.

To one side of the store and office, wooden steps led
up to two lines of houses. Those would be for the white
families who lived here all year round. These houses
had small lawns, with flowers, and they looked down on
the bay and the cannery buildings. Victor pointed to a
square, white building behind the store which he said

was for white workers who did not bring their families. Melissa, June, and Bert were ahead and Victor told them to follow the walk behind what Cy took to be the cold storage building.

This walk led to the main cannery building, which had a wharf of its own and was set broadside across the head of the bay. A good catch of fish must have come in this morning. Plumes of white steam rose from many pipes in its corrugated iron roof and there was the hum of machinery. The wide doors at one end were open and Cy saw lines of women and girls in white work clothes, and with white kerchiefs around their heads, working at tables or machines. The wet smell of fish and steam came out, a good clean smell. This was where Miriam would be working, but there must have been a hundred girls in there, and he was unable to pick her out.

Along from the cannery building was the reduction plant. Its far end rested on the rocky shore, but most of it was on piles. There were huge, silver-painted tanks for the oil which was saved from the fish scraps, and there was a shed piled to the roof with sacks of fish meal.

From here on the walk ran over the rocks which at high tide would be mostly covered with water. Some lumber piles stood to one side of it. The walk curved outward and, looking back, Cy saw the boat repair shed in a slip between the cold storage building and the main cannery.

The native quarters were in two buildings at the end of the walk. Against the wooded mountainside these seemed almost as large as the cannery, but narrower and with smaller windows. Ramps led up to them and they, too, stood on piles over the water. They had doors, thirty or forty in rows on either side and a gallery, like a narrow veranda, ran around them. So many doors and windows, all the same, gave the building a severe, unwelcoming appearance. But at their shore ends, on either side of the ramps, several lines with white clothes and brightly-coloured dresses lessened this severity.

Victor stopped the truck at the first ramp. "Caleb's is out at the end, this side. We'll unload here."

"Whereabouts is yours?" Bert asked. Victor's mother was some kind of relative of his, about the only one he had, and he was to stay with her this summer.

Victor showed him where to go, round the corner and a little way along the north side. Some older children, who had been left to mind the little ones, came over. All of them crowded around to watch the unloading. June and Melissa took up their suitcases, Cy hoisted their bedding bundle to his shoulders, and they started in single file for Caleb's door.

Nettie, Caleb's wife, had dinner ready for them. With the sun beating down into the enclosed bay and little Nettie chattering away all the time they were eating, and popping stick after stick into the already heated stove, Caleb's room was like an oven. The rooms Caleb led them to after the meal were on the north side of the building, back to back with his. They got no direct sun and were therefore cooler. Caleb let it be known that, with fishing under way and the row crowded with native people from all the north coast, it was lucky that his name stood high with the cannery manager. Otherwise they would have had to take one of the shacks behind the cold storage plant. Caleb said the people there were a mixed lot, and indicated to Melissa that that would be no fit place for June.

But in the matter of the promised jobs Caleb had not been so lucky. Their mother would start work in the morning, as arranged, but jobs for Cy and June were, it turned out, not so certain. They were kept busy until after supper time, helping their mother settle in. But after they had eaten, Cy came out and sat on the bench by the door to think things over.

Caleb's heart is strong for us, Cy thought; I only hope he can find us something. June had felt badly all afternoon, but the manager was expected to visit Caleb this evening and perhaps by bed-time they would have better news. Just the same, Cy felt uneasy. He would sooner not talk with Miriam until he was sure the manager wanted him. Paul Leget's rooms were farther along on this side of the row, and it stirred Cy to think of Miriam so close. Miriam and her grandfather had been the first to leave the village for the cannery, and after they had left, Cy had missed her more than he had thought he would. Yesterday on the train, and last evening in Rupert he kept thinking that every hour he was getting nearer to Miriam and that soon they would be close again.

Cy got up from the bench and went to the railing. The tide was full and he saw small fish swimming between the piles. He worked up some spittle and let it drop but the fish did not rise to it. Maybe it would be safer if he and Miriam were not so close. What if, as so often happened among their people, their natures got too strong for them and they came together, found they were suited to each other, and the binding arrangement was made between the families? He knew what his mother thought of Miriam; she thought Miriam was the one for him. Their crests were different so he could think of her in an intimate way. One hint from him and his mother would approach Old Paul about the arrangement. Then, if Miriam still was willing, he would go to live under Paul Leget's roof and under his authority, and the mould of his future would be set.

Behind him, in the room, Melissa was getting after June about the shoes again. Cy wished she wouldn't. Before supper June had given in and put on her old ones, but now apparently she wanted to change.

"But such heels! And no leather to protect the toes in front! I wonder the *gum-see-wa* women do not trip and break their necks."

"Native girls wear them too," June said in English. "I saw some wearing them last night in Rupert. Besides they're in the catalogue."

"Miriam would never put such things to her feet. Miriam is not froth. Nor are you froth, my young sister," Melissa said severely.

"But everybody's wearing them, Mama, all the white girls."

"Let them. What do we care what white people do?"

There it was again, thought Cy, white people. At home, up in their valley, it was true they had no need to care. The village was all right while you were living in it. A few, such as Bert Silas and Uncle Matt's don't-care daughter Dot, had tired of village life and gone away to Rupert to be among the whites, but these were the exceptions. Mostly the people were contented there, and so would June be, he thought, once she went back to it.

Cy moved farther along the rail. He did not want to hear more: he had his own troubles to think about. The air was beginning to cool and it had the land smell in it, the smell of evergreens and of sun-warmed rocks. Smoke from the cooking fires along the row lay teased out on the water, drifting off-shore and blending with the deeper blue of evening. Perhaps by now the manager had come.

Cy walked around the end of the building where he could keep an eye on Caleb's door. Beyond Caleb's, all along the rail, people were cooling off, standing, or sitting on the benches. The snatches of their talk which drifted to him were in languages he did not understand —Kitamaat with its tight-throated, clicking forceful-ness: the more flowing Haida: Tsimpshean, whose intonations, and some of its words, resembled his own. These people, though strangers, were of his race, and it gave him confidence to realize how many of them there were.

His feeling of being out of place came partly, he supposed, from the contrast between the surroundings here and those he was accustomed to. At home there was the wide and sunny freedom of his valley, with birches and white poplars between the belts of jackpine. The woods were stippled through with shifting light, while here the hemlock and cedar forest was dark and choked with undergrowth. These mountains, towering above the bay, lacked the soaring, shapely grace of those at home, where one could travel through many summer days or over the dazzling snow and never feel shut in or limited.

Being at the coast is not bad for a change, he thought, as he strolled toward the reduction plant, but I would not want to live here all the time, no matter how good a job I had. He stopped at the reduction plant and was about to turn back when he noticed several men on the wharf in front of the office. A big fish-packer was mov-ing slowly toward the head of the bay and more men came from the office to watch it. People from the row began passing him, talking excitedly in their different languages. He was starting to follow them but a whistle halted him and he saw Bert and Victor coming on the run.

While he waited, Cy wondered if there had been an accident. The packer had a gillnet boat tied alongside, bow and stern, with only its pilot house above water. More people from the row hurried past, and one of the white men in front of the office shouted some question to the packer. Everybody was heading toward the slip and boat repair yard between the cold storage plant and the cannery building.

Victor caught Cy's arm and hurried him along. The packer was nosing in very slowly, and by the time they reached the slip, a line had been thrown and men were guiding the wrecked boat into the cradle of the ways.

The cribbing on both sides of the slip was crowded with native people, looking down and not saying much, just watching. Somehow their silence made Cy uneasy.

Bert nudged him. "Let's go."

They found a good place on top of the cribbing abreast of the boat shed. Paul Leget stood in the water beside the slip with his hip-boots pulled up, helping a white man centre the wrecked boat on the cradle. A big, baldheaded white man was shouting orders. Victor said he was the boss of the shed, the man Old Paul was working under.

Paul felt under the water with his feet, then made a sign and the boss started the winch engine. As the boat was hauled slowly up the sloping track, water poured from a hole near the bow, and when it came higher and the winch stopped, Cy saw other holes punched through the planking and ribs almost to the stern. The boss beckoned Paul to him.

"Take a look at that!"

Old Paul Leget, big headed, his massive jaw sullen as a cod's, moved along the hull, thumping the planking with the heel of his palm to test it.

The boss swung around and his blue eyes searched the line of faces above him. "Where is he, the bloody Siwash? He come off the packer yet?"

"Siwash" was the ultimate in white contempt but the faces of the Indians remained passive, blank.

The man kept staring up at them but no one spoke or changed expression. His hostility had united them on some sure ground of withdrawal which long experience had taught them could never be invaded by whites.

The boss turned on Paul Leget. "I'll have him black-listed, by the hubs of hell I will. He'll never work for this company again."

Paul gave no sign that he heard.

The boss hitched his coveralls and put his head inside the hull. "What a mess!" he stormed when he stood up. "Bilge stringer buckled eight inches; a good eight inches. Don't stand there! Look inside, see for yourself."

Cy watched Miriam's grandfather bend stiffly and look inside. He knew that grim, unyielding old man as all in their village knew him—knew him so well that he could imagine what he was thinking, and it was something the enraged white man would never know. Every summer Old Paul came to this cannery and took the white people's wages, earning good money because he was skilful with his hands and knew the ways of wood. He came not as most of the others came, in response to the nomadic urge, but for the money only, giving his labour and nothing of himself, and remaining loyal to the past. No single thread of his life deviated from the old, old pattern; he was contemptuous of those who changed and of the whites who wanted them to change.

With heart and head, with every part of him, he withstood the whites and their treatment of his race. "I hate the white man's guts," Cy had heard him say last winter, translating the words spoken in English into a Gitkshan idiom even more biting.

"Well, say something!" the boss demanded when Paul finished his inspection. The unbroken silence behind him, the feeling which weighed the air, was having its calculated effect. Paul took his time in answering. "It can be fixed," he said woodenly, in English.

"A good, sound cannery boat, the fish starting to run and he gets pie-eyed and rams her. He better not lie to me. I seen him last night so full of brew he didn't know was he coming or going."

Deliberately Old Paul folded down the tops of his hip boots. He had said all he had to say. In the morning the devising, the cutting away, and the shaping of the new parts would begin, and he would be put in charge because he was better at the work than any, better certainly than this noisy white, and knew it.

Now he was going home. He did not hurry, nor did he stand waiting for permission to go. All those others of his race on the bank above were not mere onlookers. They too were participants, but his was the principal role. They knew that all his movements had a significance which the white could not read—contempt, hostility, derision, cunningly indicated by the set of his head and shoulders, the immobility of his face, the way he held his hands. All had meaning, as each movement in their people's historic dances had meaning for the initiated but escaped the eyes of outsiders.

Paul mounted the ladder and walked away, not deigning to look back, his exit a telling one, and the

more so because of the white man's inability to see in it
what all the Indians saw.

The other white, a lanky, grey-haired man, came from
the far side of the boat. "He sure rammed her," Cy
heard him say. "Which one had this boat anyhow?"

"That Johnny what's-his-name. You know him.
Been shacked up with that Rupert woman. Her where
the trouble was last night."

The second man took out his pipe and lit it. "They
can bring the Japs back any day for all of me," he said
wearily. "Them Nips was at least reliable. They took
decent care of company gear, not like these we got now.
The Company can transfer me back south any time.
I've sure had my bellyful of natives."

"You and me both. They got no respect for property
—their own or anybody else's."

"Shiftless, same's the ones we got on the prairies.
But till I come here I been led to believe these coast
ones was better. More the educated type."

"Education's got damn-all to do with it. Once an
Indian always an Indian."

"You said it. Something in their blood, I guess."

They spoke not so much in anger as with a kind of
superior disgust and objectivity, like men at home
discussing the bad habits of certain work dogs and
horses. Bert and Victor had moved with the crowd to
watch the packer tie up, and Cy wished he had gone
with them, yet he stood self-consciously, held by a
perverted curiosity.

What was the matter with him anyway? He did not
have to listen; they could not make him listen. He
tried to anchor his thoughts on other whites he knew:
the ranch family down the valley at whose table he had
been made to feel welcome last summer while he was

helping with the haying, and later, at potato digging time; or the white fellows from the Junction who played baseball against the village team, arguing and joking as equals.

Surely these two were exceptions. But could he be certain of it? Suppose the friendly ranch family was the exception. Aside from a few games of ball, he was never with Junction fellows, so how could he be sure of them? Suppose that what these two said was what all whites secretly thought of Indians?

This possibility brought a desolating sense of exposure and peculiarity, as if what they said had been said directly to him. But he was not ashamed of being Indian, and no one could ever make him ashamed. Thinking of Old Paul made him feel better somehow. His vague hostility toward that rigid old man gave way to admiration. Paul was mad, too, but he would not help the boss by showing it. At home Paul got after the boys, and men sometimes, for leaving a good dog-sled or snowshoes lying in the slush or for mistreating any of the fine dugout canoes he made. Paul knew the work which went into a piece of wood, and along the row, away from the whites, he would say biting things about what had happened to the boat.

Everyone else was crowding around the packer, waiting for this Johnny to show himself, but Cy did not feel like waiting. He was past the reduction plant when Victor overtook him.

"I guess Johnny drank too much last night. I guess he went to sleep at the wheel," Victor said. "The manager will fire him and he'll have to go back to Rupert." He hesitated. "I guess you don't know who he is, that you never heard. It's him Dot's living with."

Ahead, along the row, lights were beginning to come out in the windows, and on the gallery somebody was playing a lonely cowboy tune on a guitar. The music was drawn thin in the gathering darkness and the windows looked hard and impersonal in their regularity.

"We never heard from Dot for years," Cy said. "Half the time we don't know where she is."

June was sitting on the outside bench when Cy got back.

"I talked to Caleb at the water tap," she said directly. "Mother's in his place now. It's all settled about the jobs." She pushed her sweater impatiently from her shoulders. "Am I ever mad at Caleb!"

Cy sat down beside her. Somebody was bound to tell her that Dot was here, and he wondered if he hadn't better, now. "No use getting mad at Caleb," he said.

"Well, I am mad. He shouldn't have promised. I never would have come down if he hadn't promised. Miriam has a job and I don't see why I can't. It isn't fair. Caleb says it's on account of I'm under age, but I could have asked for a job at the Junction, at the hospital. I could have told them I'm sixteen. I almost am." She got up and went to the rail, then turned to face him. "I can't go on wearing just any kind of clothes, the ones mother picks for me because they're cheap and wear well. Anybody can see they're not suited to my style."

"I guess it's the law, about under age. Did Caleb say about me?"

"Oh, you're all right. You're all fixed up to work in the boat shed. And you know why? Because Old Paul asked for you. You're going to be his helper."

"Caleb didn't say that? He didn't say Paul asked for me?"

June shook her head. "But I just know. Anybody can see he wants you for Miriam."

"Don't talk like that," Cy told her uneasily. "What about the can loft job? That's where Caleb wrote I'd be."

"Bert got it. He starts tomorrow. You all do, all but me."

With her bare forearms on the rail June glanced down at the new shoes which had brought her such unclouded pleasure and which she had put on after Melissa went to Caleb's. She swung one straight, plump leg, pointing her toes and turning her supple ankle this way and that to admire it. The shoes gave her a grown-up, confident feeling. She enjoyed the sound of their high heels as she moved, and she remembered the assurance they gave her, strolling the lighted streets in Rupert last evening, with Bert's arm through hers. Even yet she could hear their brisk, feminine tapping on the floor of that swell café, and their echo coming to her from shadowy doorways.

Cy came and stood beside her. "Never mind. I'll give you some of my money. A few dollars anyway." He was relieved about getting work, but he did not want to talk about it. He leaned over the rail and watched the black, undulating reflections of the gallery. "What do you want to buy? What do you need?"

"Oh, I don't know. It's hard to say." June spoke impatiently, and immediately felt ungrateful. "It's all right, Cy. Skip it. Nothing much I need, I guess; not right away."

Always, in his slow gentle way, he had been protective toward her, and she supposed he was like that even before their father died. It embarrassed her that he offered the money so readily. Hinting for it had not been in her mind at all, not like it sometimes was.

She shifted her arms on the rail so that their shoulders

touched.   Letting on she was trying to see what he was looking at in the water she wriggled her fingers under his arm and gave it a little squeeze. "You're good," she said impulsively. "I'll always remember how good you were to me."

She glanced at his face, seeing the wide, straight mouth, the profile of his nose, his strong, short jaw. In repose his face had an unresponsiveness which made it appear stern, like Matt's, but it was softened by the openness and steady patience of his eyes which, for some reason, made him look older than he was, and sometimes defenceless and unaccountably sad.

She could not imagine why she had spoken so, as if before long they would be parting. Their life at home seemed obscured by the flow of new experiences which had caught her up during the last day or so; and yet, this very minute, she could picture the village clearly. The two streets, the lower of them descending to the graveyard, the totem poles, the swift river, and the steeple of the church white against the sheltering ridge.

Cy straightened, looking over her head along the row. "Too early for bed, so I'll walk around a while," he said.

June looked into his face and smiled. "Miriam will be glad for you," she said. "Well, do not get lost, my brother."

She watched him sauntering past the lighted windows of the gallery. Cy's tall for eighteen, taller than any of them, she thought. That slow, stalking gait, the rigid back and the loosely hanging arms—she would recognize these anywhere.

And then she thought of what Bert Silas had said last night after Cy left them. But he better not call Cy a stick Indian again, she thought affectionately. He just better not.

4

THE FOLLOWING EVENING BEING WITHOUT WIND, AND
warm, Caleb was on the bench at his door, taking his
ease after an exacting day. The last vacancies for people
from his village had been filled, Melissa Pitt and her
children were settled in, and this afternoon the manager
had commended him for his thoroughness in carrying
out the involved arrangements. He regretted being
unable to find work for June, but the girl's age had not
previously been made clear to him, and because of the
law, his hands were tied.

"I am sorry about that," he told Cy, who had come
to the tap for water. "But I have it from the lips of my
good friend, the manager, that her age is not enough.
Sixteen is the age for working, different than before, and
my white friend will not go against the law."

Because his hearing had become so faulty, and also
because in his prime he had been a deep-chested and
hearty man, Caleb spoke loudly, filling his lungs and
bearing down on important words. He wanted to make
it very clear that the new law was none of his doing,
and as he did so the phlegm in his throat bubbled and
crackled unpredictably, causing sentences to begin with
booming vigour and sometimes end in a husky, adoles-

cent quaver. Being fond of talking, Caleb found this something of an affliction, but he bore it as he bore his other afflictions, including failing sight and hearing, without complaint.

Cy turned off the water and stood holding the pail. "We know it is not your fault. But June is disappointed. We still hope you can find work for her."

"My heart is in a steep place because of our young sister," Caleb said, blinking up at Cy. His sleeves were pushed up, and his faded shirt open down to where the bulging fat encased his navel. The skin on arms and chest was hairless and youthfully smooth.

Caleb was so sunny and helpful a man, and disappointing people so against his nature, that Cy felt he should say no more about the job for June. He picked up the pail and was turning to go when Caleb thumped the bench at his side.

"Sit with me, young brother. I have heavy words to speak." Caleb felt for Cy's arm and patted it. "One of our village has made trouble for the manager. I learn from Victor you know of it."

"Yes," Cy said. "He told me. It never crossed our minds Dot would be here. Five years since Matt saw her. More than five, I think."

"Has word of it come to the ears of Melissa, or to June?"

Cy said he believed not.

"At the shacks was wildness from the drink, and fighting. Later, without shaming Melissa and when this trouble is somewhat drifted over, I will speak to her of Dot, to see what can be done in Christian brotherhood to strengthen the feeble knees." Caleb cleared his throat and patted Cy's knee. "Let not your heart be troubled," he said in his strong, pulpit voice.

But Caleb's heart was troubled, and after Cy left he asked himself what was coming over some of the village men and women of late years. While she lived at home Dot was a good girl, unruly at times, but good. Her face was seen inside the church, but now she was not on the Lord's side any more.

"Who is on d'Lord's side?" Caleb demanded. "Dare to be a Daniel." Oh, how he used to stir up the back-sliders with words like these! But nowadays what was happening to the church? He was the last of the native lay preachers Mr. Lloyd had trained, and where were the young men to take his place in the years ahead?

Sometimes, what with the back-sliding and the home-brew, the church having no more missionaries to send, and teachers not wanting to come, a wave of dark despair swept over him, so that he thought of his dear village as little better than the Sodom and Gomorrah he sometimes preached about.

It was Sunday before Caleb managed to have his talk with Melissa. The salmon ran well that week, the women made overtime pay in the cannery and cold storage plant, Cy seemed to be fitting in well at the boat shed, and Caleb had many things to attend to. However, with Sunday here, and the people idle for the day, he was pleased to have Melissa drop in as he and Nettie were having breakfast. He still did not know if Melissa had heard about Dot, but if so, he now had a surprise for her which should offset that unpleasant piece of news.

"Ho! Melissa, my friend," Caleb called out when Nettie told him who was at the door. "Come in; sit down, have coffee with us."

Melissa thanked him and sat down.

"You are up early; you are getting old like us,"

Caleb chuckled asthmatically. "Old people cannot lie in the bed when they get the chance. Different from when we had the young blood in us, eh?" Then, jocundly, peering at her: "Dressed for Sunday, I see. After I eat, I, too, will dress for Sunday. It gives a good feeling to be well dressed on the Lord's Day, do you not think?"

"You will be holding service today then?" Melissa inquired, smoothing the folds of her black dress.

"I no longer hold service at the cannery, my sister. I am too old, and the people no longer ask."

Nettie poured coffee and nudged Caleb to push the cup within Melissa's reach. Melissa had made herself breakfast, leaving June and Cy to sleep; she felt no need for more, but it was poor manners to refuse what was placed before you, in a home or at a feast. The skin on her hands was bleached and tender from washing fish, and the cup's warmth was pleasing to the touch. "Since there is to be no service I have it in my mind to go over and see Dot this morning." She spoke casually, as if the idea had only that moment come to her.

Caleb moved his big head up and down. "That is good, very good." He, too, managed to make it seem a natural and understandable act, quite without significance. Each was now aware the other had the facts about the trouble, and each appreciated the other's tact in avoiding putting it into words. It was a heavy thing to have a woman of your village disgrace her name and family, and Caleb was thankful that he had other and better news.

"One of the store men visited me last night," he went on. "His name is Haney and he is also the first-aid man. He is new here, and his wife needs help in her house. The woman is not sickly, you understand, and the husband gave me to think she is doing work outside the house. School lessons for the manager's children was what he said. However, it may be that the woman is carrying a child. Unlike us, white men draw back from speaking of such things. Many of their women are weak and sickly at that time. But what do you say, Melissa, my friend? Would you say June would care to help the Mrs. Haney?"

Melissa studied the cup between her hands. Now here is a chance one must seize, she thought. It will bring in money. What better could we ask for? "The wages will be the same as cannery wages?" she inquired with no hint of eagerness.

"No, not the same."

"How much will the wages be?"

"The wages will be two dollars a day. She will be fed by Mrs. Haney, though, and that is to be taken into account with a growing girl."

"June is not a big eater. You would be surprised at the little she eats."

"She is a healthy eater, however. And the food, all of the best from the store, costs a good deal."

"You have spoken of this to June?" Melissa knew he had not.

"You are the mother. The dealings should be through you."

"I would agree if the wages were cannery wages."

"But there are no cannery wages for girls below sixteen. You already understand this, Melissa, my friend."

"That, I will say, is a foolish law. It is the size and strength, not the number of years which count. Why, when I was twelve I was doing a grown woman's work at Angus cannery."

"Angus cannery is not this cannery, and things have changed," Caleb remarked pleasantly. "Two dollars a day and your food would be an important person's pay when you were a girl, Melissa."

Melissa dismissed this with a flip of her hand. "When I was a girl was a long time ago," she said with a shrewd smile.

"You are still a healthy, good-looking woman."

Melissa declined to be influenced by the flattery. "I hesitate to mention such low wages to the girl. We all of us have our pride, Caleb."

"June is a big girl. Let her go," Nettie advised. She felt that Melissa was pressing her argument to her own disadvantage. Nettie had no desires in this matter, either way, but Melissa had been so uncompromising that she could not now accept without losing face.

Watching from the shadow of her kerchief, the canny Nettie knew what was in her friend's mind. It was understood by all that Caleb had a long head, he was expected to make careful bargains with the village people and in this the manager had rarely been disappointed. Yet in this case two dollars was the actual wage Mr. Haney was prepared to pay. Melissa had the name of being a skilful trader, but she could do no better. If Paul Leget had his way, there was to be a marriage feast in the village before next fishing season, and the family would need all the money it could get to pay for its share of that. The helpful thing was to give Melissa this opening through which she could gracefully withdraw.

"She is indeed a big girl," Melissa admitted. "A grown woman, almost. There is not work enough in the house to keep her busy. I will think on what you say, my friend, and by evening I will let you know."

"Good. Very good."

"You will not make the offer to others until you hear from me?" Melissa asked. "Not even at the two dollars which, as you must know, is very low?"

"That is agreed. I will not so much as speak of it."

It was now accepted between them that June would go to work at the Haneys, probably to-morrow. And though the wages could have been better, Melissa was well satisfied. Without Caleb knowing it, she too had scored a point, for with June across at the white side all day, the likelihood of a summer friendship with Dot would be greatly lessened.

5

A SUMMER SOUTH-EASTER WAS BLOWING UP BY THE TIME
Melissa left Caleb's. Ragged clouds scudded across the
face of the mountain above the white side, threatening
rain. Because she had on her good dress Melissa
wondered if she had not better return to the room for
her coat and a kerchief for her head. But several con-
siderations complicated this otherwise simple decision.

There had been a neighbourly gathering, with singing, in the rooms of Victor's people last night, and, up
until the time she left, June and Cy were still asleep,
June in the double bed upstairs and Cy in his bunk at
the end of the main room. Cy had not stirred while
she quietly got the fire going and made herself a bit of
breakfast. Her coat hung on the back of the door and
she could reach it without entering the room. But if he
was up and about she would be faced with explanations
she would much rather not have to make.

On their side of the building, out of the wind, Melissa
paused to consider. Perhaps she should wait and slip
away later in the day. Unless Dot had greatly changed
her ways, morning was no time to call. Women of
Dot's sort lay abed until noon and, if she came to the
door at all, both her person and her room would be in
such disarray that the visit would embarrass both of

them. On the other hand, Melissa reasoned, if she postponed her visit until afternoon, June would coax to come. It would be unfeeling, having to discourage the girl from meeting this cousin she had not seen since she was small, but under the circumstances it would have to be done.

Perhaps, Melissa thought, I had better risk a drenching and go without my coat. She considered it unlikely that either June or Cy, being new here and having no outside friends, had got wind of this latest trouble which their cousin had brought on herself by her headstrong, don't-care ways. Of course everyone in the row knew about the wrecked boat, but not until yesterday had she herself known that Dot was connected with the accident. The man, Johnny, had been sent away. Everyone knew this, too, by now. What had shaken her, when she heard it yesterday from the lips of a Kitamaat woman working next to her on the cannery line, was that this Johnny had a girl by the name of Dot living with him as his woman.

Luckily the Kitamaat woman had no idea Dot was a relative. Dot had lived away from the village for years. The last time Matt travelled down to Rupert to plead with her to give up her careless ways, Dot had told him to forget it, that she would never go back to village life. "Not while I'm conscious," she had said, giving that husky, half-mocking laugh of hers. Right to her own father she had made a big thing of how little of their language she remembered.

Melissa decided to risk getting wet and go to the shacks without her coat. But at that moment Cy opened the door and came out.

"I was not asleep," he said. "I knew you were up." He looked down at her and she saw in his eyes that

same sad, determined expression which came to his
father's when there was some serious thing between
them. "I thought this was the day you would be going."

Melissa's heart beat faster and she drew in her lips,
pressing them together. He had on his hat and windbreaker and she knew why. "Some other time will be a
better time for you. This time it will be mostly women's
talk."

"We are a family. Would you have me stay away for
shame of her?"

Melissa shook her head, and her eyes, maternally
defensive, looked into him. The question was one his
father might have asked. "No, not for shame," she
answered.

"June does not know, and I will not be the one who
tells her. Is it for June you would have me stay away?"

"For June—and for you." But how could she tell
him? How, without hurting him, could she make him
understand the danger? Quite apart from the trouble,
Dot stood for a breaking with the old ways, and
Melissa was determined that Dot's influence should
not touch her children. Years ago when they were
small, when their father was alive, such a break had
almost occurred. But those days, with their love and
sorrow, were of the past and she must keep them so. Cy
was intent on coming, and since there was nothing she
could do to stop him, she stepped inside, a square, solid
figure, but light on her feet, and got her coat. "Very
well," she said. "We may be rebuffed but let us remember to be kind."

Because on Sundays the gillnet boats did not start
fishing until evening, more people were about than on
working days: men leaning on the rail, and girls and
fellows in their good clothes walking back and forth on

the gallery, talking and joking with one another. The door of Paul Leget's room was closed, but as Cy and his mother neared the end of the row they came upon Miriam. She had a large, spring salmon head in a pan, split ready for roasting, and was washing it under the tap.

"A fine, rich Sunday dinner you have there," Melissa greeted.

Miriam shook the water from her hands and straightened. "I did not see you coming," she said, smiling her slow, calm smile. Last evening at Victor's she told Cy that the native girls she worked beside spoke mostly English, and that she was trying to learn more of it. She used English now, but awkwardly and with an accent. She was shorter than June, but stronger, with filled-out shoulders from packing on the trail. Her hair was worn long and straight, native style, and to-day she had it tied behind with a red ribbon. Two Haida girls, wearing open-toed shoes, like June's, and with short, brightly-coloured coats around their shoulders, strolled past. Cy saw an amused look pass between them and he knew it was because of Miriam and her salmon head. He felt ashamed for her, and angry with himself for being ashamed.

Further on there was a plank walk up from the rear of the reduction plant. The walk had cleats, and steps at the steepest places. Above, the shacks seemed pressed into the hill-side in haphazard tiers. The Kitamaat woman had told Melissa which shack was Dot's. She knocked, and after a long wait they heard vigorous, striding footsteps and the door opened slightly.

"What's the idea?" Dot asked, seeing only Cy. "What do you want?" She kept her hand on the door, ready to close it.

Melissa stepped in front of Cy. "Do you not know me?"

Dot gave her a sharp look, then her face broke into a smile. Her features were heavy, like her father's and, like his, had in repose a sort of self-disparaging melancholy which gave her an aloof and rather striking appearance. "Melissa! Well, what do you know! Come on in."

Melissa wiped her feet and entered. Dot placed a chair for her, then pointed Cy to another against the wall. There was a double bed under the window and Dot sat on that with her forearms on her knees and her long hands dangling.

"Gee, it's good to see you," she said heartily. "I heard you came down and I've been meaning to look you up, but you know how it is. I ran into Fat Marie's girl, Bella, last day in Rupert. I was asking about Dad and everybody."

"Everyone is well," Melissa said.

"That's nice," Dot said. She leaned back across the bed and took a cigarette butt from the window-sill. "Sure has been a long time." She struck a match with her thumb nail, and took a deep pull on the cigarette.

"I was going to come this afternoon but instead I changed my mind and came this morning," Melissa said in Gitkshan. She smiled. "I did not think to find you up and dressed so early."

Dot lifted her head and laughed so that the gold in her front teeth sparkled moistly. "I was really on the ball this morning, Melissa. I got a wash out already." She pushed herself up from the bed and strode to the stove to dip water into the kettle and set it forward. She was tall and large-boned, with broad, flat hips and a loose way of holding herself.

"Now tell me about yourself," Dot asked, coming back to the bed. "What work they got you on, Melissa?"

"I am washing fish. The pay is less than for other work but Caleb did well to get me on."

"Washing fish, a woman with your experience? What's the matter with old Caleb? He can do better for you than that!"

"We came down late. He did the best he could for us."

"The old apple-polisher. Is he ever the good company man! But as long as you're satisfied." Dot pinched out her cigarette and lay back across the bed, resting on one elbow. "How about the kids? Did they get jobs?"

"Cy is at the boat shed with Paul Leget."

Dot glanced across at Cy and winked. "My old bigshot friend. How do you like it?"

"It's all right," Cy said.

"Well, don't let him ride you. I mind the time he—"

"June will start work to-morrow over on the white side," Melissa said quickly. "She will be working in a house."

"That'll be nice," Dot said. "She'll learn things. She always was a cute kid. It won't be long before she's out on her own. I wish you'd brought her along, Melissa."

"She was not up when we came away. She was to a party last night."

"Oh-oh!" Dot's laugh was rich, indolent. "Your troubles are just starting, Melissa." She looked up through the window at the scudding clouds and seemed to be studying them. "No girls for me, thank you."

There were a number of answers Melissa could have made to that, and some of them would have been acutely personal. Scarcely a man of Matt's age in the village who was not a grandfather many times over, nor an aunt much younger than she who had to be without little ones around her. They rarely spoke of it, she and Matt, but it need not have been had Dot not turned her back on her village.

"Mine's a boy," Dot said casually, after a heavy pause.

Cy took this for some sort of joke but he saw his mother staring.

"Sure." Dot reached and rubbed some steam off the window. "Didn't you know?"

"It is wrong to joke of such matters," Melissa said, stiffly.

"I'm not joking, Melissa. Lots of times I wish to God I was. He was on the way that time dad came looking for me in Rupert."

Cy watched his mother rub her hands slowly, one over the other. "We never knew that, Dot," she said, quite matter-of-factly. "We did not hear a word of it."

"Well, that's something. Nice to know not everything gets back to the village, not all the dirt." Dot got up and took Melissa by the hand. "He's in the back room if you want to take a look at him."

Dot opened an inner door and the three of them went in, Melissa with a caution which was almost stealthy. A cot stood where the shanty roof sloped down, and she bowed her head, not to avoid striking the rafters as Cy had to do, but rather with a sort of engrossed rapture.

The boy lay on his back with his arms uncovered, and he was beautiful. His face was toward them, a long face like his mother's and like Matt's, but delicate, with sweeping lashes resting on his cheeks. His body beneath the blanket seemed to Cy unnaturally large, for his existence was still unassimilated in Cy's mind and it was as if he had come into the room expecting to see a newly-born.

Melissa wiped her eyes and her tender, prideful smile made her look young again, Cy thought. Had the little boy not been beautiful it would have been the same to her. For here, within reach of her arms, was the first new life to come into the family since June's birth: not Dot's alone, but belonging to all of them, a continuing and a flooding forward.

Cy did not suppose Dot had been married white-style to any of the men she lived with, and if you went by a movie he saw this spring at the Junction, that was bad. There was this white girl who had a baby and her family felt disgraced by her. But among natives it was the mother who counted. It was the mother they traced descent by. The child belonged to the wide and enduring family group and crest, and if you believed in the native way, you need never be ashamed of any baby as those whites had been in the movie.

"It was not right to keep this from us," Melissa said, without reproach, as she returned to her chair. "Think of it! Had we not come we would not know of him, even yet."

Dot reached for a cigarette box on the bed, and finding it empty, she crossed in front of Cy and took a fresh one from the table drawer. "How did I know what you'd say?"

"You know us better than that," Melissa said gently.

"I wasn't thinking so much of you. Or of dad either. I was thinking of ones like Old Paul. You might as well know it, Melissa. The kid's half white."

"So? Well, you are not a white."

Dot gave a short laugh. "Hard to say what I am, eh, Cy?" She slit the seal of the package and offered him a cigarette.

Cy shook his head. "He looks like you. What do you call him?"

"Stevie. But don't run away with the idea I called him after his so-and-so of a father. I picked that name myself."

"What native name?" Melissa asked.

"Now, Melissa, what would he do with a native name?"

Melissa leaned back and folded her arms. "Everybody has a native name. That is the custom. You yourself have a native name."

"Have I, now?" Dot said lightly. But Cy noticed she did not say she had forgotten it. "Anyhow, he's bright. He's good company for me in a way, though of course I can't have him with me all the time. Last year I boarded him with a friend, the same one kept him for a while after he was born." She said that this fall or next, when Stevie was old enough, she would try to get him into the Indian residential school down south. Then, for the second time, she said she was glad he had not been a girl.

"Boys can make work for you, too," Melissa said. "Cy is a great help, but girls are easier in some ways."

"A girl's the last thing I want. I'm telling you, when I knew there was a baby on the way I was scared stiff it would turn out to be a girl."

"Why do you feel so?" Melissa asked.

Dot put her hands behind her and looked down at her aunt with sombre frankness. "I'd hate like the very hell to see any girl of mine go through what I've been through. With a boy it's not so bad. At least in some ways, the worst ways, it isn't. He can live in Rupert or the South and if his skin is thick enough he can take it being Indian. But look at me. I'm Indian all right, and I couldn't pass for anything else suppose I tried. That was fine so long as I was satisfied to be stuck on a reserve. But I wanted to have a little fun, nothing bad you understand, and what happens? Old Paul starts throwing his weight around. Cy knows how he is. He's the worst, but he's not the only one, and I just couldn't take it."

"Matt, your own father, is not one of those," Melissa argued.

"Let me finish," Dot insisted. "I've had all this bottled up inside me for a long time and now's my chance to spill it. I want you to listen to me, and I want you to tell my father how I feel. It's not his fault. Maybe it's not anybody's fault. Maybe it's because most of you are satisfied to keep on being just Indians and living like Indians. But why do you think I left up there?"

She knocked the ash off her cigarette with an angry snap of her fingers. "I'll tell you why I left, Melissa, and believe me there's no offence intended, because I like you and I always will. You'll find yourself up against the same thing with Cy here, and June, too, one of these days, so you better know. Smoking fish and living off the country may be all right for ones like you and dad because you like it and you don't know anything different. It may be all right for Cy and June, if you can keep them from knowing different. But you can't, Melissa. You just can't. You just can't keep standing in their way."

"I do not understand you," Melissa said, severely. "Why do you say I am standing in their way?"

"Because you are. You don't know it, but you are. Don't kid yourself. Young Indians aren't so dumb. They know the score."

Melissa turned on her chair and looked at Cy. "What does she mean? I do not understand what she is saying."

Cy tried to turn the slang terms into Gitkshan but could not. "She means we want to get ahead," he said, not taking his eyes off Dot. Her words, and the passion behind them, gave him a strange, exciting sense of release.

"I too want you to get ahead," Melissa said forthrightly. "I am a mother, I want the best for my children."

"That's what you think; that's what you honestly do think," Dot conceded. "But whether you like it or not, before long those kids are getting out from under. They're not going to live and die in the village. And before they do get out, it's up to you to let them know a few things. But instead of that you hold them back. You and the rest—"

"That is not true," Melissa objected. "I do not hold them back."

"You don't help them fit in, that's for sure. But please, Melissa, don't get sore. How about seeing it my way for a change? You take June and Cy. At school they hear some teacher telling them they've got to have good English. And what do you get at home? Gitkshan —and nothing but. At school they're taught about a whole world you old folks don't even know exists, and between the two they're pulled first one way and then the other. Like me. I was pretty bright in school, if I do say so myself. I had a teacher getting me all steamed up about getting out in the world and making good.

Well, I got out. And what happened to me I'd hate to have happen to June; and I honestly don't think it was all my fault. Let June go to the city and ask some white for a job behind the counter in some decent store, for instance."

Melissa picked at a spot of mud on her skirt. "Was that what you did?"

"It was only one of the things I did. I got the crazy idea of getting on as a telephone girl, but when they tested me they found I had an accent you could cut with a knife. Once in Vancouver I tried for a job in a nice tea room. I like shows, and I like good clothes, and I damn near cried my eyes out when I got turned down."

Dot tossed her burning cigarette to the floor and flattened it under her slipper. "This is for you, too, Cy," she said unexpectedly. "If ever you want to get out, you take it from me you've got to have your eyes open. Don't be like I was. Don't ever let them lead you to believe this country's falling over backwards to give an Indian a break, because it isn't. Any kid growing up in an Indian village has strikes against him from the start. I'm not saying you've got to be a regular ball-of-fire, but you've got to know white ways to get away with it. And if you're a girl you've got to have more in looks and education than a white girl can get by on. The Chinks will let you work in their cafés, and the second-class hotels will use you for a chambermaid."

Dot laughed, harshly. "Did I say use you? The guys that try to paw you round and get you into their rooms! If you're a native girl there is only one thing they want from you and they keep at you till they get it. Then comes the time when you figure you might as well get a little of your own back. And you do."

Dot looked down while she moved the flattened butt

back and forth with her toe. Cy thought she was finished, but she wasn't. She asked him to put a stick of wood in the stove, then she went on.

"I don't suppose I would have done so very different if I had known what I would be up against. Village life is like the dark ages and I want no part of it. I guess none of us can have it both ways and I'm telling you, Cy, that's a thing you better make up your mind about. If staying a stick Indian suits you, fine. But be sure you stay one. Don't try playing it both ways. If you want to make the grade you've got to fit in. Don't let the old people hold you back. If you do you'll find yourself on the outside looking in, like me. And one more thing. If June's got any big ideas, you tell her from me she's got to know the score. Because if you're just another native girl in any white man's town they sure have got you taped."

6

THAT NIGHT'S CATCH OF SALMON WAS SMALL AND AT noon the women left the cannery earlier than usual. Melissa returned to the row with Miriam and had the fire going and the meal ready to serve by the time the quitting whistle roused the echoes in the rocky bay. She went to the door and when she saw Cy striding along the gallery she was about to go in and make the tea when she saw Miriam come out as if to speak to him. She thought, as she often did, how well they looked together and how suited they were to each other. But Cy did not stop, and after he washed and came to the table she made bold to ask what the matter was.

Cy answered that nothing was the matter and kept on eating.

But Melissa saw into him too well to accept this. His nature was strong, like his father's, and several times since leaving the village she imagined she sensed in him the stirring of that forward-reaching restlessness which, at the end, had brought his father to disaster. "Is it the work, or is it something else?" she asked with singular gentleness.

"Oh, I don't know," he answered in English. "Maybe it's the work."

"Does the boss find fault with you?"

Cy helped himself to more of the boiled fish. "It's Old Paul."

"It is not to be expected you should feel at your ease in your work so soon. When we begin a work which is new to us we try the one who is teaching us. That goes the same for all, my young brother."

Cy did not want to discuss Old Paul—least of all with her—but whenever she used the affectionate form of address, calling him her young brother or June her young sister, she made it hard to go against her wishes. "That is not my meaning," he said, switching to Gitkshan.

"What then is your meaning? Does Paul speak to you harshly? His ways are fixed and he has a temper, that I know."

"It is how he feels about the whites. They get me between them. That causes me to make mistakes. He takes it I am always on his side. And I am not. Before them he is like a man behind a mask."

"Masks have their uses," Melissa observed.

Cy wiped his mouth and looked across at her in a way which had something of challenge in it. "I do not like it."

"You should be pleased, as I am pleased, that Paul wanted you instead of another. There is none better than Paul Leget with wood, and you must learn from him all you can. I would not have you go untrained."

"Yes, and there is another thing," Cy said angrily. "Dot came to the shed this morning to speak with me. Old Paul saw and he put a name to her."

Melissa pulled in her lips. "Paul goes too far."

"He goes too far in lots of ways," Cy declared.

"Paul Leget is in his years. Such men see deep." Melissa hesitated, but sooner or later the question must be asked. "Would you not say he has his reasons for putting the name?"

"He should not put such foulness on his tongue about her. If he were in his youth I would have struck him. He does not own Dot." Cy pushed his plate away from him. "And he does not own me either."

This talk was not shaping as Melissa wished, but it had gone too far to turn it. As had his father before him, he failed to realize—or if he realized he refused to accept—the fact that harsh words must be spoken and harsh things done if a village was to be kept whole and strong. Had not Dot herself cautioned him he could not have it both ways? He could not follow after the whites, or yield to them in things which mattered, and at the same time be one with his own people. His father had imagined he could change their village and its time-proven ways. His father had tried and had failed, and knowing he had failed, he had not only turned his back on it but had wanted her to do the same. Deeply though she loved Eli, she could not cut herself off from her village and become a woman apart. Countless times, in the procession of lonely nights and days after the wartime accident in the Prince Rupert shipyard, she had blamed herself for not yielding to her love and going with him where he went. But if she had, would not she and her children now be among the rootless ones on the fringes of that white man's town?

Fortunately for her, Cy's agitation passed and they allowed their silence to cover the threatened misunderstanding.

"Dot is going back to Rupert to-morrow," Cy said presently. "It was that she came to tell me of. The man, Johnny, has a job up there. He sent for her."

"I should have seen more of her while she was here," Melissa said. But she did not say she was sorry Dot was leaving. Secretly she felt relieved.

7

CY'S OUTSPOKENNESS ABOUT OLD PAUL WAS PROMPTED
not so much by any definable and conscious hostility
as by a sense of being invaded, an invasion which he
must at all costs resist. At the boat-shed their relationship might continue for days without any particular
tension; the old man was skilled at his work, and in his
blunt, uncompromising way he was an instructor that
a young man should be grateful to have over him. But
then would come some gruffness, some impatient
gesture or humiliating words of correction, which
caused Cy to feel he was being placed in an unfavourable light before the boss and the other white man. And
always in a thousand ways—some subtle, some down-
right belittling—Cy was made to feel that he was inten-
tionally being kept apart. Any man-to-man friendliness
between him and the two whites was resented, and,
without their knowing, he was later made to pay for it.

One such incident took place just before quitting
time. The second white man had paused in his work to
fill his pipe. He had come to the end of the bench where
Cy was, but as soon as they started to chat Old Paul
had ordered him in Gitkshan to stop talking and pay
attention to what he had been sent to do. "Tell him to
keep his shirt on, why don't you?" the man advised.

51

He got his pipe going, stood a moment, then went back across the shed. There had been similar incidents and they left Cy feeling resentful and insecure.

After the meal he went out and sat on the bench. He felt ashamed of his curtness when Miriam spoke to him as he passed her door. Old Paul was to blame for that. It was not her fault she had Old Paul for grandfather, but more and more he was seeing that by being put to work in the boat-shed he had been manoeuvred into a narrow place. It was like travelling the frozen *k'Shan* north to your trapping ground when you came on a place where the ice looked safe but the premonition seized you that it was not. If you were wise you backed off quickly and got your dogs and yourself on to solid ice and around by a different way.

He had some such premonition now. Miriam attracted him strongly and he was sure she was the one village girl not of his crest who was suited to his nature. Elora, Jonathan and Lala's daughter, had attracted him when he was younger, but she was of his crest and to feel toward her as he felt toward Miriam would be as shameful as sleeping with one's sister.

Toward the far end of the gallery he met Miriam.

"Too bad I was in such a hurry," he said, awkwardly. "Bert says the picture is a cowboy one, if you'd like to go." It was this she had come out to ask about.

"I would like," she said in English. "What time?"

"The second show. We'll have to go to-night. To-morrow it's white night, only for them."

Miriam asked if June would come.

"I don't know about her. She stays late over there some nights, talking with the Haneys."

"Bert does not like it when she stays. Last time she kept him waiting, but June says she likes it over there."

Miriam put her elbows on the rail and looked down. The sunshine reflected up from the water touched her throat and neck with golden light. The tide was low and on the rocky beach some crows were teasing a large white gull. From the woods a raven mimicked the crows, and she caught his eye and smiled.

The clothes she wore were her working ones: denims and a boy's blue shirt open at the neck and bleached from many washings. It seemed to him that, no matter what clothes she wore, Miriam was not changed by them as were June and the other girls. Always she was the same. Her sturdy shoulders drew the shirt tight and her arms, bare to the elbows, had a tapering strength and suppleness. Her blue-black hair was mostly hidden under her white head cloth. It made her rather broad face seem smaller and gave her a grave and mature appearance.

When Cy looked into the boat shed no one was there, so he hoisted himself on to the lumber pile outside and lay back with his shoulders against the higher part of the pile. Just then Dot's Stevie came along. His face looked thinner than when Cy saw him lying down. Also he was taller than Cy expected.

"I know who you are," Stevie said. "You're Cy. My mother told me. You saw me when I was asleep, didn't you?"

"That's right," Cy said. The little fellow spoke rapidly, like a white kid, with no trace of accent.

"Lift me up. I want to sit where you are."

Cy put down his hand. "Climb up, then."

"Not like that," Stevie said. "Lift me up. My back's sore. I fell out of a wagon."

Cy lifted him up. "No wagons around here."

"My own wagon. Johnny gave it to me for my birthday. In Rupert. We're going back to Rupert to-morrow. Did you know?"

"Your mother told me."

"Are you glad?"

"What for would I be glad?"

"Are you sorry?"

"Yes," Cy answered, "I'm sorry."

While they were talking, the boss went past. Cy saw him inside the shed, getting into his coveralls. Then he came to the doorway and motioned with his head for Cy to come.

"I'll wait for you," Stevie said.

"I've got to get to work." Cy got down off the pile and helped Stevie down. He felt in his pocket and held out a nickel. "For a cone," he said, and went into the shed.

The boss was over at the bench.

"Better watch your step, boy," he said. "The old man'll take it into his head you're after his job, showing up for work ahead of him." He brushed some shavings from a timber and motioned Cy to sit beside him. "Take a load off your feet. I want to talk to you."

Cy did as he was told, wondering what was coming.

"I take it Leget's a big shot where you come from," the boss went on. "A chief or something. Right?"

Cy nodded.

"Well, he best forget that old crap around here. Chief or no, he's working for wages, same's the rest of us. I'm in charge here, so anything you want to know all you got to do is ask."

"He tells me in our language," Cy said.

"Maybe he tells you more in your language than he has any call to. How about it, all his ki-yi-ing? What all does he talk about?"

Cy's throat felt dry. "About the work," he said. "He tells me what to do."

"He sure must find a lot to tell you. He sure must explain everything down to the last sixteenth of an inch. You mean to sit here and tell me that's all he talks about?"

"Mostly," Cy answered, uneasily.

"Look, boy," the boss told him, "I'm not doing this to make it harder for you; I'm doing it to make it easier for you. I've had natives under me in a lot of places, and I don't mean just your kind of native. South Africa, Burma, and et cetera, I never seen the native yet could put one over me for long. I've looked down a lot of necks in my time, black, yella *and* brown. I know what's been going on and you damn-well know I know. I know, don't I? What I'm getting at is, long as you work for me you got no need to let any native push you round. I don't care who he is, chief or no chief. This Leget, how big a chief is he? Is he a pretty big chief?"

Cy nodded, not looking up.

"I thought so. Well, I want you to get this and I want you to remember it. Us whites, we don't go in for chiefs. You don't have to let him bull-doze you while you're with me. As long as you keep doing your work like you been doing it, your job's safe as in God's hip pocket. Pay no attention to him; tell him go jump in the chuck. Another thing. You'd get ahead faster around here if your English was better. And to get it better you got to speak it instead of all this back-and-forth with old Leget. Take that young fella friend of yours, that Bert, him in the can loft. Know what I heard at table this noon? I heard he'll be upped to tallyman next week, and you know why? I'll tell you why. Because he's got good English. I bet if old Leget tried riding him, he'd tell him where he could put his chief stuff. And fast, too."

"I try to learn," Cy said. "I pick up words."

"Sure you do, when Leget gives you half a chance.
I've had my eye on you and there's not a lazy bone in
your body, that I'll say. But you got to remember
English is the language of this country. As long as
you're not at home in it you build a fence around yourself. Maybe that's what ones like Leget want. I
wouldn't know. But I figure it suits his book to keep
you young natives ignorant."

It seemed to Cy that the boss was not so much
condemning him as he was befriending him and taking
his side against Old Paul. His mother had not done
this. His uneasiness lessened and he felt a strange
excitement.

"You take my own people," the boss was saying,
"take my own father and mother. They didn't know
no more English than Billy-be-damned when they
landed in this country. But right off they got busy and
mastered it. They had ambition, see? They saw that
you need English to get ahead.

"Reason I'm talking like this is I'm a good union
man and I don't let it influence me about a person, the
colour of his skin. A man plays ball with me, I'll play
ball with him. You young bucks want to break away
from these old chiefs of yours. They hold you back."

Old Paul was at the door. "Down here at the canneries you pick up quite a bit of English every summer,"
the boss continued, plainly meaning Paul to hear, "but
soon as they get you herded back on to the reserves
they have you cluck-clucking like the rest. Your
language is old stuff now. It's dead. Forget it, boy.
Then soon as you're of age get yourself enfranchised;
get to be one-hundred-per-cent Canadian. That's the
only way you young Indians can expect to get ahead."

8

THE HANEYS' WAS THE FIRST WHITE HOUSE JUNE HAD
been in. At the start she felt strange, although with
the strangeness there was a stimulating feeling of
adventure. This feeling was heightened when Mrs.
Haney arranged for her to sleep on the glassed-in sun
porch at the side of the house. There was a cot and
some brightly-painted furniture, and Mrs. Haney gave
her some pretty material for curtains.

June could smile at her timidity now. When she and
Mrs. Haney were chatting while she went about the
now-familiar tasks of waxing floors or putting a wash
through the machine, she wished she could have
explained how she felt at first. It looked as if you gave
me those jobs just to show me up, she might have said.
What she did say, when Mrs. Haney asked her one
morning, was that she liked it here. "I'm glad I come,"
she said.

"Came," Mrs. Haney corrected. "You've a head on
you, June, and you're not one to be easily discouraged.
That's important for any of us who want to improve
ourselves."

Mrs. Haney often gave good advice such as this. She
was strict, but she went out of her way to encourage

57

you and she said she wanted any girl who worked for her to feel at home.

Another pleasing thing that came from living in the Haney house was having Cy notice how her English was improving.

"Guess what I did yesterday when I was through my work?" she asked him one Sunday afternoon as they stood in the crowd watching the steamer unload. "I ran Mrs. Haney's sewing machine. An electric. She helped me send away for material and a pattern. Patterns are hard to make out, but she showed me. The material is blue, copen blue they call it. It will look swell on me, I think."

It surprised him how rapidly she spoke and how easily she got the words out. Mrs. Haney must be teaching her every day. That was what their mother said, that Mrs. Haney was helping June with her talking all the time. If June could not think of the right word Mrs. Haney would tell her. She made June keep a book and write down the new words. She even made her practise them, over and over, while they were doing dishes. If June made a mistake, right in the middle of what she was saying, Mrs. Haney would make her go back and correct it. Mrs. Haney was all the time friendly to June, their mother said. She said that Mr. Haney was, too, and that he had been lamed, fighting in the war.

But then Cy knew that June had a way with people which he did not have, and even as a little girl she could find fun wherever she was. He believed she was happier since she took this job than she had been for months.

When the people and all the freight were off the steamer June asked Cy to come up and see her room. "Mrs. Haney said to bring you any time. She's met

Mama and now she wants to meet you. She says you understand a person better when you know their family."

"I don't think I better." He looked at his wristwatch. It was shiny new, with a wide, plastic clasp, and he had bought it out of his first pay. "I better get back. I got wood to split."

"Aw, you!" She gave him a slight push with her shoulder and laughed up at him. "There's nothing to be scared of."

He wanted to go, but, although there were no notices, Indians were not supposed to be on this side except on business. The movie house was on this side but that was as far as any of them went. Of an evening when they went up to the lake which gave the cannery electricity and water, they took a path behind the shacks and did not use the short-cut up the street where the whites lived. Even the dogs knew there was a boundary, and when an Indian's dog or a white person's dog crossed to the wrong side there would usually be a fight.

"Aw, Cy, come on. Mrs. Haney said." They were walking slowly toward the movie house and she took his arm.

But Cy held back.

"Don't be like that." She frowned. "For goodness sake!" It was just as Mrs. Haney said, one time when she was giving good advice on how to behave and talking about what she called the Indian problem. She said the mistake most native people made was thinking they were not as good as whites. Bert thought they were and now, thanks to Mrs. Haney, she did, too.

She wished she could make Cy see it was a mistake always to be conscious of the differences. Like Bert said, if you were Indian you had strikes enough against you, without acting as if you thought whites were better than you.

She released his arm. "I don't like people always wanting to be coaxed." She had been looking forward to showing him the pretty things Mrs. Haney let her use, and to having him see how thoroughly at home she was up there. "Are you coming or not?"

"If you want." Anything to make June happy. White side, Indian side. It worried him to realize the extent to which the differences were colouring his thinking. But why build a fence around himself, as the boss carpenter put it. He should be more like Victor, not think about it either way and enjoy himself as he went along. He did not want to be like Bert, who said things against whites which were unfair.

Cy knew which was the Haney house, but not until they went up the walk did he realize how nice a place it was. In fact, all the houses up here were nice. They had flower boxes at their windows, and the Haneys had a small plot of grass in front which June said she kept cut with a machine.

"It's not part of my job, but I do it anyhow," she explained. "It hurts Mr. Haney's leg to push. One day he brought me the swellest box of chocolates. He said it was my pay. He's nice."

She led Cy up the side steps and opened the glass door to her room. There were flower-boxes here, too, and the door and big windows had curtains with yellow birds on them. She made him take the easy chair while she showed him her bed and a table with three mirrors where she could sit and do her hair.

"I love this room," she said, fondly. "And look what else I have." She snapped on the shaded lamp at the head of the bed. "Some nights I lie here hours, looking at magazines and catalogues." She laughed, cozily. "I can see across the bay. The lights on the row are mostly out and I think of all you asleep in those old rooms and here I am like this, having a good time. Then when I get sleepy . . ." Without getting up, she turned off the lamp and smiled her warm, contented smile.

The bed had a pink cover and she smoothed it on both sides of her. "It's all right for Miriam and them, working on the fish, but I would not want that now, not for anything. Do you blame me?" Her hands caressed the soft, pink cloth.

He shook his head. She looked so pretty, her rich black hair and the brown of her face and arms set off by the tinted wall behind.

"But what about when you leave here?" He was thinking of the place in their house where she slept; her cot at the head of the stairs with magazine pictures pasted over the stained boards; their mother's bed on boxes at the far end close to the stovepipe hole, and the dog harness, snowshoes, and bunched nets hanging from the rafters.

"I'm not worrying," she said. "I'm happy now and that's the main thing." She rose and smoothed her skirt. "I'm going to tell Mrs. Haney you're here."

He wanted to call her back, but she was already past him and was closing the inner door behind her. He heard voices, then she came and beckoned.

After the strong sunlight on the porch the living-room seemed dim and he could not see Mrs. Haney's face until she came close.

"So this is June's big brother," she said, briskly. "June tells me you're rather shy, but you needn't be, not in *this* house." She led him to the couch and motioned him to sit down. "June's going to make us some tea. My husband will be home presently and then we're all going to sample the chocolate cake June made yesterday. It's getting to be one of her specialties."

Cy sat with his back straight and his feet drawn in. As June passed toward the kitchen, her confidence in this beautiful room made him proud of her.

"This is our first summer here, and I understand it's yours too," Mrs. Haney said. "Are you enjoying it? I mean, generally speaking, how do you find conditions?"

Cy was not sure what reply was expected of him but he said "All right." Mrs. Haney was a strong-looking woman with light brown hair. Her voice was vigorous. She told him they had been here since early spring. Cannery life was new to them but they found it interesting. She said it was "revealing". Then she asked about his village, what the country was like up there and how the people lived.

She piled the questions together, and he felt she was asking them more to make talk than for the answers. He had noticed this before with whites. They seemed to think two people could not feel at ease unless they talked back and forth all the time. She could get the answers from June any time, instead of piling them all on him.

"And how far did you go in school?" she asked. When she spoke to June her voice was different than when she spoke to him. To him she spoke louder and slower, as you do to a person who is hard of hearing or who is not very bright.

"Grade six," he told her. Then, knowing this was low by white standards, he tried to make it sound better by explaining that some years their school could not get a teacher, and also that, when he should have been going, his Uncle Matt took him to the trapping grounds.

"I quite understand."

"I wanted to go on—read books, speak good English. My father did." Her earnestness encouraged him.

"Of course you wanted to, and it wasn't your fault, none of it. Really," she said, as if to herself. "*Really*, I had no idea."

She rose. "This is something we must talk about. We certainly must. We'll talk about it later."

They were having tea when Mr. Haney came in. Cy had seen him several times in the store. His face was lean and would have been tired-looking except for his eyes, which were humorous and thoughtful.

"Hello", was all he said. He took his cup and a sandwich from the tray June passed to him and lay back in the armchair at the window. After taking a big bite and a swallow of his tea, he asked his wife to guess who came off the steamer. "Charlie Vipond. He's coming over."

"How nice. You haven't seen him since you got out of uniform, have you?. Whatever is he doing up here? I thought he'd gone back to selling insurance."

"Biscuits. Some firm or other." Mr. Haney held his sandwich in front of him and looked at it, before he took another bite. "You may not think it's so nice when you see him. He's pretty mellow."

Mrs. Haney set down her cup quickly. "Oh dear! Then we don't want him coming here. Not just now, not in *that* condition."

"It's my fault, I suppose. I told him where we live. He's gone to get a room, so perhaps he'll change his mind and have a spot of shut-eye." Mr. Haney grinned. "He could do with some sleep."

Mrs. Haney began stacking the empty plates. "I suggest you phone the hotel, Bob. Make some excuse; tell him to come this evening."

"You phone him." Mr. Haney motioned June to pass the cake. "Only I'm warning you he's got a talking jag on. That's how it hits him. He'll talk your leg off."

"Doesn't this sister of yours make good cake?" Mrs. Haney asked energetically. "Are you quite sure you won't have another piece?"

It was good cake but Cy said no. He did not understand all that was said, but he knew Mrs. Haney wanted him out of here. He let her take his cup and got to his feet.

"Why all the rush?" Mr. Haney asked.

"Don't urge Cy, if he feels he must be going," Mrs. Haney said. She wheeled the little table so he could pass. "Now you've broken the ice, I hope you'll come often, Cy. I'll find out more from June about that school of yours, and I want to talk to you about it, too."

Mr. Haney winked at June. "Once a teacher, always a teacher. So we're on that track again."

"Yes, we are. I've always been interested in the Indian problem and here is one aspect of it I can put my finger on."

Mr. Haney took a quick look out the window. "Here comes something else you can put your finger on." He hoisted himself from the chair and limped to the front door.

"It's *not*!" Mrs. Haney went to the window. "Bob, for heaven's sake, go out and talk to him. We simply do not want him inside."

Mr. Haney gave her an odd look. "I'm not so sure of that." The humour had left his eyes. "We hear a lot around this place about Indians not being able to carry their liquor. I'm for letting these kids see what a horse's neck a white makes of himself when he gets a few too many under his belt."

"Bob! What an attitude!"

"Well, some of these top-lofty Joes brown me off. You've heard them. Their wives, too." He opened the door and a man's thick voice drowned whatever else it was he said.

Mrs. Haney drew June to the back of the room.

The man was not as drunk as some Cy had seen, but just the same he was pretty drunk.

After the sunshine he could not see well and he bumped into Cy. He drew back with a puzzled frown, then he took Cy by the arm and turned him to the light. "Brother, I salute you," he said thickly, grabbing Cy's hand. "Unless these old eyes deceive me, you're Indian. Right?"

Cy tried to get his hand free.

"Friend to friend. Straight question deserves straight answer. You Indian? Yes or no?"

Cy wet his lips. "Indian."

The man was big, as tall as Cy, but heavy. He pulled Cy against him and flopped an arm across his shoulders. "All brothers under the skin. That's the way I look at it. That's the way you look at it?" He waved his other arm toward Mr. Haney, who was leaning on the back of his chair. Cy thought this was his chance to get away, but the man kept his arm around him. "Do I or do I not believe in brotherhood?" he wanted Mr. Haney to tell him. "Answer yes or no."

Mr. Haney said yes.

"Correct. Indubitably correct." The man turned

to Cy. "Spoken like a gentleman. Bob knows and I know. Some of the best men in the outfit were Indians like you. The original red man, of whom it has been truly said—"

"All right, Charlie, all right," Mr. Haney said.

The man bowed, swayed, and steadied himself. "I thank you. If I have offended, I apologize. Apologize profoundly. Spoken like a gentleman." He scowled. "What was I saying when I was so rudely interrupted?"

"Indians," Mr. Haney prompted. He gave Cy a straight, understanding look.

"That is correct. Lo, the poor Indian. Normandy, Holland, all the way. Good comrades, good soldiers. Fine body of men. Best in the world. The tumult and the shouting dies. What happens? The captains and the kings depart, anybody knows that. But to hell with them. My friend and my brother, here's what happens. They give their precious blood for Canada, the last full measure of devotion and all that crap. In Flanders fields the poppies gorge upon their blood. Heroes and gentlemen, every one." He waggled his finger under Cy's nose. "What does it get them? Does a grateful nation stop treating their sorrowing mothers and fathers like second-class citizens? It does not." He gripped Cy's shoulder. "You're Indian?"

Cy hesitated, nodded.

"Then what are we arguing about? You're Indian, anybody can see that. I can see it, you can see it, he can see it. *Amo, amas, amat.* Breathes there a man with soul so dead? Lo, the poor Indian, as our friend here so truly said. Blood, sweat, and tears. After me the deluge. Taxation without representation, if you know what I mean. There comes a tide in the affairs of men—"

"Cy," Mrs. Haney called sharply. "Your sister is waiting."

Mr. Haney got in front of the man and kept him talking and when Mrs. Haney left them at the side door, her lips were white. "It's disgraceful," she said. "It should never have happened."

At the gate June started giggling. "Boy! Was he ever loaded! Wait till I tell Bert!"

"What you want to tell Bert for?" But he knew what she meant. Any time a white was made to look foolish in front of natives, Bert got a kick out of it. He would hide it at the time, but later, when they were by themselves, he would ridicule the white.

"Why not?" June asked as they started down the sidewalk.

"You want to make Mrs. Haney look foolish?"

June stopped walking and stared at him. "For the love of Pete! I didn't say that."

"It sounded like that."

"What's the matter with you anyhow? She shrugged and walked on. "You make me sick."

"You go with Bert Silas too much. You go too much on what he says."

June walked faster. "I don't want to talk to you," she said with a toss of her head.

"It would be better if you got some other fellow. One like Jasper Gawa. You should let him be your fellow when you get home."

"You better mind your own business, Cy Pitt, that's what you better do." Tears of anger came to her eyes. "Jasper Gawa—that stick Indian. I don't tell you what girl to have, do I? You go too much on Miriam; you let Old Paul boss you. I don't get after you about her and you have no right to get after me. I know what I'm doing!"

"That's what you think." But his anger died and

suddenly he was afraid for her. Was this how it began with Dot years ago?

He tried to take her arm, but she pulled away. "I'm going to my room and don't you dare follow me." Then as a parting shot: "You should get some other girl, that's what you should do. One like Bella. At least she wouldn't hold you back, like Miriam does."

9

LATER CY WISHED HE HAD LEFT JASPER GAWA OUT OF IT. If June was still cross with him next time they met, he would take that back.

What he was not going to take back was what he had said against Bert Silas. It was so unlike June to say unkind things that he was sure some smart remark of Bert's was the cause of her slighting remarks about Miriam. Bert acted very friendly as long as a person did what he said, but when you opposed him he could say some pretty cutting things.

It is not Miriam's fault that she has little English, he thought one night as he sat at the table looking at a comic book Victor had passed on to him. June would be the same if she had to live with someone who discouraged her from learning it. Discouraged? This was much too mild a word. Paul had English enough when he needed it, yet in his presence Gitkshan only must be spoken. It was not that he forebade its use. He did not have to. All he did when you spoke to him in English was refuse to answer. He would ignore what you said, and you, too, with a contempt more stinging than any out-and-out prohibition.

The boss carpenter's friendly talk about the advantage of good English, and Bert's being promoted to

69

tallyman, showed what a native person could do if given a chance. And the more Cy thought about this, the nearer he came to believing that it was not so much the whites as ones like Old Paul who were holding back the young. Let Old Paul stick to Gitkshan if he wants to, he thought defiantly, but he has no right to keep Miriam from learning.

Melissa had gone to bed an hour ago. He put away the comic book and turned out the light, thinking of Miriam, and of how it would be if their friendship kept growing until something binding happened between them.

If I could get her away from Old Paul, it could happen right now, to-night, and I would be glad, he thought with yearning. But what chance had he of ever getting her away?

Below the doorway, the lights of the next building scrawled their reflections on black water. A tanker across at the main wharf was unloading. He heard the whine of its electric winches slit the velvet hush of the bay. Unless I am going to give in to Old Paul all my life, I must stay away from her, he warned himself. After they came together it would be too late. The thought gave him a desolate feeling and made him want her the more.

Two girls idled past, their arms around each other's waists. Their English sounded so natural that he would have taken them for whites, except that there was no trace of the nasal harshness which the speech of many white women had to native ears.

Resentment brought him to his feet. They could go anywhere, those two—on the train and steamer and to Prince Rupert—and not draw attention to themselves. By their speech you would never know. But see what

Old Paul had done to Miriam, so that her tongue sounded thick. Some of the English sounds, most noticably the "th" and "sh" ones, she could not make at all!

When the girls moved on, he went out and stood with his large angular hands gripping the rail. He was thinking of his last talk with Dot, the evening before she and Stevie left for Prince Rupert, when he and Melissa went to the shacks to say good-bye. Dot spoke even better English than those two girls, and Stevie, young as he was, was so at home in it that no one would know his mother was Indian.

"It's the only language he hears, that's the reason," Dot had explained. And when Melissa scolded her for that in a friendly way, Dot told her not to worry. "I'm not like some; I'm not dead against him knowing native. But when you get right down to it, where's the sense?"

"I like my children to have English too," Melissa argued. "But not to know their own language, that is doing them a wrong, my sister."

"For my money I don't see it. Look at it this way. It's not as though a person could write it or read it. Besides, if you're talking English all the time and then go back to native, you make slips and your own people laugh at you. That's why I think unless a person is going to stay cooped up on a reserve for the rest of their natural, it's better to forget the whole business. Take me. Long after I stopped speaking Gitkshan, I would find I was still thinking in it. Even thinking in it holds a person back, believe me."

Thinking in Gitkshan. He and Miriam did that all the time. Even in their thinking they were, as the boss said, building a fence around themselves.

As the days passed, Cy noticed that he was often

called from helping Paul and told to lend a hand with other work.

It encouraged him when the boss trusted him to get a new strake or fender strip out of the steam box and handle the clamps, working swiftly, as Paul had taught him he must do, to bend the piece into place before it cooled. It had been a busy week, and on Saturday forenoon, with the ways clear, a cannery collecting boat was hauled up to have a new skeg fitted. This was a rush job; Cy was under the stern cutting away the drift bolts with a hack saw when the boss shouted from the bench for him to come.

Cy untangled his legs from the cross braces of the cradle, and when he got to the bench he saw Paul and the boss facing one another.

"He claims he can't understand what I want done. He wants to wait and use the old piece for a pattern; but the hell with that. We got net guards to put on a couple of boats from the south, after this one, and they got to be ready by to-morrow night. Tell him that. Tell him does he want us to get behind." The boss was mad.

Cy knew that Old Paul understood well enough. He avoided the white man's eyes. "I think he knows."

"I damn well know he knows, but go ahead and tell him anyhow. I'll show the old coot he better not come that dumb native stuff with me."

Cy glanced at Paul. His eyes were veiled, his face stiff, his jaw clamped so that the creases at the corners of his mouth showed outside his scraggly moustache.

"You know all he said, do you not?" Cy muttered, wanting to get away, get under the boat, stay out of this.

Old Paul spoke. "The thing he wants done is a

stupid thing. It will not save the time he says." He
stood with his long arms slightly bent and drawn back,
in a position which could be taken as either hostile or
mockingly submissive. "He is a stupid, low-class
person. You are into your manhood and should be
able to know that the mere fitting of a piece of wood is
not his reason. He wants to humble me and he is using
you to do it."

"Who's doing the talking around here, you or me?"
the boss shouted. "What's all the song and dance about
this time? Let's have it."

Cy felt the boss was testing him. He scuffled one
foot in the chips. "Nothing much."

The boss banged his fist on the bench. "I've had
enough of him standing there, looking like the wrath
of God. I'll rub his nose in it, that's what I'll do."

A tremulous feeling took hold of Cy. His heart was
thumping and he kept looking at the chips. He says
you are a stupid low-class person, he says you do not
know your job. How would that sound in English?
Here was his chance to defy the old man, and he was
disgusted with himself because he did not seize it. What
was the matter with him? Where was his courage?
"You know it would go badly with you if I told the
gum-see-wa what you said," he muttered in Gitkshan.

"Have I forbidden you to repeat it?"

It was maddening to see Leget so confident of his
authority over him. Leget could not conceive that any
young person would challenge him, least of all one he
meant to have as son. This is your time to stand up to
him, Cy was thinking; this is the chance you have been
waiting for. The thought was a smashing, liberating
weapon, yet here he stood lacking the resolution to use
it. He felt trapped between their opposing wills.

"You taking your orders from him or me?" the boss asked icily. "Make up your mind."

But the degrading part was that he could not make up his mind and knew he could not. He resented Paul but knew with absolute certainty where he stood with him. Paul would never change. In his hatred of whites, in his determination to dominate, in his adherence to tradition, in nothing would he change, and to that extent he could be trusted.

But where did he stand with this white and how far could he be trusted? *Once an Indian always an Indian . . . Not a lazy bone in your body . . . Shiftless . . . I'm doing this to make it easier for you . . . Look at the way they live.* . . . Shame at white condemnation and yearning for white approval were struggling for first place in his mind.

Deliberate thought became impossible. Instances of white approval eddied to the surface of his mind, then sank out of reach in a welter of uncertainty. In their place, Paul's unwavering belief in Indian superiority rose and offered him back his self-respect. "He knows what you said," he told the boss.

"Well tell him again, see he gets it into his thick head."

Cy approximated the instructions in Gitkshan and Paul grunted the word to tell he understood.

"He knows," Cy said.

The boss slapped his rule against his leg. "Then get on with it. Not you," he said sharply as Cy started back. He waited until Paul was out of sight on the far side of the hull, then he put his face close to Cy's and spoke from the corner of his mouth. "You know damn well you didn't translate all he said," he accused. "Not the half of it. He was sounding off about me, wasn't he?"

Cy wet his lips. "I don't know."

The blue eyes became chilling. "What all did he say? Out with it."

"I don't know," Cy answered obstinately, without a trace of expression.

"I give up," the boss spoke with disgust. "Here I offer you the chance to get some of your own back but you just haven't got the guts to take it. What a hope! But if that's the way you want it—" He pointed with his rule to the stern of the boat. "Get on with it."

Cy stayed out of his way for the rest of the morning. He thought the noon whistle would never blow and when he left the shed he wished he did not have to come back, ever. He wished he could send word he was sick, or could just not show up for work, like an Indian who has the name of being unreliable. Bringing the boss's disgust down on himself had not just happened. Paul had planned it to find out what he would do. Well, now the old man knew and Cy knew if he went on working in the shed there would be other humiliating scenes, each leaving him feeling more degraded and insecure.

I have to get away, he thought, I have to. For if I let myself go farther with Miriam, and the arrangement is made, I will lose what is left of my self-respect, and surrender my very manhood.

10

STRICTLY SPEAKING NEITHER CALEB NOR ANY ONE ELSE
was allowed to operate a store on cannery property.
However, Caleb's status with the company was no
ordinary one. Frequently a native man tried to benefit
himself by going over to one of the rival canneries,
providing, of course, that he could pay up his store
bill, but both now and in his active years Caleb had
remained loyal, and his name stood high with the
company. The workers whom he, as hiring man,
selected gave the manager very little trouble and
Caleb saw to it that any disagreements which arose
were smoothed out in a manner which usually satisfied
his village's people and which certainly left the manager
with very little to complain about. And so in the course
of the years, though not officially, Caleb was allowed to
have his store.

To look at, this pleasant little enterprise was not
imposing. It consisted of a few shelves along the side
wall of his and Nettie's lower room, a set of scales which
he brought down each season from the somewhat larger
establishment he conducted in the village, and an
untidy array of cartons and tin boxes on the floor. But
the good will that went with it was extraordinary. Few
people along the row would think of walking as far as the

company store when, about to sit down to a meal, they found they were short of something Caleb sold. Also they liked to drop in at Caleb's for an evening's chat, or for candy or tobacco.

And Caleb liked having them come. His failing eyesight, and the puffiness in his feet which came from walking, prevented him from getting out among the people as he used to. Having the people come to the store kept him in touch with happenings and trends along the row—and over at the shacks, too, as Dot realized by the time she left. Without people dropping in for pilot bread and biscuits, cornflakes, and flashlight batteries, and the children wanting candy bars and bubble gum, he would not have been able to glean those bits of news and gossip which, when pieced together by a man of his discernment, kept him extremely well-informed of what was happening, or about to happen, among the native employees. It was never suggested, except by the occasional malcontent, that any stories confided to Caleb reached the manager's ears, and yet it was remarkable how often a legitimate cause for complaint was removed soon after Caleb came to hear of it.

How he saw to these and other matters was Caleb's secret. "I make a few dollars; I help the people," he would explain. Oolichan grease from the coast villages was exchanged for the up-river people's dried soap-berries or beaded moose-hide, Melissa being the only one who still persisted in doing her own trading. Island people brought their dried halibut and seaweed for Caleb to buy outright or handle on commission, and from these he was able also to secure at times some of the cockles, dried and smoked on little pointed sticks, as a special treat for up-river people. These and the other native delicacies, as well as the sale of packaged, white man's food, kept the people coming, and the baking-powder tin under the mattress filled with silver and bills, and, equally rewarding, kept Caleb floating in the full, deep stream of native life.

The people came; they bought; they told him things. But in listening to their talk he did not jump to conclusions. However, by a broad, sure stroke here, a judicious toning down there, and by enlarging or diminishing what he heard according to the reputation for veracity—or lack of it—among his many informants, Caleb was able in most cases to build up a remarkably accurate picture of how the wind was setting.

Among the rumours which reached him in mid-August was one which, if true, would call for careful handling. In spite of Paul's wish, and Nettie's having Melissa to dinner so the two young people would be thrown together during the noon hour, little had come as yet of the arrangement concerning Miriam and Cy. In fact, as long as two weeks ago, Victor hinted that Cy was looking for other work; any work, providing it took him away from Paul.

This must be kept from Paul's ears, for it would not make for harmony between the houses. More recently it was indicated things had come to such a state that Cy was thinking of quitting the cannery altogether if he did not get a transfer. This would be unfortunate for all concerned. But it could not be ruled out, for the young man had a mind of his own, and Caleb had hoped that when the sockeye season ended, and the cannery went on to fall fish, a transfer could be arranged, with Paul left none the wiser, of course. Unfortunately, it had become evident to-day that this was not to be.

That evening, when Cy came to the tap, Caleb invited him inside.

"The manager was here this afternoon," Caleb said, after he covered his purpose with small talk. "Usually at the end of sockeye fishing we may expect changes. The lazy ones are sent away, the good ones asked to stay for the fall work. You will be pleased to learn that all our people will continue working. This speaks well for our village. It makes my heart strong."

Having provided the opening, Caleb hoped his young brother would take advantage of it. There were other canneries, and worse still, at this season there was always work for such a strong young man in Rupert. Going to a rival cannery would be bad enough, but to Rupert would be worst of all. Many a promising young man, and woman, too, had been held by the flesh pots of that town, and village life had been weakened by it. No discontent must make the village lose this young man to Rupert, for Caleb had a secret hope that, if it were the Lord's will, there was a village need which Cy would one day fill . . .

When Cy did not speak, Caleb cleared his throat and felt under the bed for the can; not the large one which crabapples came in, but the small one which Nettie fixed with paper, for spitting. In a month or so they all would be going home, the village would be gathered in, and already he was beginning to be troubled about the church.

In the old, old days, the first native lay preachers that Mr. Lloyd raised up trained younger ones, and Eli, Cy's father, had been one of those who followed in the steps of the first preachers. Even away in Rupert, Eli had remained strong for the church. At the start of the summer he had dared to hope that Bert Silas would prove to be the one, but a few chats with that young man had shown that the Lord's hand was not on him, for all Bert's good English. He had no certainty that Cy would be either, but he was steady and willing, still pliant and possible to mould. This discontent must not be allowed to grow until it diverted him from the continuing stream of village life.

Caleb felt for Cy's shoulder and placed his hand on it. The time had come for open dealing. "It has reached me you are not satisfied with your present work. Has the talk been twisted in the telling, or am I to believe it?"

"You are to believe it."

"I did believe it and I have tried to place you else-where, but the luck has gone against me. It will not be for long. Promise me you will make the best of it."

"I promise nothing." Cy took the pail and went outside, but after filling it he looked in the door. "It is not your fault," he said. "It is Paul's fault and I have had all of him that I can bear."

Cy took the pail to their room and felt relief that his mother was not there. The pan of salmon heads, split and baked, that she had taken from the oven after supper, was missing, and he concluded she had gone to share the treat with Victor's people. Victor and Bert were at the early show. It would be out soon and he did not want to talk to them or to anyone else. He wanted to be alone, to walk and keep on walking until it came to him what he must do.

Passing the cannery building he stopped to watch a big seine boat being emptied of its catch. Most were chum salmon, hook nosed, dark of belly and soon to spawn, but the cohoes among them were fine, fresh-run fish. Watching them going up the conveyor to the bins, he supposed that by now the cohoes would be running strong in the river at home.

In spite of his disappointment, he did not agree with

Dot that Caleb was afraid to go against the company; but it seemed strange that, with all the cannery jobs, a different one could not be found for him. The few times he had been in the cannery he had noticed that by no means all the jobs there were done by women. There were men sorting in the bins and tending the machines which gutted and washed the fish and keeping an eye on the conveyor belts which took the filled cans to the ovens and later to the big labelling machine; men running the stapling machine where the tins were boxed, and other men in the shed where the boxes were stored until the steamer took them south.

Victor was helper on the stapling machine since they moved him from the can loft. Fellows being moved and never having to ask, but only the boat shed for him, right to the finish. As Cy passed the shacks and started up the trail to the lake, he was positive Paul had told Caleb he must stay. Well, Old Paul would soon find out he was mistaken if he thought he could use Miriam to hold him.

Miriam had been brought up by Old Paul since she lost her parents. She never seemed aware of his domination, or, if she was, to object to it. June, no doubt repeating some jibe of Bert's, spoke as if Miriam lacked spirit. But this was not a fair thing to say. June would be submissive, too, were she in Miriam's place. Even the slightest move toward independence would take great courage for everything about Paul Leget, not least his silence, showed how sure he was of his authority. Left to herself, would Miriam ever realize this domination, or be able to get free of it?

After the heat of the bay it felt cool under the cedars and, as Cy was nearing the lake, he heard the voices of girls. He stepped aside to let them pass. Some carried pails and others the proper native berry-picking baskets. Miriam was among them.

"I thought you were going to the show with Victor," Miriam said. The other girls kept hurrying down the trail, laughing and calling out, apparently not noticing she had dropped behind.

"I said I might, but I did not care to go." He tilted her spruce-root basket and looked into it. "Not many."

"The bushes are mostly leaves; different from at home." She smoothed back her hair. "Nobody's at the lake. Are you going on up?"

He pretended he was undecided. "I was only going for a walk."

The great cedars made a roof over the path. Clumps of fern as tall as a man narrowed it and Cy let Miriam walk ahead of him. She did not hurry. "I hope the girls don't go around saying a bear has got me," she said, smiling at him over her shoulder. "But I don't think they will. They know about you."

It excited him in a peculiarly gentle way, noticing how her English was improving since she had been moved from among the older women to work beside coast girls. They called this work "patching". It was to make up the weight of filled tins as they passed her on the conveyor, and to do it a person must be quick to know in a second what size piece of fish was needed. Only the more alert girls were put on this job, and when the forewoman picked Miriam, his mother said that showed how well the company thought of her. Yes, he thought, and it shows how quickly she can learn English, or anything else, once she gets the chance.

Following her and watching the erect, supple movement of her body, he hoped she would say more of what the girls knew. They must know how it was between them, for they did not wait or tease her.

He knew from the movies that when a white girl felt ready to yield to a fellow it was done differently than among his people. For one thing, when the two first met, bumping together in a doorway or at a drinking party, they would never have seen one another before, whereas in the village all the girls and fellows had known one another since they were babies. Also the white girls acted more like Bella. A white girl led the fellow on, then pretended she did not care for him and went off with some other fellow until almost the end, although it was plain all the time that the first fellow was the one she wanted.

Such girls as Bella would not be ruled by the native way but they would not let the proper white way rule them either. But these, as speakers at marriage feasts frequently pointed out, were froth. That was what they called them—froth. Of course not all white girls were froth. The last teacher told the girls in school that, a long time before, a girl should sew and lay away things for the house against the time when she was, as the teacher called it, "decently married". That teacher was all against the native way and she let you know it.

By now they were at the flat rock where the trail passed above the falls out of the lake. Miriam went to her knees and looked at the churning water in the pool directly below. She said something to him but the noise of the falls kept him from hearing.

He stood beside her, looking down. The noise was louder here, an enclosed, hollow sound, and the foam very white between the rocks. Miriam shrank back and touched his knee, warning him away from the edge.

She looked solid and small and beautiful in his eyes. An upward puff of air lifted the ends of her hair. He saw the rounded strength of her neck and shoulders and the outline of her breasts, tight and alive beneath her thin dress.

A surge of glorious assertiveness swept over him. They were alone up here, the arrangement could be made, so why should they not begin this that was between them? Instantly his lonely discontent was obscured by desire, and what he wanted most was immediate and real. For all he knew this was what she wanted most, too, this instant.

With tremendous effort, like a pouncing and a grappling within him, he choked the imagining. He dared not imagine, for it would be degrading to act as though he thought her froth.

They were still on the edge of the rock, on the edge of this consummation, too, and she must have known it, for she rose and went quickly down the trail.

Miriam was out of sight before he permitted himself to follow. What was in his mind must have been in her mind, too, and already a loyalty and pride in her was taking away some of the willed, constraining pain of the denial. Let Bert shoot off his mouth and June stay on the white side if that was what she wanted, but what had almost happened at the rock carried more conviction than anything they could say. His longing for Miriam was a delicious, enfolding fire in his body, making him feel uplifted and sure of himself again. What did Old Paul matter compared to being sure?

He was running now, driven by his longing for her and knowing she would be waiting. She was standing, her back to him, looking at some ferns, and they walked down in silence for a little. When the trail widened he walked beside her. They walked slowly and he hoped she felt as he did, not wanting to go home.

"We can go to the show if you like," he suggested. "The second one will be on soon."

She considered, then shook her head. "I told grandfather what time I would be back."

He broke off an alder switch and began tapping it against his leg and whipping off overhanging fern fronds with it. Had she denied him herself or had the old man made her promise, he wondered. But the intensity of those soaring moments remained, and he meant to keep his thoughts of Paul from clouding them.

"Caleb called me in after supper," he said. "All our people will be asked to stay."

"Two of those girls, Naas river ones, were not asked. It is their last week. They got told to-day." They were within sight of the cannery, and the lighted windows of the row showed through the treetops. "Are you glad all of us are staying?"

Something in her tone made him suspect she knew he had asked for a transfer. "It will give us more money," he answered, "but I will be glad to be home."

Miriam nodded, gravely, "I know. Grandfather told me the boss all the time makes trouble for you."

He tossed away the switch. "I do not want to talk about it."

"All right, but that is what grandfather says."

He knew Paul would have twisted things, and that his reluctance to give his side of the trouble was placing him in an unfavourable light. "Did your grandfather tell you why the boss got mad at me?" he asked, abruptly.

"Because you're Indian. He gets mad at grandfather, too."

"Both of them make it hard for me, and I do not want to talk about it." These moments were being spoiled, and Cy felt cheated.

"The boss makes you ashamed of being Indian."

"Who says I am ashamed?"

"Grandfather says you are ashamed, and sometimes I think you are ashamed." Then with a tenderness which struck him to the heart, and using his native name: "You must not be ashamed."

"You make a big mistake to think I am ashamed. Do not talk foolish." His voice hardened and he began speaking wildly against all whites.

She caught his hand and held it. "Grandfather only wants to help you, but you will not let him help you."

"Help me?" He stared at her.

"He says you would go over to the white side if he did not hold you."

White side, Indian side—the clear, uplifting promise of the moment gone, misunderstanding rising between them, and all because of an uncertainty which had scarcely entered his head until this summer.

"I am not his slave. I will not have him saying what I am to do." His mouth was working, spitting the words with explosive force. "All must put knees to ground to him, but I will not. He will see."

Miriam drew away. "You are one of those who weaken themselves by trying to go two ways."

"I will not go his way; I will go my own way."

"But your way is the Indian way. Do you think you can be two persons and follow both?"

"Why do you let him fill you up with lies about me?"

"Think what you are saying," she warned. Her eyes flashed. He had never seen her angry before.

"So I am weak, am I? Is that a lie or not? Tell me what you think," he demanded. "I stand here waiting for your answer."

"I will tell you this. You have been bending before that white man but you will not bend to what grandfather knows is right." She stood proudly. "I will tell you something else. I could never give myself to a person who turns his back on his village and who acts ashamed."

She pushed past him. He wanted to follow her but he held himself and when he reached the shacks he caught sight of her passing under the flood lights at the conveyor. She was running.

11

TIME AFTER TIME DURING THE NIGHT CY TOLD HIMSELF
he was not going to show his face at work that morning.
If Miriam's parting words meant that their intimacy
was ended, Old Paul's hold on him was ended, too. I
have money enough, he thought, as he lay on his bunk
in the dark. There is a steamer this afternoon. I will
pack my things and go to Rupert, and if I cannot get
work there I will go home.

If it was over it was over, and ones like Bert and Dot
would say it was better over. As long as it went on
there would be involvement and humiliating com-
promises. Once they came together, his love for Miriam
would cause him to make one surrender after another
until he was confronted with one he could never make.
A break then would be a thousand times worse than
now, for to lose her after having had her would be
torture.

June's retort that Miriam would hold him back still
smarted, yet if only he could quell his desire he would
see the truth in it. But each time his thoughts dwelt on
that moment of withholding, up there on the waterfall
trail, he wavered. Until that moment possessing Miriam
had been a wish, languorous, dream-like, blurred and
warm behind a curtain of postponement. But no longer.
The welcoming readiness he had sensed in her, the urge

to comply which prompted her flight, and her shy waiting a short way down the trail, gave consuming immediacy to the wish and made him positive she shared it. Then Old Paul had come between them.

At breakfast he scarcely spoke, leaving Melissa to make what she could of his silence. She was usually among the first to get to the cannery, and almost as soon as she was out of the room he went to the gallery, hoping to see Miriam before she was lost to view among the hurrying groups of women. That was the craziest thing I ever heard, me ashamed of being Indian, he imagined himself telling her.

And until this summer it would have been the truth. Until this summer the differences between Indians and whites had not greatly affected him. All his life he had been more or less aware that some native ways did not make sense to whites, any more than some white ways made sense to Indians. But here he saw the balance constantly upset. An Indian had to ask the whites for a job or a chance to fish, but what did a white need to ask an Indian for? What had Indians to confer or withhold?

Bert told of eating places and hotels in Rupert where Indians did not feel free to go, of storekeepers who attended to a white woman first and made an Indian woman wait. But Cy refused to believe his father had ever found it so. His father had not allowed chiefs like Paul Leget to hold him back. His father had learned to fit in, as Dot had warned Cy he must do.

Cy wished now, that in spite of Paul's low opinion of Dot, he had told Miriam this. If he had, then she could not have accused him of wanting to go over to the white side in everything. But a person was foolish to turn his back on white ways which could help him.

Yet even here, with many whites around, Miriam held herself intact. She was as sure of herself as his mother was, and as he had been before he left the village. He needed her! Without her, the life he wanted for himself would be an empty thing. He must make her see that because he would not bend to her grandfather in everything he had not turned against his people.

That day, puttying seams in a gillnet boat as Paul caulked them, Cy wondered if Miriam had told of their quarrel. But throughout the day, nothing in the old man's words or bearing indicated that he knew.

After work, Cy returned to the room by the gallery on Caleb's side of the row in the hope that Caleb had word of a transfer. But customers kept coming, and after waiting outside in the rain awhile, he went on.

As he took his place at the table, Melissa set his plate of good fat stew before him and remarked she had felt cold all day. "At work the coast women joked me about it. They said the blood of up-river people must be thin."

"What did you say?"

"Oh, I joked them back. I told them I am not a seal. This damp gets in my bones; I do not like it." Melissa came from the stove with her plate, and her moose-hide slippers made a soft, home-like sound on the rough floor.

"I do not like it here, either," Cy said.

"The rain is the cause. We people miss the sun."

"I have had my fill of it here." He thought of the dry, autumnal warmth of their groundhog-snaring meadows with the heather brown between the rocks. "We should go home."

"Only a few weeks more," Melissa encouraged. "The money comes in; the days pass quickly."

"Already the fattening snow is on the peaks. We have money enough and there is much to do before cold weather."

"You are thinking too much of home, my brother. Also you know Caleb told the manager we would stay."

"I say we should go." Cy spoke bluntly. "Frost may be early. We may lose our potatoes. We can finish out the week and leave on the steamer, Saturday."

"And find ourselves named with the shiftless ones? The manager counts on us to stay."

"Why should we put ourselves out for him?" Merely naming Saturday as the day gave a feeling of purpose, of release.

Melissa was aware of a smouldering here which it would do harm to fan. Life was becoming no easier for the young, in spite of higher pay and much talk of better education. "It is not a question of staying to please the manager," she said. "We stay to please ourselves."

Cy went to the stove for more stew. "The work is too wet for you," he said, as he continued eating.

"Tomorrow I will wear more clothing."

"If you get the cold-sick you would have to stay in bed. Where will all this money go if you fall sick?"

Melissa's chuckle made her gold earrings twinkle in the light. "I do not get sick; I am not the sickly kind." She sat back, fingering the rim of her empty plate and watching his face, which was bent over his food. "Something has gone against you, my young brother," she said, persuasively. "Would you now care to tell me what it is?"

"Nothing. Nothing at all." He kept on eating. "I am merely saying what I think is best."

"We wish to return here next season, do we not? We have done our work, given no trouble. We are not drinking people and our names stand well before the company. Will you, because of a twinge of home-sickness, throw that away?"

Before he could think of a convincing answer, June entered.

"Hello, everybody," she said cheerily, taking off her raincoat and hanging it on the back of the door. The coat was new, one of the blue plastic ones Cy had noticed in the cannery store.

"You're some guy, you are," she told him. "When you're at the store you should ask for mail. Look at this letter. It's been in the post office for a week. It's a good thing Mr. Haney saw it and brought it to the house."

The only mail Cy ever got were circulars from fur buyers, telling him fur prices were sure to go up and that all trappers should go out and make big money; these, and a farm weekly some fellow at the Junction talked him into taking. "It is nothing much, I guess," he said, holding out his hand. "Let's have it."

"It's not for you," June said. This was their first meeting since the Sunday at the Haneys, and she sounded a little cross. "It's for Mama, from Fat Marie."

"What has Marie to say to me?" Melissa asked, quickly. "Has she made herself more trouble?"

"Nothing like that. She's back in the village. I read it before I came over." Then because Mrs. Haney said it was not polite to read another person's mail, even though native people saw no harm in it, she went on to say she knew it was all right to open this letter because she or Cy would have to read it out anyway.

Melissa put her hands inside her apron. She was wary of letters. Few came to her, and those which did brought bad news more often than good: somebody far gone with T.B. in the Indian hospital at Miller Bay outside Prince Rupert and pleading to be brought home; papers from the government which must be taken to the Agent's office to have explained—usually a string of big words which threatened you because you had not paid this thing they called the Income Tax. On the other hand there were the monthly letters with family allowance cheques, but these would stop next month when June became sixteen. All in all, letters were not a good thing, and as she saw June spread the sheet of paper on the table oilcloth she prepared herself to hear that Marie was in home-brew trouble again and wanted her to pay the fine.

Melissa drew in her lips. "Start to read. I am ready for it."

June burst out laughing. "Gee, Mama, no need to be scared. Wait till you hear." She began reading:

> Dear Friend, thought I drop you a line to say hello. You be surprised I home so soon but that alright because I here to help Matt till you get here.
>
> Matt got Dot's boy with him, Stevie his name and going to live with you and Matt looks like. He playing very hard and to beat the band so like it here I guess.
>
> The way it happen this way. Dot come out in taxi to Angus and in some kind trouble so hard to have the boy with her all the time, the place she living with that fellow closed by the police and they going to Vancouver. But not for Stevie so she ask me take him to Matt and I do. They living your house eating my house, Stevie eat much as bird so not hard to cook for ha-ha. Well that all I got to say so will ring off till you get here. Keep smiling from Friend Marie.

Melissa eyed the letter as she would a person trying to trick her. "Tell me again what it says. Turn it into our language. I understand you better."

June was finishing the translation when there was a rap and Bert walked in. He ran both hands over his hair and shook the rain off them. "What a night!" Then to June: "You wouldn't be standing me up, would you? I waited where you said since seven. We'll miss the first show if we don't hurry."

"Just a minute," June said, over her shoulder. "Whatever are you going to do?" she asked her mother.

Melissa took the letter and balanced it on the flat of her hand as if, by its weight, she would judge its contents. "I am thinking on that."

"What's up?" Bert inquired, looking from June to Melissa. "Bad news or something?"

June explained.

"That's Dot for you," Bert said. "Why doesn't she look after her kid herself?"

"Do not speak so," Melissa reproved. "He is of our flesh and blood." She returned the paper to its envelope and put it very carefully in her apron pocket. "My mind is made up. I am going home."

"And pass up a month's wages?" Bert protested.

"That is how it must be."

June's full, soft lips quivered. "But I promised Mrs. Haney I would stay till after fall fishing," she pleaded. "I can't go back to the village right away, Mama. Honestly I can't." Tears came to her eyes and in her agitation she appealed to Bert. "It's not fair, is it?"

It irritated Cy, seeing her turn to Bert Silas for support against her mother.

"I do not mean we all should go," Melissa said. She motioned June to stand before her. "Listen closely.

You are not froth and you are in good hands at the Haneys. I will speak to Nettie and Caleb. They will bring you with them at the end of fishing. But, for myself, I leave here Saturday. Do not say more. All is settled."

"Aw, gee, Mama, thanks," June exclaimed, her face brightening. "I was hoping you would let me stay. Cy can look after himself. Miriam will be glad to cook for him," she added teasingly.

Bert guffawed. "Sure she would."

Cy sprang to his feet. "You close your mouth!" The Gitkshan idiom was never used to humans except in anger, or to provoke a fight. It was for dogs.

"Don't get sore," Bert said. "I can see Melissa might have to go, but you don't. The kid doesn't need you to look after him."

"I'm going anyhow," Cy retorted. "I don't need you to tell me what to do."

Bert smiled uneasily. "What's the matter? Miriam give you the brush-off?"

"I told you to shut your mouth," Cy shouted.

Bert backed away. "All right, I will. But I can't see why all of a sudden you don't want to stick around."

June went for her coat. "What's the matter with you two?" she scolded. "The last few times you argue about nearly everything." She put an arm around Melissa and kissed her. "I know how you feel; you're just dying to see the little fellow. Cy, too, I guess."

After the door closed, Melissa sat quite still, her elbows on the table and her small, neat hands clasped in front of her. They were bleached from two months of cannery work and showed white against the oilcloth covering the table.

Cy put a stick of wood in the stove, quietly replaced

the lid, and stood studying his mother. The drop light drew shadows under her eyes, cheek bones, and mouth, making her face seem heavy and giving it the timeless, impersonal look of a totem carving. The drip of rain and the lapping of water around the piles emphasized the stillness of the room.

"I told you before that I wanted to go," he said. "I cannot stay here, and if you ask me I will tell you why."

"Let us not speak of that."

A hastiness in her voice, a kind of wariness, gave him the idea that she knew. She had never concealed her wish that, when the time came, he would take Miriam for wife, and while he had been careful not to reveal to her how intolerable working under Old Paul had become, he had said enough to make her understand there was friction. Miriam was the one she wanted for him, the only one. She would reason that if he left now the friction would pass and that in the village Old Paul's authority would be easier to accept.

He knew that once she made a decision she put it behind her, and that she had done so now. Her mind would be moving ahead to deal with the practicalities facing her: telling Caleb, packing, what food to parcel for the trip, the time the train left Prince Rupert and when they would leave it at the Junction station. He could never recall her being hampered by indecision. For a long time after his father died she had been enclosed and quiet, but she had kept busy, finding food for them, and teaching them little ways to bring in money. In spite of hard times her life had appeared to him orderly and settled.

I have got to be like that, he thought, make up my mind and not be pulled this way and that by what people think. In this, too, Miriam was like his mother and would be more so as she grew older.

Only until Saturday and then they would be away from here! He pictured what the village would be like on the day of his return. The first frosts would have touched the hazel bushes and soon all the cottonwoods and then the poplars would turn so yellow that it seemed more than a colour, more like something floating in the air. Every morning would be so calm that the cool smoke spilled from cracks in the smoke-houses and seeped along the ground until it became tangled among the fluffy stalks of the fireweed or was lost in the flat, silver mist spread on the river.

Evenings when he walked home after sacking potatoes in their patch below the ridge, the clear silence magnified small sounds as smoothly as the reflection of one reed is magnified at sunset on the face of a sheltered pond. This time of year, in the pause of summer's fulfilment, voices of jays and squirrels carried far and without harshness. And sometimes, following one of the paths leading to the village—paths pressed deep by the feet of generations of his people—he would hear the padded thump of a rabbit signalling through the firm, dry ground.

At home all was proven and familiar, and any white who came did not matter much. The place was the same, and surely he could be the same. Being able to see it so vividly proved he had not turned his back on his village. Miriam would see.

He must keep his mind on this and not let it dwell so much on the cause of their quarrel. But many times during the remainder of the week it did so. Old Paul and what he stood for had got between him and the girl he wanted. Each time Cy thought of his parting with Miriam he felt thwarted and, in some deep way, defeated.

12

MATT WAS COMING DOWN THE SMOKE-HOUSE PATH. THE
weathered faces of the totem poles beside the river were
moist from the night mist and appeared knowing and
less austere against the widening translucence over-
head. The air had the nose-tingling smell of the mist
in it, and the sweet spice of fallen leaves. Another fine
day in the making, Matt thought, a true fall day; one
of the first, and in a matter of weeks the bell of the
village school would ring again.

The few people now in the village had talked much
about that since the Agent drove out the other day and
told them that some white couple would likely be here
before September was out, to open the school and live
in the mission house. The final papers had not been
signed, but chances seemed bright for a teacher this
year, the Agent said.

Some concluded it was the man who was going to
teach. Others thought it would be the woman; but you
never could be sure about white people. Jonathan
Tate only yesterday returned with his family from
Angus, believed it would be the man, but old Minnie
Moose, who had a secret way of knowing what people
were up to without leaving her bed, prophesied it would
be the woman. The teacher who cleared out because of

the home-brew trouble had been a woman. The last
man they had was young, just right for the war to take.
Few, since the old, old days of Mr. Lloyd, had stayed
more than a year or two, and there had been stretches
when no teacher came at all.

Matt's knees were stiff and unpredictable on steep
ground, but after he was below the crabapples and onto
the close-cropped grass, he walked briskly, for on the
level the knees were as good as anybody's. *The* knees
was how he spoke of them, when the doctor down at the
Junction hospital asked how he was feeling. I am a good
man yet, he had told the previous doctor, and if the new
one should ask he would answer the same. I am a good,
strong-hearted man, he would answer, and give his
chest the flat-handed, approving thump one did to a
faithful horse which could always be relied on to pull its
weight. Only the knees. And here Matt's curling lips
and disavowing, downward glance would place the
blame squarely where it belonged.

Smoke was spilling through the chinks of the family's
smoke-house when Matt reached it. It took knowing to
build fires that would keep in all night, one in each
corner, burning low and ripening the split salmon on
the racks. But Fat Marie, for all her foolish ways, was
almost as good at it as Melissa. Too much wet wood
and the fires went out, too much dry and you got heat
which in a single night would ruin a winter's supply of
fish. Some kinds of wood gave off bitter smoke, other
kinds sweet. You had to be taught young to know.

Matt went to the door and peered in. Marie and
Stevie were at the far end, moving back and forth below
the layer of smoke. They were talking away, and in
English. It still sounded strange in his ears when a
child chattered like a white person, but every day he

was teaching the little fellow words in their language, and it would not be long before English between them could be forgotten.

"Stevie, I am on my way to pull the net," Matt called. "Do you want to come?" He used the simplest Gitkshan words and it pleased him when Stevie understood. Matt took his hand and they walked side by side to the bank.

It was many years since the people moved to houses on the bench, but even yet the turf dipped and swelled where the earth had been banked against the walls of the old communal dwellings, in one of which Matt had been born. One of these evenings he would tell Stevie more of how it had been with their people then.

When they reached the low cut-bank Stevie took away his hand and went ahead across the shingle to the edge of the big eddy. In other places up and down the Skeena the channel changed with the years, but here it stayed the same. Things were slow in changing in this village and valley; perhaps it would be better if they did not change at all.

The mist lay close on the water, but only the outer end of the net was hidden and Matt saw that most of the floats were pulled under by the weight of fish. Fairly in the bight there was a swirling where a heavy spring salmon fought the net.

Such a fish must not be lost. "See him, young brother?" Matt asked. "Heaven is near us this morning." He went to the dugout canoe and began to drag it down, motioning for Stevie to help.

Stevie dug in his heels and tried so hard to pull that Matt's long upper lip folded in against his teeth as he suppressed a smile. "A big one, eh?" he grunted, heaving away.

"You bet." Stevie could not keep his eyes off the net. The moment the canoe was afloat he crawled to the bow and picked up the small paddle Matt had whittled for him. He was even more excited than on previous mornings.

"We go after the big one first," Matt said, as he pushed out to where he could pull the canoe hand-over-hand along the float line. "Get ready the club. This fish is yours. It is you who must kill him."

The tarred cedar floats rattled against the side of the canoe when they were over the place, and while Matt hooked his fingers into the web until he found the lead-line, he could not take his eyes from the boy. The thin little face had an eagerness which warmed Matt's heart. This was the seed of his seed and he felt an inexpressible gratitude and acceptance toward all which had gone before—Dot as she once was, and as she was now, the separation and the long, endured loneliness. No matter what she had done to put his heart in a steep place with her wild ways, he could, and did, thank her for this moment. And there would be other moments for him, years of moments, and a lifetime filled with them, in his valley and among his people, for the grandson who had come long after he had ceased to hope for one.

"I see him! I see his tail!" Stevie yelled. He gripped the raised club in both hands. Matt pretended it was all he could do to hold the net, although by the time he rolled the salmon into the canoe it actually did not have much fight left in it. But it was a good fish, close to thirty pounds, fresh-run and white bellied.

Stevie got astride it and smacked the club down on its head until a dying tremor ran along its flanks and it lay still. Then they went over the rest of the net and took twenty lesser salmon.

Back on shore, Stevie leaned against the arched bow of the canoe while they admired their catch. "Marie will have a full morning's work from this," Matt remarked, stroking his wispy moustache with his knuckles, one side and then the other.

"Say it to me in English," Stevie asked. "That's easier." He got over the side of the canoe and squatted beside his big salmon, sliding his hands proudly along its sides.

"You understand those words, surely," Matt said gently. "Morning, and work; I taught you them. Your ears are quick, and your tongue. Do not let them forget."

"I talk English and your words are hard to say, Matt." Stevie spoke impatiently but Matt let it pass. It was merely that the child was tired, which was to be expected when so small a fellow had only a street to play on. Here where he belonged, he would soon become strong and filled with life.

When Stevie got out of the canoe Matt placed a hand on his head. "They are your words, too. They are in you. They will come back."

"I'm going to tell Marie," Stevie said suddenly. He made for the cut-bank and Matt followed him but, by the time he eased first one leg and then the other over it, he decided to let Stevie go on alone. He went to the fallen totem pole of the Grouse people which lay with its rotting faces pressed into the turf and sat down stiffly on its butt, rubbing his knees and watching until Stevie went inside the smoke-house. Then he turned his face toward the river.

Soon the school would open and Stevie would have to go. They would not have much of the day together then and the learning of the little fellow's language

would move more slowly. The school came first, many
people said. They said education was the thing.

The mist twisted itself, devising shapes over the
strongly flowing water. When he was Stevie's age he
used to stand at the house door a few yards from where
he now sat, watching the river on a fine fall morning
such as this. Ghost faces, and the shapes of things to
come, formed and swayed and dissolved there. Obscured by the white breath of *k'Shan* they performed
their ritualistic dance, recalling the dead and fore-
shadowing the good and evil that was to be.

Presently he found he was thinking of his own first
days at school. The village had no white man's houses
then. The big split cedar ones, each with its group of
families and often four generations under one roof,
stood so close to the river that at high water the noses
of the canoes were nearly inside the door openings.
Mr. Lloyd, who opened the first school, had come in
late summer, almost exactly at this time of year, in the
moon month known as When-groundhog-goes-in-hole.
The big Tsimpshean canoe had landed where the Fireweed people's pole used to stand, before they raised
their new one in what was now the village.

Mr. Lloyd's wife was with him and he brought his
own canoe men and a Tsimpshean interpreter. Mrs.
Lloyd was small and she did not talk as much as others
of the long-nose women. The Lloyds stayed a week,
telling the people the Good News. Then they went away
down river, but sure enough, as they promised, by the
time the fattening snow was on the mountains they
came back to stay.

For a time they held school in the smoke-house
dwellings. You sat on the earth floor around the fire
and learned to say A-B-C. If you kept at it you were

given a slate to use, and later still you were taught to say words, all together, out of the reading book.

By the time the Lloyds had their own log house, the ice was on the river. The house was not much, judged by those even the native people had to-day, but it was a big thing to talk about then. It had fire in an iron box instead of on the ground, and the snow did not blow through the walls as it did through the cracks in the native ones. And that first window! People found it hard to believe you could stand inside and look through a wall. Some thought the glass was ice and expected it to melt. Mrs. Lloyd taught the little ones and showed the smartest girls how to cook, white style, and to wash with soap and understand the use of flour. A few more years and Mr. Lloyd could preach to you in your own language and Mrs. Lloyd, though she never put it to her tongue, understood every word a person let slip, make no mistake of that.

Matt got slowly to his feet and turned to see if Marie was coming to dress the fish. She had not left the smoke-house yet. He could hear the two of them inside, talking back and forth in English.

Resting on the pole again, he recalled how first one family and then another built separate houses for themselves, back from the river. That was when the mission house was built. The people liked the Lloyds because they did not act too big to learn the native language from people who could not read or write, and because they did not turn up their noses at good Indian food as most of those who came after them had.

More years. The way some people told it latterly, it was in the big 'flu that Mrs. Lloyd died, but it was before that, years before. Mr. Lloyd was getting old, but when the head men of his church wrote letters offering to send a younger man, Mr. Lloyd said no. He said this was his home. Some of the women baked bread for him, and the men brought him fish and wild meat and shovelled his roof and paths in deep snow time.

At the last Mr. Lloyd said he was happy to go, and when they put his body beside his wife's, there in the old graveyard overlooking the river, the people built the finest grave-house, all jigsaw work, with a spindle fence and doves like from the Gospel, carved from cedar and standing on wire legs on the corner posts. Everyone put in fishing money or trapping money and bought a white, Christian gravestone.

Matthew Hecate—Mr. Lloyd had found those white man's names for him—was remembering with regretful tenderness and self-reproach that he had not gone to the grave in years. The trail became overgrown when the new graveyard behind the church was started. It was clogged with windfalls now, and, the knees being what they were, he had excused himself by believing he could not get through. Cy told him last year that the doves and the fence were down and that a spruce, big as your leg, was growing through the grave-house roof.

There had been a succession of other teachers and preachers in the old mission house, but why, Matt wondered, did the people forget most of them and still feel close to Mr. Lloyd and his quiet little wife? Was it simply because they were the first? No, there was more to it than that. Although Mr. Lloyd worked hard to turn them into Christians he did not boss or scold, but took them and liked them and spent his life among them, good and bad, just as they were. The big thing was that he had something in his heart to make an Indian feel he was as good as anybody else. But to-day very few whites could do that, for all their friendly talk.

In the sound of the water out there, swirling past under the mist, it was as if he were hearing voices: Mr. Lloyd sitting here on the grass beside you, talking to you in your language, asking the women how many fish they were putting up for winter; Mr. Lloyd in church praying for the sick ones, or his voice choking when he would be standing at the head of the grave as they buried some little child; Mr. Lloyd's voice leading with "Rock of Ages" or "Do Not Pass Me By".

But did Mr. Lloyd know how much had passed his village by since he went away? Did he know that the Better Day he was sure was coming, when he got after them to learn their letters and numbers so they would be ready, had been so woefully long in dawning?

"A better day is coming," Mr. Lloyd had promised. Yet to-day when children not much older than Stevie could do two-and-two and read out to you about Dick and Jane; when some of the people had cars and trucks and washing machines run by gas engines; when you could turn on choir and cowboy music any night in winter—with all this and more the Better Day had not dawned. Who or what was to blame? Was it government or village, the go-ahead, grasping whites or the half-ashamed, don't-care Indians? Was it too much money or not enough, too much of the white man's education or not enough of it, even yet? Or was it simply because, though his hair was as black as when he was a young cedar, he was growing old and much was happening that he did not understand.

All he was sure of, sitting here on the rotting totem pole, was that the bell soon to ring for the children of his village could not renew the hope which he had lost.

13

THERE WAS A MOON THE NIGHT CY AND MELISSA LEFT
Prince Rupert. Already the evenings were closing in.
They were early at the station, and while he waited for
the train, Cy strolled to the little park above the tracks.
Out across the sea the islands of Alaska were faint in
the silver light. Behind him, on the little hill at the top
of the park, the three totem poles showed against the
street lights. Cy sat on a bench for a while, admiring
them; then he went back to the station.

The train was not crowded the way it was when they
came down at the start of fishing. Fishing would be
nearly over on the Skeena, although as the train skirted
the river mouth he saw the lights of fishing boats drifting with their nets. In the moonlight their reflections
in the water seemed more solid than the boats themselves.

But soon the mountains shouldered in and for most of
the night, both train and river ran through darkness.
Later, the ranges fell back and jackpines began showing
against the sky at the top of rock-cuts. At one stop,
where Cy took a walk on the platform, he thought the
stars looked closer and that the air tasted more alive
than at the coast. It reminded him of the lively feel of
bubbly water in his mouth when he drank below a

certain falls on their hunting ground. At dawn, birches gave airy perspective to the track-side woods, and then he knew for certain he was nearing home . . .

The letter his mother asked him to write to Fat Marie must have reached her because Matt was at the station with the team; but Stevie had remained in the village with Marie. On the five-mile drive north to the Junction, Melissa asked all about him, and of how it had gone with their friends this summer. She was pleased to hear that enough salmon were being taken to keep their smoke-house going, and that the potatoes had grown. Not until they were in the Chinaman's having coffee while waiting for the stores to open did Matt think to tell them a teacher was expected.

"Good, very good," Melissa said. "June will be pleased."

This about a teacher was no doubt good news, but as Cy walked behind the wagon, up the big hill and along stretches of river bottom, he did not think much about it either way. It was good to pass through miles of familiar woods, to be able to stretch your legs after being cooped up at a cannery all summer.

In his village nothing had changed much. The leaves of the big cottonwood across the corner at Caleb's horse trough now had a dry, tired sound when a breeze moved them; grass and the seedy heads of the nettles stood high inside the fences, but the cropped grass was still green and the horses were sleek after ranging all summer. All was so right and familiar that the first night in his own bed, had it not been for Stevie beside him, he could have imagined he had not been away at all.

It gave Cy a protective feeling those first nights when Stevie stirred in his sleep and snuggled closer to him. He understood the way Dot had gone, but because Stevie had come to them so young they should be able to keep him from finding out the whole of it. For all her talk against the village, he believed Dot would feel better having her child where her family could care for him.

Melissa's arrangement was for the two to share this bed all winter, but when Cy told her that Stevie turned in his sleep, as if he could not get comfortable, she had Matt build a small bunk against the opposite wall. The room was off the kitchen and it was nice to look across it in the first light of morning and see the little fellow lying there.

"I guess you like it with us," Cy said one morning when Stevie got into bed with him.

Stevie did not answer. He pretended he wanted to go back to sleep, but through his lashes he kept his eyes on Cy. So Cy pretended he was sleepy, too, then suddenly he grabbed Stevie and began tickling him.

"Cut it out," Stevie protested, laughing. "You hurt."

"Where do I hurt?" Cy smiled and held him fast.

"You hurt my back."

"That's from picking potatoes yesterday. We picked sacks of them, eh?" Stevie tried to pull away, but Cy held him. "You're not fooling me? Your back really hurts?"

"I was standing in my wagon and a kid pushed it. I told you that, down at the cannery."

"It shouldn't hurt this long."   Cy slid his hand inside Stevie's shirt. "Hold still. Now, show me the place."

Stevie snatched away the hand and rubbed it up and down on his ribs. "Dot says my ribs are like a washboard. Feel."

"You better eat more, then you'll get fat."

"Marie doesn't eat much and look how fat she is. Cy, what makes Marie so fat?"

"She was always fat. That's why everybody calls her Fat Marie." While they talked, Cy got his hand inside the shirt again. He was not sure, but he thought he felt a small lump low on the spine.

Melissa came in. "Do you two think you are great chiefs who can lie in bed while others work? Your food is waiting; Matt is eating; we are going to the river." She helped Stevie dress and when she sent him out to wash, Cy told her about the lump.

"To-night, when I wash him, I will look for it," Melissa said. "An insect may have bitten him. There were blackflies among the potatoes yesterday."

"It did not come from a bite, I think. It hurt him at the cannery; you had better look at it."

"Children often have such little pains. If the swelling remains I will ask advice of Minnie. She makes a good medicine for swellings."

"Maybe you should take him to the doctor next time at the Junction."

"Minnie's native medicines do as well as any doctor. I know doctors. Once they get you in their hands there is no end to what they want to do with you. All they think of is the knife. Minnie has many cures. All have had great faith in her."

Breakfast that morning was one Cy was very fond of. It was salmon heads, split before the smoking, eaten with hot baking-powder bread and all the tea you wanted. Matt had coaxed Stevie to try one, and after the first taste he forgot to ask why wasn't there corn flakes. He sat there, chewing the crisp skin and jellied gristle from the jawbone, holding it in both hands and sucking it as he saw Matt doing.

Cy was the last to leave the table and as he rose he saw Fat Marie waddling into the yard. A puff of wind filled her flowered-cotton dress from behind, showing her massive legs and making her feet in their canvas shoes seem much too small to carry her. She walked with short, quick steps, her feet moving with a heel-and-toe motion like the feet of a mechanical toy. She wheeled off the path and came to a stop at the bottom of the steps where Melissa sat, touching up her fish knife.

"Bro-*ther!* Am I ever hot!" Marie fluffed out her tightly curled hair with one pudgy hand. "Big fool me, I dig few rows potatoes before I come."

"I too like working in my garden in the cool," Melissa said, "but we did not get up early this time. Minnie Moose and John visited us last night. We sat late."

Marie eased herself to the step. "I seen your light. Well, it okay dig potatoes this morning. But those parsnips! Nettles and everything. Some job."

"We do not eat parsnips at our house," Melissa said.

"Bella neither, but I like to try some." Marie fanned herself. She felt no need to mention that a Haida woman at Angus had told her there was a good wine the whites made from parsnips. "Seen Jasper this morning?"

Cy was sitting on the top step lacing his boots. "He said last evening he would ride to the Junction to-day. He will ask for mail."

"I sure hope he brings that home permanent stuff I sent away for," Marie said. "I sure going to need it when the girls get home. They all be after me."

Melissa tested the edge of her knife with her thumb and picked up her oilskin apron. "Bring your axe when you come," she told Cy. "More wood for smoking will be needed."

Cy was the last to leave. As he turned the school corner opposite the house he saw Matt and Stevie hand-in-hand below the hall. Matt would miss the boy when he started school, but with his good English Stevie should do well, and it was right that he should go. Beyond the hall and the crabapple thickets, the wooded ridges between the river and the distant mountains seemed close in the clear air. It was like a picture on a calendar.

At the hall corner he saw a car coming up the road. It was the Agent and he said Cy was the very fellow he was looking for.

"It's final about a teacher coming," the Agent told him. "I've a couple of days' work for you tidying up around the yard. Get in and we'll see what needs doing."

They drove back up the street, went into the yard and took a look around.

This Agent was youngish, different from the one they had before, and although some did not like him because he would not do for people what they could do for themselves, most of them said he was the best they ever had. His yes was yes, and his no was no, so you knew where you stood with him.

"Brush out the weeds and split wood enough to get them started. You may see other jobs as well. I'll leave it to you. Let me have your time and I'll mail you the cheque." The Agent closed the gate and they crossed the school ground to the car. "I understand the husband's a war disability. Maybe you and Matt would carry in their trunks and sort of get them settled. Their name is Haney, in case the people ask."

Cy gave no sign that he knew the Haneys. But while he was riding back to the hall corner, knowing them was the one thing in his mind. Before he went down the bank, something stopped him and made him look back.

He felt a sudden need to see his village objectively and this was difficult because he had never tried to see it so before. What if he were standing here for the first time and facing the rows of houses, some neat, some run-down, and able to disassociate them from the people who lived in them? How would the scattering of sheds and outhouses, the meat caches gawky on their tall posts, strike people like the Haneys who had no under-standing of their very real uses? He saw that one side of the hall was only partly painted and thought he must be blind not to have noticed before.

Well, it was not his problem what the Haneys thought. They should have learned from June what they were coming to. The village could be better, but mostly it was nothing to be ashamed of. In fact, had they been strangers, he would not care at all what they thought.

Melissa took the news calmly, but she seemed pleased. "These are the ones June works for," she told Matt, "the ones I spoke of."

"You mean you know them?"

"I myself have sat in their fine house and eaten of their food. Also Cy. They deal fairly with June."

"Tell me of the man," Matt urged. "And have they children?"

"No children," Cy said. "I only talked with him the once."

"Did you like him?"

"Oh he's all right, I guess."

"We know little of them, nor they of us," Melissa said. "But I am ready to believe we can live as neigh-bours."

After Cy and Matt, with the excited Stevie in the bow, went over the net, Melissa and Marie set to work on the fish. When people are getting salmon for winter food, especially cohoes whose backs are thick, they must be skilful with the knife or the fish will spoil. The flesh must be pared to exact thickness, and as Melissa did this with her Indian fish knife, a touch here and a long, sure stroke there, constantly testing for thickness with her fingers, Cy stopped to watch. Some winters native people who were too busy or too lazy to put up their own, offered Melissa a dollar each for good fish such as these. June could talk of the fine food she ate at the Haney house, but on the trapping grounds or at the pole camps, dried salmon made a food which stayed with you in cold weather, especially when dipped in the oolichan grease Melissa traded for her soap-berries.

The split fish were spread on the turf away from the sand, and as Cy passed, Melissa asked him to bring an armful of the flowering raspberry stalks growing behind the smokehouse. The furry undersides of the broad leaves were better than cloth for wiping the slime off salmon. When he came back Marie was giggling.

"I bet the Haney woman laugh her head off to catch us like this, guts and flies all round," she said.

"I believe Mrs. Haney to be a common-sense person," Melissa said firmly. "She knows the need of food as well as anyone."

Marie's hands were covered with blood and slime and she pushed back a curl with her wrist. "I bet she don't like to eat it."

"Different people have different foods," Melissa observed.

"I try her, take her one for a present, see what she do." Marie winked at Cy. "You think I got the nerve?"

Melissa reached for another fish. "The sooner we

finish here the sooner we have coffee." She did not lose
patience with Fat Marie, but Cy supposed she felt as he
did—that making sly jokes about the Haneys was a
poor way to start.

After all the partly-cured salmon were turned on the
racks and the morning's catch laid saddle-wise over the
poles to drip, they followed Matt and Stevie back to the
house. Jasper Gawa must have ridden past because
Matt had found a letter on the top of the gatepost, held
there by a stone.

"From Bella," Marie said, very pleased. She spread
herself on the chopping block and tore it open. Matt
was making shavings for the outside fire. Cy stretched
full length on the sun-warmed chips. Stevie climbed
astride of him and started playing horse.

"I'm Jasper. You try and buck me off," he urged.
"Go on, Cy. Try and buck me off."

"What you know!" Marie called out, a delighted
smile creasing her flabby, small-featured face. "Victor
and Teresa start living together, man and wife."

Cy lifted Stevie off him and sat up.

Melissa paused with the coffee pot in her hand. "I
was prepared to learn of this in the course of time,"
she said. "I know how it is with the young. But so
soon! Nothing was said by Victor's mother this
summer." She turned to Cy. "You had nothing from
Victor?"

Cy shook his head. Stevie was trying to climb on his
back but he held him off.

"Bella says Victor and them come up to Angus, boat
after you," Marie explained. "But I hear nothing
before I come away."

"I conclude Clarice was waiting to learn Teresa's
wishes," Matt replied. "She is not froth, that one."

He kept on drawing his knife toward him methodically, cutting more shavings from the stick of spruce held endwise against his chest.

Cy believed that what had been between him and Miriam was stronger than between Victor and Teresa, which must have come suddenly when their natures got the best of them. He should be feeling glad for Victor.

"It will be helpful for Clarice and her husband to have Victor living with them," Matt said. "He has the name of a hard worker."

Melissa agreed. "When June's time comes may we have so good a one."

Fat Marie snickered. "I sure hope they get all fixed up before them two come," she said piously, glancing across at the mission house. "Maybe those Haneys the same that other teacher, they think we bunch of animals when they find out Victor and Teresa not decently married."

"They are already married by native custom," Melissa said. "Your joke is not in keeping."

Marie shrugged. "Oh, well, be all right I guess, if nobody put them wise. Be lots of talk but we can hide behind our language."

The water was boiling and Melissa asked Cy to bring the coffee. He had no way of knowing whether or not Mrs. Haney was against native marriage, as was that other teacher. But he was pretty sure she would be, and as he went to the house he wished the Haneys were not coming. It made him feel ungrateful, but it would be better if they were strangers, whites whose opinions he need not care about.

14

MINNIE MOOSE EXAMINED STEVIE'S BACK AND PRO-
nounced pus to be the trouble. She had Jasper Gawa
go to the head of the valley for a poisonous plant which
was to be heated over the fire and its vapour inhaled.
This was to cleanse the blood. She also supplied
Melissa with a piece of hairy bulbous root which grew
in swamps. Melissa was instructed to hang the swamp-
root where Stevie would brush against it as he got in
and out of bed. Once, many years ago, Melissa had
seen swamp-root work a miraculous cure. She told Cy
it had the power of absorbing certain types of sickness
and that she had great faith in it.

"How can it help a person?" Cy argued. "Stevie
does not take it inside, nor do you rub it on him."

"Minnie knows ways of curing which we ordinary
people do not," Melissa told him. "Perhaps she does
something to the root to give it power. We do not
know."

"I know it did not save Elora from being sent to
Miller Bay with the lung-sick."

Melissa raised a warning hand. "Do not voice such
doubts, or think them. It is not wise."

"I am thinking only of what is best for Stevie," Cy
answered, uneasily. He was not so superstitious as to

117

believe Minnie had it in her power to get even with anyone who went against her, as some village people believed. But on the other hand it would give you a queer feeling to discover she had hidden a piece of your hair or clothing in the coffin of a dead person. The story was that she had done this against a man who scoffed at her healing powers, and that the man had later sickened and died. This was sheer chance, of course. The man would have died anyway. But knowing Minnie had it in for you would be a bad thing to have hanging over your head.

Some mornings, waking early, he looked across the room at the piece of swamp root and wanted to jump out of bed and yank it from its string. Such ignorance! During his last year in school he learned from the health book about germs. How could that wizened bit of root kill germs? Not that he was against all native medicines. When he was small he had burned his hand quite badly when he and his father were camped out. His father used an outside native medicine made like tea from alder bark. It eased the pain, and the burn healed with scarcely a scar. But swamp root was different. His father would call it superstition. No, the sensible thing was to get Stevie to the doctor.

A week or so later, the four of them drove down to the Junction. Stevie's refusing breakfast that morning had Matt worried, so Cy suggested that, since they were down here anyway, they stop at the hospital on their way out of town. To his relief, Matt agreed.

Melissa did not strongly oppose the idea. "But no word of native medicine," she warned. "All white doctors are against it."

Now they were waiting in the hall. It seemed a long time since a nurse took Stevie away, but at last the door opened and the doctor looked out at them. He was not angry but he was not friendly either. He took them into his room and told them to sit down; then he closed the door to an inner room where Stevie lay on a high, white table. The doctor went behind his desk.

"Why didn't you bring this child in sooner?"

They had no suitable answer. It would be hard to explain about Dot and of how they came to have Stevie. It was easier to take the blame.

"When did you first find the lump on his back?"

Melissa told him, and the doctor said it was strange they had not noticed it before. "Do you bathe him regularly? It must have been there a long time. You should have reported it before this."

Cy did not like hearing the blame put on his mother. "We just got him. His mother lives at the coast."

"I see. Well, there must have been neglect some-where, because a condition such as his should not have been allowed to develop. We've X-rayed and I'm sorry to tell you that the trouble is quite advanced. It's Pott's disease—TB of the spine."

In the intensity of her rejection, Melissa's face lost all expression. This man did not care; he must be against them to put the dreaded name to Stevie's illness. She felt affronted.

A numbness went through Cy, and as from a distance, he heard Matt speaking.

"This man calls himself a doctor but I do not believe he knows his business." Matt's voice was deceptively free of the emotion and outrage he was feeling. "The boy does not spit blood. He has not taken to his bed. Under such a body lump there is always pus. The man has hands; let him cut to take that out. That is all we ask. We did not come here to have such wild talk tossed at us."

The doctor caught Cy's eye. "What's he going on

about? For the sake of this boy, they've got to realize how serious this is. The old man doesn't believe me, does he?"

Cy wet his lips. "They don't understand," he answered, in a flat voice.

"Well, they've got to understand. You and I must make them understand."

"Ask him how long?" Melissa urged. "I see his scheme. His mind is set on holding the boy here. Ask him how many weeks?"

"It's not a case of weeks—or months," the doctor informed them after Cy translated. "It may be years." And then he said a thing so devoid of human feeling that it outraged them still further. "I want you to sign papers allowing me to send him to Miller Bay."

Melissa stared at the floor, then her gaze crawled slowly up the side of the desk and across it to the doctor's face. "We like him here," she said with firmness, in English. "We like to see him; cheer him up."

"He cannot get proper treatment here. We have neither staff nor facilities."

"Did he find the pus?" Matt blurted. "The pus is the trouble. Minnie knows. He is twisting words. I am telling you to ask him."

At the same time Melissa began talking vehemently. "These whites! You fall in with them in a small matter and they demand you go all the way with them. The boy is not to go to the coast; I will not hear of it, ever. We up-river people cannot thrive in the coast winters, even when we are healthy. It would be sending the boy to his death. We will sign no papers, and if he will not cure him we will take him home with us, now, to-day."

"Good," Matt agreed, "very good."

Cy knew this was no way to get on the right side of a white person, talking back and forth before his face in native. He knew what the doctor wanted and what his family wanted, and the two were very far apart.

He stood and moved closer to the desk. Doctors knew sicknesses which Indians did not understand, and his mind was being forced to accept the fact that Stevie's trouble was no passing one. "I guess they'd like a few days to think it over," he ventured. He stressed the "they", giving the impression that he, at least, was standing with the doctor.

"I know it's no easy decision for them to make, but it's the only safe one. You realize that, don't you?"

Cy's face was a blank. "It's up to you."

"But that's exactly the difficulty; it isn't. If he were my child I'd have him away on the next train. As soon as the film is dry I'll try and explain, but my point is that without written consent of parent or guardian my hands are tied." The doctor removed his glasses, folded them and turned them end for end between his hands. "I can see I'm going to need your help in this," he went on after a glance at Matt and Melissa. "You're younger; you've been to school. I want you to make them see the plain common sense of what I'm advising."

"They want you to fix him up here."

"You want him to get better, don't you?"

Cy nodded. He had learned in school that there were other kinds of TB than the one Matt had spoken of, and if Stevie had one of those other kinds it was an awful thing. Melissa had just sent away, mail order, for a little winter coat with a parka hood, and Matt had promised to take Stevie up the valley to get vine maple for a small pair of snowshoes so the two of them could run a line of rabbit snares when winter came. There were so many things they planned to do for Stevie, but if he had to stay in hospital, perhaps for years—

"You must make the old people understand the boy's not going to fold up and die simply because they can't fuss over him every few days," the doctor was saying. "He'll miss them at first, naturally; but Miller Bay's a cheery place and in no time at all he'll find other interests and make new friends. Try to make them understand that giving their consent is the kindest thing they can do for him. Besides, every so often one or another of you can go down and visit him. Explain to them that his case is not hopeless, not if we act at once."

Cy could think of no way of getting out of this. His mother's and Matt's hearts were set on the boy, yet he did not doubt the doctor. "They're afraid for him at the coast," he said. "They're afraid they'll lose him."

"I realize all that; I've had to contend with it before. Now, what we've got to do is make them face facts, so tell them this from me. Just about the only chance that lad has is to get to the coast for treatment. If they refuse to co-operate I don't mind telling you I'm not in duty bound to admit him to this hospital. Actually I will, for the time being, but you're not to tell them that. We've got to jolt them; throw a scare into them if necessary." The doctor leaned back in his chair. "Is that clear? Then go ahead and tell them."

Cy hesitated, then turned and faced his mother. "He says Miller Bay is the place. It is a different sort of TB and—"

"If you are simple enough to take that down, I am not."

"It is what he says."

"Do you believe it?"

Cy looked away. He could not meet the wild terror in Matt's eyes. "I believe it."

"Lies, all lies!"

"The man is a doctor."

Matt half rose from his chair. Such yielding by one of his own flesh and blood was too much. "He calls himself a doctor, but I have other names for him."

Melissa stood behind her chair. "I am thankful to say that the law is on our side, for once. Without the paper he cannot send him, and there will be no paper. We should never have come." Deliberate and solid, she turned her back on the doctor. "Ask for the boy's clothes. Say that I will dress him myself. Say we are taking him with us."

With one long stride Cy got between his mother and the door. "Understand me," he entreated. "The boy has a deeper sickness than we know. Take him home and we may finish him."

Matt's sinewy hand clamped on Cy's arm like the jaws of a trap. "The boy is not going to the coast," he said, each word separate, and violent as a hurled stone. "Since this man does not choose to cure him here, what can we do but to take him home?" And again, with passionate determination: "He is not going to the coast. He is *ours*."

The doctor had told him not to reveal it, but Cy was cornered. "He let it slip that he will keep Stevie here if you continue to refuse," he said.

"Will he cut out the pus?"

"Do you mistake me for a doctor?" Cy jerked away his arm. "How am I to know what he will do?"

"I want you to ask him."

Cy stood away from them. "I have tangled him with

enough of your questions already." His face was drawn, twisted by the anguish of unavailing protest. "I believe this man. What has he to gain by deceiving us? If you will not let Stevie be sent to the coast, you should leave him in the hospital. It will be on your heads if we take him out of here."

"I must have my answer about the pus," Matt insisted.

"Ask him yourself. Why do you put it all on me?" Cy cried out. Why should he allow them to corner him like this, they and this man? Either he should come out strongly for the doctor or else he should stand squarely with his own people. This was as bad as at the boat shed when Old Paul and the boss got him between them. No, it was worse, far worse. They loved Stevie and wanted him cured, and this was what the doctor wanted. Cy knew, with self-accusing certainty, that he should support the doctor, but if he did, Matt and his mother would think he had yielded and turned against them.

"Perhaps we should not force this," Melissa said. "I now see that this man has been saying two things at once. From one side of his mouth he tells us the boy must go to the coast. From the other side, he lets drop that he will care for him here, if we will not have him sent away. It is he who yields, not we. The boy will stay. We have gained our point."

"He will keep him only until you make up your mind," Cy warned.

The shadow of a smile crossed Melissa's face. "When it serves my purpose, I can be a long, long while in making up my mind."

This was evasion, but Cy must be party to it, for his fears for Stevie left him no alternative. "They are all worked up," he told the doctor. "They need more time to think it over."

"How much time do they think they've got? I'm worried about that boy, and I know you are, too. You do agree he should go to Miller Bay? Right?"

"Yes," Cy answered.

The doctor came and stood before Matt and Melissa. "You heard him? He would not say the coast if he was not sure it is the only safe thing. We'll care for the boy here until you give consent. But you must promise me you'll make it soon."

The two of them nodded, promising. But Cy knew how little that promise meant.

15

AFTER A NURSE PUT STEVIE TO BED IN A ROOM UPSTAIRS,
the matron took them up to visit him. This matron had
been at the hospital for many years; she was friendly
and native girls who worked here liked her. She was so
brisk and cheerful, making jokes with Stevie and the
two other little boys in the room, that some of the sting
was taken from the words the doctor left in their ears.

"He will do well there," Melissa said when they were
in the wagon and starting home. "The woman has a
good heart and that counts a great deal with the sick."

Matt agreed with her. "On top of that, we know the
parents of the two boys. One is of our crest, from
Kitwancool. Stevie will learn his Gitkshan in their
company. They have been there many weeks and no
talk of sending them to the coast. I am proud of us for
standing together. We will hear no more of that coast
nonsense."

Their satisfaction suggested that, except for the
immediate cutting out of the pus, they had won their
way in the entire matter. Out of all the doctor said they
apparently chose to remember only what they wanted
to remember; but their talk did not lessen Cy's fears.
Some English words lost meaning after he held them in
his mind for long, but this would not happen to the

doctor's words. In a few days they would not miss Stevie so keenly. That would be his time to remind them of their promise about Miller Bay. That evening he wished he could say some little thing to prepare them. But in the lamplight the unaccustomed stillness of the house left a sadness which he went to bed with and wakened with, and which the sight of the empty bed across the room did nothing to dispel.

As he dressed, he looked at the swamp root. It hung where Melissa had placed it and he was about to take it down when something seemed to stay his hand. It was a foolish thing, a token to him of an ancient superstition, but it could do no harm; you never could be absolutely sure of such things. Many of the old beliefs, told at night around the fire, were beyond explanation. They frightened you, but they held you. The old people believed them and you never knew.

After breakfast he took his axe and crosscut saw and put in the morning at the woodlot. When he returned at noon he was astonished to find June in the kitchen. She must have arrived some time before because she was in an old dress and was peeling potatoes while she chatted with her mother.

"I'd have dropped you a line, only Caleb didn't say what day until too late to write," she explained to him. "How are you, big boy? Not so crusty now you're home, I hope." She lifted one hand from the pan, pretending she was going to splash him.

Cy stood at the table smiling broadly.

They paused, enjoying one another with their eyes, and then June said, "That sure got me down, that about Stevie. I've been counting on seeing the little guy."

"He will not be long in hospital. You will see him next time we go," Melissa told her, from the stove.

"Yes, but it's tough just the same, a kid his age."

Cy hated to tell her how tough, and when she asked if they knew what day the doctor would operate, he felt relieved. Hearing right away that Stevie must go to Miller Bay would be a sorry thing to come home to. Here at home not everything was turning out the same, not as he had imagined the last time they were together. But June was her same warm, happy self, he thought with the old, affectionate protectiveness. It was good to have her in the house once more.

"I guess you were surprised about Mrs. Haney coming to be your teacher," he said.

"In a way. She never let on a thing to me until it was all settled."

"I guess you feel pretty good about it, eh?"

June shrugged. "In a way."

Her casualness surprised them both.

"It is a new thing in this village for a girl to have a friend come to teach her," Melissa said.

"I thought you would be excited, the school opening," Cy said.

"Well, sure. But gee whiz! School's nothing new to me. I'm not a kid."

"Hear the girl talk! Secretly, she is as pleased as anyone. This winter we will find her across the road gossiping with her new white friends when she should be at home, working."

But Cy was puzzled and when June took the pan of water and peelings to throw on the garden, he followed her out. "That's a funny thing to say about the Haneys," he remarked. "What's wrong? Don't you like them any more?"

"Don't be so serious. Sure I like them. I owe a lot to Mrs. Haney, and Mr. Haney's tops with me. Bert says he is one swell guy."

So that was it! "What does Bert say about Mrs. Haney?"

June giggled. "He says she gets in his hair. But that's just his talk. You know Bert."

Cy waited while she shook the last of the peelings from the pan. Perhaps he was jealous of Bert. He did not know. But the resentment which overcame him at the cannery that last night returned strongly. Jasper Gawa might be only a stick Indian, but you always knew where he stood, which was more than you could say of Bert.

"Did Bert get that Rupert job?" he asked, abruptly. "The one he talked so big about?"

June fingered the clasp at the side of her hair. Here in familiar surroundings, it was more noticeable how much like a woman she had grown this summer. Her nearness quickened the tenderness he felt for her, and if Bert Silas had turned her against Mrs. Haney—

"He's at the Junction, if you want to know." June started for the house, her head high, but at the steps she set down the pan and came back to him. "Aw, Cy," she asked appealingly, "Do we have to quarrel about it?"

"I'm not mad at you."

"I know you're not, but let's skip it."

"All right. But I don't like him to say things about Mrs. Haney."

"You should have heard what she said about him!" A twinkle came to her eyes. "But I guess at that he had it coming. I'll tell you about it sometime."

Cy had hoped that she would give him word of Miriam, but she did not, and he wondered if she had heard about the misunderstanding. Some nights, before he went to sleep, he tried to create a picture of Miriam in his mind, but although he could make her feel near, he could not visualize her. The harder he tried, the more her appearance became obscured by feeling. Sometimes unexpectedly, when he was not concentrating on it, the slanting lines of her eyes, or the expression of her mouth, or the poised set of her head would come to him. But when his longing for her was strongest, any mental image of her eluded him. This troubled him and he thought it must be a bad sign. One night he had got up and gone through June's boxes at the head of the stairs, looking for a snapshot of Miriam he knew was there. Later he found it and was disappointed. The warmth of her in his mind was the better likeness.

Victor and Teresa and their family came home the following afternoon; the next day's train brought others. As the week went on it was fine to see house after house being lived in again, and lights in the windows until late at night. All things considered, it had been a better-than-average season for native fishermen and workers at the various canneries, although, as Caleb commented when Matt and Cy were about to leave to meet the Legets early that Saturday, as usual some of the foolish ones had left most of their money in Prince Rupert, and at the wrong places.

"But not Paul," Matt said, looking down from the wagon seat with an enigmatic smile.

"Not him," Caleb agreed. "He comes home with one of the richest seasons behind him for many years. Overtime pay almost every day this month. I am not speaking against our friend, you understand, but can we expect the church to come by any part of that?"

Leget's two contemporaries looked at one another and left the question to answer itself.

"That one will be raising his pole in this village in a year or so," Matt remarked to Cy as the team trotted past Fat Marie's house and started down the hill. "Police or no police, what a potlatch that will be! He will give away thousands to make his name memorable."

As elders of the village—as well as ones who wanted no trouble with the authorities—Matt and Caleb professed to favour the law forbidding this ceremonial bestowal of extravagant presents for the sake of prestige. And since a pole could not be raised without this and the accompanying period of feasting, neither could lay claim to names which stood high in the ancient heraldry of crest or band. In these times of closer contacts with Indian Agent and the Mounted Police, the risk would have been too great. Besides, Caleb's frugality and Matt's lack of means prevented them. But for all that, their roots went as deep as Leget's, and his avowed intention to wait his chance and adhere to the old customs compelled their respect, and at times, a degree of wistful envy. This morning, driving down the valley, Matt would have talked at length of this, but he soon realized that Cy's attention was elsewhere.

Lean and erect at his end of the wagon seat, Cy was thinking of Miriam with an exciting sensation of newness, telling himself that her doubt of him was in the past, and trying to imagine that all was beginning afresh between them, wondrously enhanced by the weeks of separation. At first he had counted off the days as obstacles laid end to end which must be surmounted one after the other, but putting them behind him seemed to bring the end no nearer. These days, these weeks, formed one emptiness between the now and Miriam; an emptiness so inescapable that Stevie's trouble, the pleasure of June's return, and his mixed feelings over his own home-coming, had not filled it.

But this morning, driving down the road bright with fallen leaves and with the sun mild and intimate through the mists of the river bottom, this emptiness was obscured by anticipation. He could let his imagination run ahead and not have to pay for the indulgence with increased longing, whereas, even as recently as last night, visiting Victor and Teresa and knowing they were together as they had not been before, he could not.

At the Junction Paul and Miriam were waiting on the bench outside the Chinaman's. While Cy was putting their bundles in the wagon she scarcely spoke to him. Yet her nearness was more real than what his hands were doing. The new kerchief she wore matched the yellow of the poplars, giving her skin a golden wholesomeness. She is as beautiful as ever, he kept thinking, busying himself with the loading; she is the same, everything is the same. He handled the bundles with swing and vigour and when Matt said it would need the two of them to lift Paul's heavy tool box, Cy picked it up and slid it over the tailboard as if its weight were nothing.

An increased awareness of each other, amounting to shyness, came while they were driving out of town. Matt and Paul were on the seat and beginning to talk, although the rattle of the wheels on the gravel covered their voices most of the time. Cy was grateful that it did. They arranged the bundles to suit them and lay back. Once or twice he saw Miriam's eyelids droop because, sitting up all night on the train, a person could not get much sleep. Then she would rouse herself and look at him with a sleepy, little-girl smile which moved him deeply.

"Bella was at the train at Angus," she said as the

horses slowed on the long hill where the woods began. "She told about Victor and Teresa." Miriam turned from him to adjust the bundle she was leaning against. "Were you surprised when you heard they came together?"

He felt his heart quicken, for he was hoping she would speak of it. "Were you?"

Miriam settled herself but kept her eyes on the road behind. "One way I was surprised, because before fishing Teresa told me that if they came together she wanted to be Christian married. Teresa's church is different from our church and I did not think that she would turn." The bundle suited her now and she rested her head against it. "You did not tell me what you think," she reminded.

"I think it is all right for them."

Miriam partly closed her eyes against the dappled sunlight. "I think the same. All the people will be glad for them."

They sat sharing the silence while more of the familiar woods unrolled behind the wagon. Soon the road would dip between cedars to the spring which gave the sweetest water in the valley, and after that they would cross the jackpine flat where in winter people travelling on foot stopped to make tea and where, close by, rotted stakes marked the place where a body had been cremated before the missionaries taught that burial was "the Christian way".

"Melissa put up lots of fish, I guess," Miriam said presently.

"We have enough. Cohoes ran pretty good but we missed the sockeye. John and Minnie Moose stopped fishing them, they had so many. I think they will sell you all you want."

"Sockeyes are the best. That's what we miss, not staying home," Miriam said. "I wish we would stay home some year."

Cy asked if she knew about the teacher.

"Bella told us that, too. Bella knows everything that goes on, I guess," Miriam said with an odd, brief smile.

"Does she know you were mad at me?"

She lowered her eyes and smiled in a different way. "I didn't tell anyone of that, not grandfather even. I'm not mad at you." She hesitated. "But I was afraid, afterwards, you were mad at me."

"I was mad at myself."

She looked up. "Too bad for Stevie. Bella told us. She got a letter from one of the native girls working at the hospital. The one June knows."

"What else did she tell you about him?" he asked warily, thinking of Paul.

"Only that; that he was in hospital."

Cy wanted to get their talk away from this so he told her that everyone's potatoes had done well and that Caleb had his store open and that Marie had some things in hers, too. She wanted to know when Jasper Gawa had returned from his packhorse trip to the head-waters of Naas river with those surveyors.

While he was answering these and other questions he hoped she would say more about Victor and Teresa; but she did not. The noise of the wheels was loud on the gravel for the next mile or so, making talk difficult, but it was enough to be with her, to feel the composure and gentle certainty of her mind. He saw her eyes closing, then she roused, but in a little while the soft rise and fall of her breathing showed she had fallen asleep.

He leaned closer, studying her face, memorizing every feature so as never to forget again. One of the bundles toppled across her feet and he straightened it, taking care lest she waken and he lose the intimacy of this moment. He wanted her, though not as he had on the waterfall trail. He wanted to push back the yellow kerchief and kiss her forehead, yearning for the day when he could gather her into his arms while she slept, not waking her but holding her as he would a child and feeling the warm, yielding innocence of her body.

The rattle of the wheels tapered into silence on the moist clay of the road and Old Paul's voice came harshly.

"I tell you these doctors are in the same canoe with the government, all of them," Paul said scathingly. "They want us to die out. That is their secret aim. Then the whites can take the last of our trapping ground, fishing places, our land, our fur, our timber."

"I do not think you fully understood me," Matt said. "This doctor does not know it, but we will never put our marks on paper for the boy to be taken from us. He will stay in the hospital. There we can keep our eye on him and know what the doctor is up to."

"How can you know what he is up to, now you have allowed him to have the boy wholly in his power?" Paul demanded. "I know what those doctors do in that place. They try a certain cure on the body of one of our people. When it proves to be no cure and the person dies, they try another. Then another. But we learn nothing of it until the word is sent for us to come and take away the dead body. If at last they find a medicine or a cutting with the knife which benefits, they write it in a book. When the book is full, away they go to the big towns and grow rich curing whites through what they have learned on us. Our graveyards are full, but their pockets are full, too, so what do they care?"

"Our children are taught there is a reason why more native people die in hospital than white people," Matt said, uneasily. "It is because our people do not show their sicknesses to the doctors soon enough."

"Who teaches that?"

"It is in a book. Cy had it in his book."

"You sit here and tell me you believe it?"

"I tell you what is in the book."

Paul made a derisive body-sound with his mouth. "White books, white teachers, white schools! You run to strange corners seeking the truth, my friend." He brought his fist down on Matt's knee. "Now look here. You are a sensible man. Next time at the hospital watch what medicines they give our people. Are you so simple as to suppose those are the medicines given to whites? Of course you are not. When this man Haney opens the dispensary in the mission house, just you ask him to read out what is written on the bottles. You will find it is against the law for him to give those medicines to a white. The reason is the government knows they are cheap medicines with no power to cure, but any dung is good enough for Indians."

Matt let the horses walk to the top of the rise before he spoke. "We had one kind doctor in that hospital," he maintained, "one who was out to help the people—"

"Where is he now?" Paul interrupted. "Off to the big towns with his tail in the air."

"Let me finish," Matt said stiffly. "I know little of this doctor, I am not defending him to you, for I suspect he uses the TB as a club over our heads. I am asking you to not forget it is in our power to stop him from sending the little fellow to the coast. Any fool knows what the coast winters do to our people, and to that we will never agree. He is to cut out the pus and return the boy to us. It is as simple as that."

"Then why did he not cut out the pus the day you took the boy?"

Matt hesitated. "That was what we wanted," he said, defensively. "On that only we did not have our way. But Melissa hears from June that this Haney helped the doctors in the war where the fighting was. He has, moreover, the name of being friendly. When he comes I will ask his help in having the doctor do what we ask. The blood will cleanse itself; the back grow strong; the boy come home."

"You should have kept on with Minnie Moose. Her swamp-root never fails. For years your heart has been hungry for a child. Melissa's, too. Then you allow him to be taken from you."

Cy got out of the wagon. More than he wanted to be near Miriam, he wanted to be out of reach of the old man's voice. Or was it only his voice? People said Minnie could give off a power to sicken or cure, but Old Paul had a power, too, though of a different sort. What a fool he was to have forgotten it!

It is the same as at the boat shed, Cy thought angrily as he strode behind the wagon, he will not try to see another's side of it. Of course they had done the right thing. It was not what the doctor wanted, but leaving Stevie at the hospital was the first step toward having him sent to Miller Bay. That would have to wait until he could persuade Matt and his mother to give their consent. And certainly he was going to try, although Old Paul would accuse him of being on the doctor's side. But Cy told himself he did not care. This day was to have meant much to him; now it was spoiled.

He knows what I think of him. He knows that one day I will stand up to him, Cy was thinking when the Agent's car came out of a side road and waited for him.

"Is that your uncle and Paul Leget up ahead?" the

Agent asked. "Would you give them a message? It's this trap-line trouble catching up with us again. I know your chiefs are dead against the new regulations, but I can't stand off the Game Department much longer. Ask Leget to drop into my office next time he's in town, will you? Tell him we'll have to arrange a meeting."

"Will we lose our traplines?" Cy asked cautiously.

"You will if you don't have them registered in your own names. The Department won't stand for a lot of lines being held in one chief's name. Each of you must register your own line, like any white trapper. Leget should understand. He and I have had it back and forth a dozen times. Tell him I'll be in the office all day Monday."

The Agent put his foot on the starter. "You might tell your uncle I'd like him at the meeting. Caleb, too. I know they're not chiefs but they're a pretty level-headed pair."

Miriam was sitting up when Cy overtook the wagon but he did not get in. "The Agent says to see him Monday," he told Leget.

"He knows where I live," Leget answered.

"It's about the trap-lines, so you had better go," Cy said. And he thought, you will have to go the white way for once. Now we will see how big you are.

"Explain yourself," Leget demanded.

Cy walked ahead beside the horses. "I have nothing to explain," he said rebelliously. "I only tell you what the Agent said."

16

MATT GOT UP FROM HIS COT AND WENT TO THE WINDOW
again. Dawn had sharpened the eastward peaks and he
saw three of Jonathan's dogs in the yard, scavenging
and sniffing. They took turns at the chopping block,
then faded into the ground mist. He returned to the cot
and lay down to wait. Matt blamed himself for not
following Paul's advice. Now it was too late. Stevie's
little body locked inside that white cement! The
thought was frenzy. June said Mr. Haney had worked
with big doctors in the war and that he knew about
casts. She said to ask him. But if Mr. Haney would not
side with them against that hospital doctor, to whom
could they turn?

Matt must have dozed, for when he looked again he
saw smoke from the mission house chimney. He put on
his boots, touched off the kitchen fire and went to the
garden. He pulled carrots, beets and several of his
largest onions, and after washing them under the tap
at the school corner he came back and cut a cabbage.
Then he went into the room off the kitchen, shook Cy
and told him to get up. "The man and his wife will be
waiting for us to carry those boxes up the stairs," he
said. He went out and put the washed vegetables in a
pail.

Cy came to the porch, looking sleepy and combing his hair. "How long have they been up?"

"Long enough. If you are ready we will go. And should there be confusing talk I ask you to make it straight for me in our language." Matt led across the school ground and knocked on the kitchen door.

Mrs. Haney opened. "For you, to get you started," Matt said, giving her the pail.

"How thoughtful! Thank you very much." She gave Cy a brisk "good morning" and invited them inside.

Mr. Haney was sitting at the table. "Just in time for coffee," he said. "And thanks again for your help last night."

Cy explained that they were here to carry up the trunks but Mr. Haney said not to hurry. He brought a chair for Matt. "How's June?" he asked. "We were hoping to see her last night."

"She was out," Cy said. Both he and June were visiting Victor and Teresa when Matt came to say the truck was in. Matt expected her to hurry back to the mission house with them, but she said to-morrow would be soon enough.

"I'm looking forward to having June in school," Mrs. Haney said to Matt as she handed him his cup. "June has real promise; she's a girl with possibilities. And your new little boy, what about him? Will you be starting him this morning?"

Matt held the cup tightly. After his hours of anxiety, here was his opening, ready-made. "She in hospital." His agitation made him use the wrong word, but then natives with English much better than his often got the "he" and "she" mixed.

"What's your little boy's name?" Mrs. Haney asked. "What do you call him?"

"Call for Stevie. But not for school this year, look like." The trouble was boiling up inside him now, strongly, like the whirlpool below the big riffle. "One day he playing his wagon and he fall. Last year I s'pose. Now little lump his back, size of this," Matt crooked his finger to show how trifling the lump was. "That doctor say pretty bad and put in hospital.

"Last day I go for see him that doctor got in cast." Matt's voice rasped with protest. "Here to here." He made a slashing gesture across his throat and then across his hips, giving the impression of constriction and of trapped, unavailing struggle.

Cy swallowed his coffee and set the cup away from him. "It's part of the cure," he said. He felt very conscious of his uncle.

Matt got to his feet and faced Mr. Haney across the table. "S'pose you take big strong man same me. If in cast gets weak; don't want for eat; get more sick." His eyes flashed. "We want that doctor do something. S'pose my finger got bad pus. I cover up; don't wash out that pus. Pretty quick my finger rot and dropping off. You know that right." He was almost shouting, as if challenging Mr. Haney to contradict him.

"Could be," Mr. Haney admitted.

"Everybody know that. Indian people know that. I born back in hills but I know that. We know what that doctor got for do. He got to cut; wash out that pus in Stevie body. We got our own medicines for fix, but he say no. Own doctors, too. They do all right before. White doctor not only kind of doctor. What the matter that doctor? He got hands. What you think?"

"I'm sure I don't know what to think," Mr. Haney gave Cy a questioning glance. "I'm afraid I don't quite get the picture."

"You know that doctor; you hear about him? How we sure he got his papers?" Matt reached for Cy's arm and pulled him forward. "Stand by me. Paul told it to me right. I want you to tell him of the doctors who have learned on us, then gone away. Do not let him think I am talking wildly, that I am an idiot."

"Why doesn't he have a good straight talk with the doctor?" Mr. Haney asked Cy. "It sounds like a pretty clear-cut case to me. Were you along when the boy was taken in? Do you remember what name the doctor gave it, what he found?"

"Do not repeat the name," Matt commanded. "You are here to help me. You know it was a lie."

Mrs. Haney put her hand on Matt's arm. "That's what I'd do. I'd ask the doctor to explain; tell him exactly what's on your mind."

Matt asked Cy to verify his understanding of her meaning, then shook his head. "More better I not make trouble for that doctor."

"But that's not making trouble, asking the doctor to explain. He'd be glad to explain. Simply tell him you do not understand."

A shrewdness, not at all characteristic of him, stiffened Matt's face. "S'pose I make trouble for that doctor—look out."

"What do you mean, look out?"

Matt felt himself in a narrow place. Either he had said too much or not enough. "That doctor got his hands on Stevie now," he answered, warily. "I make him mad for me; he see his chance get even."

Mrs. Haney looked startled. "Cy, whatever is your uncle getting at?"

Matt stood straight, his eyelids lowered. "Good chance for him, first time he get Stevie on the table."

"Cy, please! I realize how terribly worried he is and all that, but tell him he simply must not let his imagination run away with him. Doctors are here to help us; doctors are our friends. He may be sure this doctor's doing what is best."

"I know," Cy said. He wanted to tell them the name of the sickness, and the reason for the cast and that Stevie should go to Miller Bay, but if he did he would be out in the open against his uncle and his mother. "They think the doctor is all right," he told Matt. "They think he knows what he is doing."

But Matt was not falling into that hole. "There is this doctor with his crazy talk of Miller Bay and there was that other doctor who gave me white pills that time I had trouble with my kidneys. Take them with lots of water, water until my belly bloated. That doctor mistook me for a horse. But with him it was simply a matter of throwing the pills in the bushes and curing myself with Minnie's medicine, while with Stevie we are trapped. That doctor has his hands on Stevie; every day he has his hands on him. He will not cut out the pus. I have seen the cast, and now what worse thing is he up to? But I will say no more for I see these two are with that doctor in the same canoe."

What Matt said to the Haneys, Cy had heard him say even more vehemently at home, but this morning he was made inescapably aware of the opposition he faced in getting Stevie away to Miller Bay. It towered before him and he saw no way around. His hints and attempts at persuasion would not help; they were no more use than piling stones to overcome a mountain. Now he stood under its shadow and he felt himself in a dark and lonely place.

This dark and cut-off feeling came whenever, in even

the most trifling particular, he tried to stand against the
current of village life. At the cannery he had felt confusion, while here it was the continual, one-way pull of
choices. Was this Miriam's meaning, and Dot's too,
when they warned him he had to make up his mind to
go all one way or all the other?

Like me in there with Matt this morning, he thought,
coming down the ridge from the woodlot after work. I
was afraid to go clean over to the Haneys. They would
have backed me up if I had told them it is TB of the
spine. That way they would have got behind me and
scared Matt so he would have to let Stevie go.

Matt had spent the afternoon at the river, pole
fishing, and after supper he told June she could take
some of the trout to the Haneys. June let him think
she would but when Cy left the table she followed him
outside and said she wanted to talk to him.

She caught his arm and walked him over to the side
gate across from Caleb's. "The Haneys must think
we're an ignorant bunch," she burst out, angrily. "Matt
—the way he talked about that doctor!"

"When did they tell you? When were you over?"

"I wasn't over and I'm not going over. You think I
want to show my face there after this? Matt can say
what he likes inside our own house, but to say it to
them! He must be crazy." Tears came to her eyes.
"When I came in from school he was telling Mama
about it. My gosh! The stuff he said!"

Cy kept looking at her and shaking his head with a
sort of dismayed commiseration, then he looked away
and put his arms on the top of the gate. He had no need
to ask. He knew enough, more than enough. A feeling
of physical weariness came to him, as in one of those

dreams when the same obstacles keep coming up over and over, with no hope of release.

"It makes a person feel foolish, their own family showing them up like that." June plucked a leaf and nipped its stem between her even front teeth with an exasperated kind of daintiness. "All about the doctor taking it out on Stevie if we go against him. Talk about your superstition! Now I guess they think we go in for medicine men and everything."

"He's scared for Stevie."

"Sure, but what does he think we are? He didn't have to talk like that in front of them." June blew the leaf from between her lips. "People talk too much around here. Next we know somebody'll be letting slip about Victor and Teresa just living together. That's what I hate. A person tries to do things the right way and then we get disgraced. I'm sick of this old place."

Far away, beyond the house tops, the sunset drew vast geometric patterns among the peaks. Cy felt a tender, tragic, sadness for June, for Matt, for all of them. There was no sense in blaming them, for in the end nobody was to blame. It was all a part of being Indian. His few hours with Miriam had cleared the confusion from his mind, but as long as he stayed here, as long as he resisted, he would never be free of it. Now for the first time, he fully understood why his father had not lived out his life here, and why he had been compelled to go away.

17

CY PINCHED OFF A SMALL LUMP OF SALMON ROE, IMPALED
it on his hook, and put the bait-can on the sand behind
him where his catch and Miriam's lay in separate piles.
He gave his pole an easy, under-hand swing and sank
the bait in a patch of quiet water inside the eddy, then
rested on his heels and let his cork drift. The sun was
off the river and the shadow of the old totem poles
reached across the turf almost to the smoke-houses.

The best of the fishing was over for the day and the
trout would soon drop into deeper water, but he was in
no hurry to go home, nor was Miriam, apparently. Their
meeting had not been planned but this was the best
fishing place and they had been together since mid-
afternoon. She had kept to her place, a little upstream
from him, and stood on the strip of wet sand with her
pole in one hand and the other hand resting on her hip.
Her feet were together, her body relaxed; but she kept
her eyes on her cork and was ready for a fish the instant
it took her bait. Her attention never wandered as he
allowed his to do, and she had more fish to take home
than he had.

Away from others, fishing or picking berries, she
always showed a sort of primitive absorption which
June and the other girls did not. Mostly they went out

for the fun of it, chattering and calling back and forth; but Miriam always became intent, as if what she brought home meant the difference between plenty and hunger. At the cannery or in town, people might think her old-fashioned compared to the other girls, but in the woods or along the river she had a watchfulness and a grace which gave the impression of belonging.

In one way he felt easier in his mind when he was with her. They did not see each other regularly, sometimes not oftener than once a week. She had the house to look after, and because of Old Paul, it was not the same between them when he went there. He had his chores, too; recently he had been out cruising a timber claim he and Victor were thinking of taking so they could bid on a contract for cordwood at the Junction. Fur prices were down and Matt thought they would be wise to let their fur multiply on their line this season. They could not make wages on the wood contract but it should see them through the winter. The timber claim they were after was only three miles down the road, and that suited Victor because he and Teresa wanted to live at home.

Cy's cork was pulled under but it came up before he could strike. Probably his bait was gone but he did not lift his line to see. He had trout enough, and he was reluctant to interrupt the thoughts which Miriam's nearness aroused.

He saw her lift her line and start winding it around the butt of her pole, so he took his in and went to a scrub willow growing on the edge of the turf. He cut two forked switches and was threading his catch on one when she came.

After she strung her fish she took them to the water, wetting them and wiping the sand off them. "We did well," she said. "Did you feel lucky when you came?"

Cy said he had not thought about it. He knew she kept to the old belief that some people spoiled the luck of the person they went out with while others helped it. There were many old stories about that.

Miriam scoured her hands with sand and shook the water from them. She said they must be lucky for each other. They stood for a moment, reluctant to leave. The noise of the riffle seemed louder. That might mean rain. Matt said the riffle sounded louder before a rain.

Carrying their poles and fish, they crossed the turf and came to the open shed in which Paul built his canoes, where Miriam turned up the narrow path leading to her house. She did not look back or say good-bye, as if they were parting, but as if they were a couple each with work to do and presently to come together again, a couple who would be always close.

Melissa had the meal ready, and after he had eaten, Cy took some of the trout to Fat Marie. Her house was the last one in the village, beyond Jonathan's, and advantageously hidden from the road by second-growth. Dick Dawson was there.

"I sure was lucky this afternoon," she was telling Dick. "The smell all through the house and big fool me working the bottling machine when Mr. Haney come up the path."

Dick swore. "Was he wise?"

His alarm delighted Marie. "Sure was. I had to set him up a couple."

Dick told her that wasn't funny. "I wouldn't put it past you, at that. Okay, what did you do?"

"I beat it outside and kep' him talking. He come for cigarette papers."

"If you ask me you better leave off that store of

yours. You don't want people nosing round. Us guys from the pole camp give you business enough and we don't want no Mountie on our tail. How do you know he wasn't wise?"

"Oh, I just know." Marie was giggling. "But the stuff sure smelled."

"All right, laugh. But lots of whites are stool pigeons. They sure go for the stuff themselves but it gripes them to see us get it. How do you know he won't tip off the Mountie?"

Marie had the trap door up and was packing the two dozen in Dick's sack, wrapping each bottle in paper so it wouldn't rattle. "How could he?" she asked, disarmingly. "He didn't see anything."

"He's got a nose, ain't he? You're not taking all the chances, remember. Last time they got the goods on you, you know what happened. Four of us got nicked twenty and costs for being in possession on a reserve. How do you know what he came for?"

"I told you. Cigarette papers."

"Oh yeah! You better smarten up. That guy's been around."

"I think so, too." Marie fastened the sack. "I slipped in a couple extra to show the fellas nothing stingy about old Marie."

Dick paid her and put the sack on his shoulder. He was feeling better now and said he would hate to see her thrown in the can, because her brew was the best of any. "Even the white bootleggers admit that. But you better not crowd your luck, sweetheart. You were lucky as a cut cat this time, but you got to watch your step with whites in the village."

Dick went down the short-cut over the creek and Marie closed the trap door and pulled the woodbox into place on top of it. "I kind of like that Mr. Haney," she said as she began cleaning the trout. "I don't know about her but I sure like him. What you think of him?"

"All right, I guess."

"He sure was friendly, us talking out there beside the aster bed. I sure don't like him finding out the business I'm in. If he ever asks around, you cover up, see?"

"He could ask anybody. They all know, and lots are against you doing it, don't forget."

"Caleb all the time after me to cut it out but I don't like to make the fellas sore. I'm only doing best I can but Caleb makes me feel mean about it." Marie reached for another fish. "What you think of Mrs. Haney? I hear Jonathan's little kid kind of scared of her. I sure hope she's not the bossy kind same as the one made Bella stop school."

Like everyone else, Marie excepted, Cy knew that was Bella's own fault. Bella's teacher had got after her for talking native in school and to get even Bella had written across her reader, and in ink, "I don't want to learn the damn white man's language." The teacher said she must say she was sorry before she could be taken back, but Bella was tired of school anyway, so she made Marie believe the teacher would not let her in.

Cy said he did not think Mrs. Haney was the bossy kind. June had had little to say of what went on in school and she still had not visited the mission house. Walking home, he wondered why. He was not at all sure June's avoiding the Haney's was due entirely to the wild things Matt told them about the doctor.

Turning into the yard, Cy saw Paul Leget, Caleb, John Moose and Crosby Duncan on the front steps with Matt. He went to the back door and Melissa asked him to bring water. When he came from the tap she told him to make fire in the outside stove because she would serve coffee to the men. By that Cy knew they were holding some kind of village meeting.

He was kneeling beside the stove making shavings when Caleb spoke.

"Matt will agree with me," he heard Caleb say. "The Agent's heart is strong for us. It is not for us to make it harder for him. To-morrow afternoon when we gather there, let the voice of this village be a friendly one. He will have opposition enough from some other villages."

"We have our rights," John Moose answered tartly. He was a wispy little man who had worked with French Canadians in steamboat days and had absorbed some of their mannerisms. In village affairs he took his instructions from Minnie, who was of the Wolf people and who invariably supported Paul Leget.

Chief Crosby Duncan of the Fireweeds spoke. "Wild talk will not serve our rights down there to-morrow. We must not over-reach and so turn the Agent against us. Trapping rights have always needed careful hand-ling. From oldest times friends have quarrelled and men have been killed because of them. The white trappers want our grounds; we need strong law on our side and the Agent stands before us as the law."

Leget sat on the top step with his head sunk between his shoulders. "The government is cunning and this is one more of its attempts to break down our crest system. Take away a chief's right to give to one man and withhold from another and what is left to him but the shell of his name?"

"We must go by the maps," Caleb said, persuasively.

"Whose maps? What maps? Our maps are in our minds and in our memories, and our memories are long. Whites crowd in on us but we have been here always. Not a stream or mountain, pond or draw, which does not have its ancient name and its ancient story. We are a part of this valley and it is a part of us. Separate the two and the life sickens and goes out." Paul banged his fist on the step. "Can you not see in this further proof that the government has set its face against all which holds us together as a people? Yield nothing, consent to nothing, and leave the Agent at the bottom of this dark and twisted matter."

"The Agent is reasonable; we must be reasonable," Caleb said. He spoke blandly, giving his words the shape of a suggestion.

Paul turned on him. "Because you are a Grouse man does not compel you always to sit on the sunny side of the hill."

Matt was picking his teeth with a splinter and he took out the splinter and studied it. "This will end," he said, "as things always end when the ways of white men go against the ways of Indians. You will storm and denounce, but a thing which is very old will die down there to-morrow and you cannot save it. The tree which stands too stiffly against the wind is the first to fall; the proud canoe wears thin and splits apart."

Caleb turned to Leget and his face had a conciliatory, pleading look. "Not all have the warrior's heart. And on top of that, my friend, there is the law."

Leget brushed the words away. "We can speak as one man and force them to change the law. Or we can ignore it."

"The law is the law," Matt said. He got up slowly and went into the house.

"Twenty-five hundred of us along this river and he bows the neck!" Paul's words bit. "I tell you we could make a mountain stand aside if we heaved together. I know what I am saying."

There was further talk but already Cy, still kneeling at the fire, knew that this time Paul was not going to have his way. Yet the knowing brought only a passing gratification, for the defiant words again gave the feeling of worth. In contrast to Caleb's compliance and Matt's resigned evasion of the issue, Leget's unyielding opposition made him the one complete man among them, rooted and massive and whole.

And yet to-morrow, because they would leave him to stand alone, it was certain he would lose. In former times such a gathering of chiefs would have meant feasting, oratory, historic dances, feats of magic, pageantry, and colour, and when the people returned to their villages they would have in them the talk of months. Instead, promptly at two o'clock, they would file into the Agency office with their hats in their hands and sit down to a white man's business meeting.

What would happen in there would be what Matt said would happen, with Leget and his small following seen through the government's eyes as trouble-makers because they held to the ancient rights. But Old Paul would stand there and the acquiescent, reasoned arguments would drift around him like snow around a boulder.

That night, after Cy went to bed, Matt and Melissa sat in the kitchen, talking late.

"As for myself, I know what I am going to do," Cy heard Matt say. "I will tell the Agent to put my line in Stevie's name. Then it will be held the white way until he is old enough to work it."

"I suppose it had to be," Melissa said, "but my feeling about those grounds is deep. It is a heavy thing to know they are to be dealt with in this way. They have been in our family since the beginning. See you make Stevie understand how big a thing it is to hold them in his name. Dot will have forgotten, and in any case she would not have told him."

"I will make him understand the long story of it. Get better soon, I will say to him, and if you do not travel too fast for me, one fine day we will be starting back there together. One of these days, young brother, I will say to him, one of these days . . . "

I can hear you telling him, Cy thought, as you told me when I was little. And how long ago that seemed! Matt would show Stevie their beaver ponds, and the big spruce where as a boy he caught his first marten in a deadfall, and the place where the grizzly almost got him. At night they would lie by the fire under the smoke-hole while he told the little fellow old, old stories of their grounds. To Matt, the spirits of their forebears would draw near and the past fold protectively around. The feet of their people would be on the mountains again; the forest intimate; the sky contained and close.

I remember every word Matt used to tell me, Cy thought; he made me feel I was part of it, like Paul said. But Cy was unable to feel that now. The grounds were a place on a map now, an emptiness with echoes.

18

CALEB SAT IN THE SUN AT HIS HOUSE DOOR, HEARING Cy's saw bite into the seasoned birch that would keep them warm this winter, and waiting for Mr. Haney to come.

To-morrow was Victor and Teresa's big day and Clarice had delegated Caleb to give the Haneys a special invitation to the wedding feast. The customary word-of-mouth invitation had been circulated but the two white people might fail to understand it included them. Unfortunately, because there was no missionary in the village, the young couple were to be married earlier in the day by a minister of a different church who lived at the Junction. It was too bad that the village church would not be used, but the feast was the big thing; it was open to all and Clarice wanted everybody to attend. For more than a week she and women of her crest had been preparing for it and her heart was set on seeing the Haneys seated among the guests of honour.

And little wonder, for this would be a feast to remember. Nothing skimped, nothing overlooked. Yesterday the cake, ordered well ahead from Rupert, had been delivered at Clarice's house. Bert said it was nearly as much as he could carry. For days the women had been going back and forth, collecting dishes, baking, and cooking. The village hall was scrubbed and ready, the tables and seats inside and in place. Clarice, Caleb mused, was not a woman given to pride but she could be forgiven if she held her head high after this was over.

Cy's saw kept going and Caleb began to feel a trifle anxious. "You are sure Mr. Haney knows he can buy his tobacco from me?"

Cy came to the pail for a drink of water. "I told him. I think he will come. It is still early."

"Good; very good." Caleb did not begrudge Marie her share of the Haneys' trade, but Mr. Haney had been seen going to her store more than once, and one must bear in mind that the worn trail is the easiest for the feet to follow.

"Do not fret yourself, old one," Nettie sung out from the room. "Marie does not sell his kind of cig'ret tobacco. The man is a slave to tobacco, so is sure to come. Remember the Captain?"

Caleb chuckled. "I remember." Like the vivifying warmth of the sun, the memory of those long-ago days helped him forget the handicaps of his obese, mis-shapen body. The strong light on his eyelids was like a curtain through which he could see old happenings within the sealed-off room of memory. The Captain and the pack horse, name of Blackie, which ate his tobacco!

Caleb could see the place on the old Naas river grease trail where it happened. The Captain was not a trader nor a "Boston man" seeking gold along the creeks. He was wild enough before he lost his tobacco. Chasing up and down side valleys, taking pictures with his picture box in daytime and at night hiding in his tent getting the pictures out of the box. Plenty mad sometimes; plenty strong talk. And then Blackie eating his tobacco!

In their own camp, resting and making love at nights, he and Nettie would laugh and laugh to think that a big white man would fly into tempers like a baby because he had no tobacco for sucking through his pipe.

A dog got up from the chips and flopped in the shade of the woodpile. To-day's sun had warmth enough to draw the pitch smell from the lumber of the wall, but all too soon the cold, short days would be upon them. Winters came so swiftly now. Caleb was remembering the pitchy smell the sun drew from the branches of their beds, the hundreds, thousands of brush beds on which he and Nettie had lain along the trails they could not travel any more.

Little Nettie clinging to him with desire, yielding to him, teasing him, making the nights and sometimes the noonings too, hours to look forward to. And across the divides the groundhogs whistling down at them and flocks of little birds coming and going in swirls of cheery sound, the sky pure blue and a lightness in the air and in your heart and limbs.

Caleb heard Cy's saw stop. "Mr. Haney is here," Cy called out.

Caleb hunched sideways on the bench and placed his hand behind his ear to indicate his deafness. "Sit down, my friend." He put out his hand and Mr. Haney took it.

"So we meet again," Mr. Haney said. "Good country you have up here."

"Village people glad you come," Caleb shouted. "Good thing this village have white lady teacher, white gentleman in mission house. Bad when nobody in that house for telling people right way to go. People got to go the good way, not look for bad way." He cleared his throat. "Remember Lot's wife."

Mr. Haney said "yes, indeed", then he asked for cigarette tobacco.

Out of sight in the doorway Nettie made a clucking sound. Not that she was making fun of Mr. Haney, but his weakness for tobacco made him pleasantly human, and if he had Gitkshan they might soon be having their little jokes, all in good fun and no offence intended.

After Nettie brought the tobacco, Caleb gave the invitation and then he said that Clarice would take it as a high honour if Mrs. Haney, as their teacher, would say a few words when the time came for the speech making. The village teacher was expected to speak at wedding feasts, he explained. That was the custom.

Mr. Haney rubbed his ear and thought for a moment. He turned to Cy. "You think it would be all right? I mean to say we're new here. It wouldn't be, well— horning in?"

"It's what Clarice wants. When people speak they give advice to the young couple."

"That's fine, then. If you're sure it's the accepted thing. I rather think my wife will take to the idea. We've not met either of them yet, at least not to know. They're both of this village, I suppose."

"Victor is."

"And the young lady?"

"She's from a different village."

"One of those long-range romances, eh? Do you know her? Do you think she'll like it here?"

Cy turned and drew a stick of cordwood from the pile. "I guess so." He wished someone had told the Haneys about the native way and that, if you went by it, there was nothing shameful about Victor and Teresa living together, before.

The following afternoon at three o'clock Cy, after

considerable urging from Clarice, presented himself
at the mission house and told the Haneys he had been
sent to conduct them to the hall.

Yesterday Caleb had told Mr. Haney the feast would
start promptly at two, and it was pretty obvious to Cy
that they had been dressed and waiting for him for some
length of time. From June he knew that Mrs. Haney
was a great one for promptness, but there had been a
heavy frost during the night and it took time to get the
hall comfortably heated. According to Bert, who had
driven out around noon, more people from the Junction
reserve were going to attend than had been expected.
This required extra tables, and before getting into his
good clothes, Cy had gone to different houses and
collected planks and trestles. All morning, women of
Clarice's crest kept bringing baskets of food and dishes.
Then, while bringing the couple back from the Junction
in his truck, Jonathan had a puncture. On top of all
this Teresa and her attendants took long in dressing.
However, none of the village people minded the delay,
for all the while a pleasant anticipation was building up.

Cy and the Haneys were passing Caleb's house when
they heard the band strike up and on reaching the hall
corner they saw the wedding procession coming from
Clarice's. The trumpets blared at the cold, hard sky,
the big drum thumped, and the ribbons on Dick Dawson's car rippling in the wind made a pretty sight.
Children ran beside the car and dogs raced this way
and that between the totem poles, barking. Two
young fellows in sport jackets, Junction fellows, stood
in the road aiming their cameras. Marie was on the
hall steps, giggling, and tearing at the cellophane of a
packet of confetti with her gold-capped teeth.

Chief Crosby Duncan conducted them to the head

table set parallel to the stage. It had cards telling each person where to sit. The wedding cake was midway along this table. It stood high, with pillars between the layers. Mrs. Haney's place was furthest along. Bert pulled out Mrs. Haney's chair for her and sat down between her and Mr. Haney. Cy heard him tell the Haneys that the bride's mother had asked him to sit between them and translate.

"That's very thoughtful of her," Mrs. Haney remarked, in a formal sort of voice.

Mr. Haney settled himself and looked at all the things on the table. "Very nice," he said.

"Not bad," Bert conceded.

Each place had new dishes, glass ones. There were platters of cold chicken, ham and salads, cakes and fruit in bowls and vases of paper flowers. The serving women wore white aprons, Miriam among them. This morning she said she hoped Paul would let her stay to the dance.

The blare of horns filled the hall. Everybody rose and Mrs. Haney's face had a tender, motherly look. "So that's Teresa!" Cy heard her whisper. "How composed she is. And look at June. She's *beautiful!*"

Victor was leading Teresa up the aisle between the rows of tables. "There's one guy with something on the ball," Bert said. "I keep telling him to get out on his own, not stick around the village."

"I see," Mr. Haney said.

Victor did everything just right, smiling, not in any hurry, and knowing what to do. He drew back Teresa's chair for her and waited until she sat down, and Cy felt proud of him. June had on her blue dress, the one Mrs. Haney had shown her how to make. She wore her hair a new way and looked like a grown woman. Bella, being Bella, had fixed the front of her dress lower than it should be. She had a locket and it lay in the cleft between her small, pert breasts.

When all were in their places, Crosby Duncan asked for silence. "Be Present At Our Table, Lord," they all sang.

The food was good, but Cy did not feel much like eating. Bert kept telling the Haneys who people were and making fun of some of them. When Teresa cut the cake, Victor stood at her side and guided her hand on the knife. Cy noticed the ring on her finger which Victor had sent away for.

Then the speeches began. They were the usual mixture of good advice and 'newly-married' jokes, which Bert translated only in part. "In sickness and in healt'" Caleb intoned, then elaborated in native. "Dow s'all not commit adultery." People nodded gravely but soon they were laughing at his chamber-pot joke. That was one joke Bert did not translate.

A dozen others spoke, all at length. It was growing dark. Mothers and big sisters were going out and coming back with little ones who needed attention, and with the doors being opened the hall became cool. The wind was rising and somebody put more wood in the heater. Gas lamps were brought and hung from the ceiling. Then Chief Crosby Duncan looked along the table and told Mrs. Haney it was her turn.

Mrs. Haney's speech was short, but it was a nice one, and the people listened closely. She told them she and her husband were pleased to be living in the village and that they wanted to help in every way they could. She asked fathers and mothers to see that their children came regularly to school, and that being late kept a child behind the others. "They are bright children," she said, "and it is only their lack of English which holds them back. More English spoken in the homes will help them to get ahead." Then she said thanks again for the invitation, and that she and her husband wished the young couple a long and happy married life. When she sat down, the people clapped.

Although Paul Leget's rank entitled him to be among the first to speak, he waited until last. Cy soon knew why.

"My advice to you young people is to stand on your own feet. You weaken yourselves when you lean on others," Bert translated. "Respect your names and the position of your family. Hold yourselves high."

"Good for him," Mr. Haney said, quietly.

Bert took out a cigarette but smoking was forbidden in the hall and he did not light it. "Listen who's talking!" he muttered. "He holds these people back more than any."

Mr. Haney nudged him. "Please go on."

Bert wet the end of his cigarette. "It's nothing much. He's telling them to stay away from the booze," he said.

But Paul was telling them much more than that. "We had no strong drink among us until the whites brought it. The whites want to see all Indians in the ground, put there by the drink and the lung-sick and their other diseases. They want to finish us as a people. This latest attack on our trapping grounds should make clear to all what they scheme to do . . ."

"What's he saying?" Mrs. Haney whispered. "Please do continue. We very much want to know what he is saying."

But Bert just sat there with a slighting, defiant look on his thin face.

Beneath the table Cy's hands were going up and
down over his knees and he was afraid to look up in case
the Haneys asked him to interpret. Paul had just told
Victor and Teresa it was no concern of theirs how
whites looked upon their having come together weeks
ago. He told them that from their first night they had
been honourably married and charged them never to
grow careless and forget it. "Speak only in the *gum-
see-wa* tongue to your children, this woman advises. A
sweet medicine that would be! Holding to our language
is what preserves us as a people. Our language is a
strong wall around us. We are inside that wall and we
shut the whites outside it." Paul levelled a finger at
Victor. "See that you and your woman keep it so."

The short, hammering sentences beat upon the
attentive stillness, and as Cy listened with a kind of
hostile fascination he could imagine Paul Leget holding
forth at some long-ago feast in one of the old communal
dwellings, his jaw thrust out, his face contorted in the
leaping firelight, and swaying his hearers as he was
swaying these, by the sheer power of his unshakable
convictions.

But suddenly Cy's awareness of Paul's voice and of
the rows of attentive faces blurred and he was seized by
the feeling that he was once more in the boat-shed when
the boss and Paul got him between them. Only this was
worse because, unlike the boss, the Haneys were
genuinely friendly. It was maddening to see that old
man so confident of his power, attacking all whites from
behind his wall and knowing that none of them—least
of all the young cedar he meant to have as son—
possessed the audacity to breach that wall. The
Haneys must suspect things were being said which even
Bert dare not put into English.

When Paul finished and returned to his place, Bert pushed back his chair. "I've had my fill of this," he told the Haneys.

"It must have been quite some speech," Mr. Haney remarked.

"You wouldn't like what he said. Ask Cy. No more speeches anyhow, so if you folks'll excuse me I'm getting out of here."

As Cy watched Bert edge between the tables and join Dick Dawson and some others near the door, a wave of self-disgust swept over him. He saw Bert and Dick go outside and it was all he could do to keep from following them. Paul's words were not his words, yet here he sat like a guilty person, afraid he would be asked to translate them, and avoiding the Haneys' eyes.

Chief Crosby Duncan was speaking. "He's telling the people the cake cost sixty dollars, from Rupert," Cy explained in a taut monotone. "Fifty dollars goes to the band, thirty to Caleb for the church, the same to the hall. Twenty for the orchestra for the dance right after this."

There were murmurs of admiration. "Everybody take home all the food in front of you. The dishes at this table are presents. Take them home; take everything home. The feast cost over seven hundred all together and they hope everybody had a good time. The dance starts soons as the floor is cleared. Everybody stay, he says."

People began reaching, filling flour sacks and pillow cases with the remaining food. "It's the way we do it," Cy said stiffly, seeing the Haneys' curious glances.

Clarice, tired but beaming, liked it when the Haneys thanked her. A lot of people were crowding around and Cy could not get away. Just then Bert came up.

"Everybody happy?" he asked loudly. His breath was strong, hard stuff. He tapped Mr. Haney on the shoulder. "You folks staying for the dance?"

Mr. Haney said he thought not. His wife had been watching Bert and now she moved to the end of the table where June was. She put her hand on June's arm and began speaking earnestly to her, but June tossed her head and turned away.

Miriam was at the opposite side of the table gathering up the plates. She looked across at Cy and smiled. "Grandfather will let me stay to the dance a while," she said softly, in Gitkshan.

All day Cy had hoped for this, but now it did not seem to matter. In her good dress and white apron she looked small and self-contained, and her brown, rather slanting eyes held a welcoming readiness. But, strangely, he felt that to-night he must not so much as touch her. To-night he must not think of her in that way at all; he must not think of her warm maturity and that she was a woman who could be his. Away from this place, this village, it would be different. He remembered with longing the protective feeling which came to him on the day of her home-coming while he sat beside her in the wagon as she slept. He remembered the little-girl innocence of her face and how he wanted to gather her in his arms and shield her and have her always to himself. But to-night he realized with deadening certainty that in this village she could never be completely his. In Rupert it could be different; even in the Junction it could be. But never here; Old Paul had seen to that long ago.

Cy pushed through the crowd and stood irresolutely on the steps. He did not know if he would stay for the dance or not. The Haneys were going up the side street and he had to check his impulse to follow them, to sit late in the mission house with Mr. Haney, not talking, but somehow feeling again the flow of understanding between them which Paul's hard words had marred.

Or had he merely imagined there was ever understanding? Standing in the darkness at the bottom of the steps, with people coming and going and the laughter and voices inside, he felt cut off, impotent, and terribly alone. A girl ran past him to recover a cloth left on one of the tables the men had carried out. He saw the blur of her dress and the light from the open door on her hair. If only Miriam would come out! Even if she did not notice him or speak, it would help. The mere sight of her would give him something he could hold on to. He felt confused, overwhelmed, like swirling drift when the river was in flood.

He heard his name called from the corner of the building and, going over, he found Dick Dawson and two native men from the Junction.

"Haney and his woman coming back?" Dick asked. Cy said he did not think so.

"You should know; you been sticking around with them all night," one of the men said. He held out a bottle. "Have a drink."

"Hold it," the second man objected. "How we know he ain't some stool pigeon?"

"Cy's all right."

"If he don't tell Haney all he knows, he's all right."

"Whose bottle is this anyhow?" Dick took the bottle from the man and thrust it into Cy's hand. "Don't stand looking at it; drink it. You think we got all night?"

Cy did not want to drink, but the way he felt just then it made no difference whether he did or not. Nothing made any difference. He put the bottle to his lips and held it there until the fumes rose in his throat and choked him.

"You want to knock yourself out?" One of the men held up the bottle and looked at it against the light from the window behind them. "That's rum; it ain't Marie's brew, remember."

Cy felt it hit his stomach, its numbing hotness fanning out inside him, pressing against his lungs and making his breath come short. The bottle went from hand to hand and when it came back to Dick, Cy reached for it.

"I be god-damned! The slugs you take!" The man clapped Cy on the shoulder. "I wish we had old Leget out here; I sure would like to see him with a skinful."

Dick laughed, "How about that, Cy? How'd you like to see the old man with a skinful?"

"I don't care about him," Cy answered, boastfully.

"How about that girl of his?" one of the Junction men asked. "How about getting her out here? I bet she'd like a nip."

"Bella would, that's for sure," the other Junction man said. They laughed and Cy laughed with them. He was getting on fine with them, just fine. A warming fullness was under his skin and he felt he was bigger, aglow with an expansive disregard. A narrowed-down dullness that he liked very much was coming to the front of his head. His sight became fuzzy and there was a thumping in his ears, but altogether he had an enclosed, safe feeling which made all his perplexities seem remote and inconsequential, as if they belonged to someone else.

They talked some more and then Dawson shook the bottle. "We might as well kill it before we go in," he said.

He threw the empty into the weeds and somebody passed the cigarettes. A deadness had come to Cy's lips and he fumbled the one he took, so that most of it broke off inside his mouth. He spat and stood with his legs spread and shreds of the tobacco hanging from his lips.

One of the men gave a cowboy yip. "Start running, Bella. Here I come."

Cy lurched toward the wall, and tried to steady his shoulders against it, but it listed away from him.

"What we waiting for?" someone wanted to know. A face came close to Cy's. "You coming?"

Cy tried to dig his fingers into the clapboard on both sides of him but it kept slipping away.

"I'll say he ain't coming," one voice said.

"Crazy young punk," another voice said.

Another voice was blaming Dawson; another was answering him. All the voices were mixed up, receding, surging against him, above and under him, as the world whirled faster and then blacked out.

He staggered, pitched forward. The ground was tilting, folding backward on itself, and he clutched the weeds to keep from falling off it while his brain sank into darkness.

19

MOST OF THE AUTUMN COLOURING HAD GONE; THE cottonwoods along the river were bare and stood with their great, knobby arms extended in dreary benediction over the heads of lesser trees. Puddles along the valley road had ice on them; the mud was frozen hard; and over the sides and tailboard of Jonathan's truck June saw only a few thinned patches of yellow on distant ridges. Winter was almost here, and having to spend it in the village was a prospect she did not care to think about. She was glad to be getting away from the village if only for the day.

Cy was in the front seat with Jonathan, getting a driving lesson. The other night she heard him tell Matt that if he cleared enough on the wood claim he would make a down payment on a truck. He said that a fellow with a truck stood a good chance of getting hauling jobs around the Junction, as well as at mills and pole camps farther down the river. Ever since the dance, a truck seemed to be the only thing he could think about. He said no more cannery for him after next summer. He would come home with enough to pay off most of what he owed on the truck. After that, he would be his own boss and could work where he liked. A fellow could never get ahead just sticking in the village, he said.

Well, that certainly would be nice. By this time next year they would be able to drive down to the movies and dances at the Junction any time they liked, June mused. She and Mrs. Haney were sitting on boxes against the back of the cab, with Mrs. Haney's steamer rug over their knees. It was Saturday, the only day Mrs. Haney could get to the stores, and while it was nice that Jonathan could bring her, if a person had their own truck they could get out of the village and have a little change without everybody knowing. Mrs. Haney was good, and all that. This morning when she came out to the truck, she gave Cy a colouring book and crayons to take to Stevie. June thought how kind that was and wished all could have stayed the same between them in the village as it had been at the cannery.

The truck entered a grove of birches and Mrs. Haney remarked how beautiful they looked. "When I was little, I thought birch woods were what fairyland must be like. I used to think the most wonderful things could happen in a birch woods. I wonder if little native girls ever feel like that."

June said she did not know. It would be pleasant to chat back and forth with Mrs. Haney as they used to, but somehow things had begun to change between them from the very first day of school. As she marched up the school steps at the end of the line that first morning something told her their relationship had altered. Mrs. Haney's eyes had looked into hers with disconcerting directness—almost, June thought, as if Mrs. Haney had some special claim upon her and as if special things were expected of her. She had experienced a peculiar impulse to resist which, although it faded swiftly, made her feel she was being ungrateful.

Midway through the birch woods they crossed a

shoulder of the hill and were coasting down when the horn gave a short, salutory toot and there was Jasper Gawa on his horse, a short distance up the slope, between two birches.

Jasper waved, but June did not wave back. He sat his pony with slack grace, his rifle across his arm, looking down at the truck and smiling. His hair was long and his handsome, small-featured face had an untamed look. The light reflected from the birch trunks seemed to surround him and his pony with an airy unreality, as if they had ridden out of a world of their own and would go up through the birches and into it again.

"Who's that?" Mrs. Haney asked quickly. "I don't recall seeing him before." And when June told her: "Gawa? That sounds Japanese to me. Surely he's not Japanese."

"It's just a native name," June answered coolly. "It means like staying out in the woods most of the time; like living off the country."

For the rest of the trip, Mrs. Haney did not have much to say. She kept watching the scenery, sitting straight and with her gloved hands clasped in her lap. June knew she had been a little rude and she was sorry, but Jasper Gawa meant nothing to her, absolutely nothing, and she did not want to talk about him.

The Junction, on its flat between the two strong rivers, had once been the head of navigation for stern-wheelers churning up riffles and through canyons for almost two hundred miles from the coast. Later, when the railway was built, it passed the Junction by, but the Junction lived on, a setting readymade for movie westerns, with its trading post—RAW FURS BOUGHT AND SOLD; MINERS' SUPPLIES A SPECIALTY—its two Chinese cafés, its Mounted Police post, old stopping place, its Indians, prospectors, numerous dogs, and idle pack horses wandering the streets.

Jonathan let them out in front of a trucker's warehouse with the sign "Stage".

"What time will you be starting back?" Mrs. Haney asked him. She seemed all friendliness again.

Jonathan told her around four. Or maybe five. He said to take her time; no hurry.

Cy crossed with Jonathan to the garage. Mrs. Haney was going to the post office, but June told her she would ask for mail later, that she had a few things to buy. She noticed that the delivery truck Bert drove was in front of the trading company store, so she stopped and looked at what was in the windows. Compared to Rupert there was not much. She was about to stroll on when Bert came to get something out of the window and motioned through the glass for her to wait. Native people traded at the store, and because Bert knew Gitkshan, they liked to be waited on by him instead of by the white clerks.

As soon as he was free Bert hurried out. "Let's duck in next door for coffee. It's cold out here. I've got something to tell you."

It was steamy warm in the Chinaman's and the jukebox was going loud and fast. The place was filled with natives and he put his hand on the small of her back, guiding her to the only empty booth. The table was covered with used dishes, so while he went for the coffee, June stacked them and wiped some spilled food from the oilcloth with a paper napkin. He seemed eager and excited. She wondered what he had to tell her.

"If you hadn't come in to-day I was going to write you," he began. "I just heard yesterday there's a maid's job going at the hospital."

June set down her cup. "Honest?"

"That's right. If you like I could run you up there this afternoon."

June smiled across at him. "Wouldn't that be something, me working in town and you with a car to ride around in!"

"Well, why don't you? The pay's not bad, and they feed you and give you a room. You'd sure look sharp in one of those blue uniforms."

June looked down, toying with her spoon. Frequently of late she had wondered if they would have her at the hospital. The dozen or so native girls who worked there were mostly from the Junction and accustomed to being among whites. Others had been away to residential school and so would feel at home in a big place like that. But, except for her short while with the Haneys, she had only her mother's ways around the house to go by, and since this summer she realized how very unlike white ways these were.

"What makes you think they'd have me?" she asked, with a hint of teasing in her voice.

"Sure they'd have you!"

The prospect of working in the hospital, and his aggressive confidence in her, brought a confusion which she found distinctly pleasant. "I don't know why you think that, Bert. Native girls get turned down there all the time."

"Not your kind of native. Some types, yes. But not ones like you."

With a little inward smile, June let him take her hands. "It was swell of you to think of me for the job," she said. "It really was."

The dreamy passivity of her face puzzled him. "You want it, don't you?"

June nodded. "But poor me, I'm supposed to stay in school. One more year anyway, Cy says."

"You don't have to go by Cy."

June withdrew her hands. "I'll come in and see you this afternoon. I'll let you know what I'm going to do about it."

"How about me phoning up now to say you're coming? I could ask them to hold it."

June said not to bother, that she needed time to think it over. "I'd love to try it though. I'm getting tired of school." Before they went out she promised she would let him know right after lunch.

There was no mail, and as June came from the post office Mrs. Haney called to her from across the street. She had Cy with her. June hesitated, and then went over.

"It occurred to me that after our long drive we all would enjoy a real dinner," Mrs. Haney said pleasantly. "I've invited your brother, and I hope you'll join us."

June stole a glance at Cy. She knew by his face that he expected her to agree. "Well, thanks," she said. "I'm kind of busy though, but I guess it would be all right for me to come."

"Splendid. I've been meaning to have you two for weeks and this is my chance." Mrs. Haney spoke with what seemed to June unnecessary heartiness. "You see, June, I've a plan I'd like to discuss with you and Cy."

June again had the feeling that she was being challenged.

Eating with whites was nothing new to her but to Cy it was, and she wondered what persuasion Mrs. Haney had used to get him to consent.

"How about the café next to the garage?" Mrs.

Haney said. "It looks cleaner than the other, and fortunately it has no juke-box. But I'll leave it to you to choose."

"I think the garage one," June agreed. There was less chance of meeting Bert there. June was well aware of what Bert thought of Mrs. Haney, and she did not want him to see the two of them together.

They went in, took off their coats, and sat in one of the booths. Mrs. Haney read the menu. "What do you say to tomato soup and then the roast beef dinner?"

Cy nodded, but June picked up the other menu card and studied it. She said that if it was all the same she would skip the soup and take just ham and eggs.

While waiting for the Chinaman to bring their order Mrs. Haney talked casually, but they had not been eating long before she said, "After we get settled in for the winter how would you two like to come to our house evenings and take some extra lessons? I've already suggested it to Cy."

Cy waited for June to answer, but she kept on eating, taking special care to hold her knife and fork correctly and remembering her elbows. "I don't know," she said.

"I think you'd find the effort well worth while," Mrs. Haney told her. "I've been looking over reports left by your previous teacher, June, and I see no reason why, if you worked hard, you could not cover two grades this year. That would bring you right up to standard. For a white pupil, I mean."

June avoided answering for as long as she decently could. "I'll have to ask my mother." In school Mrs. Haney had taught her to put expression into her voice, but June spoke with an exaggerated native flatness. She knew she was doing it, but she did it anyway.

"It's for your own good, June. You *do* want to learn, don't you? You *do* want to get ahead?"

The swift impulse June had to draw away was as strong as if Mrs. Haney had attempted to lay a hand on her. "I don't know," she said.

"Cy thinks it's a good idea. You do, too, I'm sure."

"I don't know."

"I'm sure your mother would approve."

"I don't know."

June's face had no more expression than her voice. Through her lashes she saw that Cy had stopped eating. He sat there, stiff and awkward, with food in his mouth, not even chewing. Why didn't he say something, anything to help her out? Instead he looked wooden-faced and scared, like—in her exasperation she allowed the thought to come—like some stick Indian.

"What is it, June?" Mrs. Haney asked in an altered voice. "Things haven't been going at all well at school, I realize that, and if it's my fault I'm sorry. I wish you'd tell me."

June did not look up. "It's nothing."

"You used to confide in me. Is it because of what I said to you at the wedding about the Silas boy? Is that what it is? Believe me, June, I did it for your own good."

Once Mrs. Haney had personified opportunity, acceptance, a scope and freedom which village life could never give. More than Bert she seemed to open doors to the kind of life June longed for. But one after another, those doors had been closing. The last one was being closed now by a solicitude June could no longer tolerate.

The words came of themselves. "I'm quitting school. I'm taking a maid's job at the hospital."

June saw Cy's head go down and up, straining to swallow the lump of food he had been holding in his mouth. "No such thing," he blurted. His eyes were angry.

June crumpled her paper napkin and dropped it into her empty cup. "That's what you think!" She kept to English because she wanted Mrs. Haney to understand. She was angry at both of them; unreasonably, blindly angry, and she was free to say things to him which she could not very well say directly to an older person, one of another race. "I know I can have the job, and I will. Mother and Matt will say to go. You can't make them go against me, so don't you try. They will be all for it on account of Stevie. I can see him every day if I go." Hotly, breathlessly, the staccato declarations came. "I'm past sixteen now and nobody can make me go to school. I need the money and I'm going, so don't you ever try to stop me."

Mrs. Haney looked greatly upset. "I think you're making a grave mistake, my dear."

"Oh, no, I'm not! You don't understand; you're not native." June was on her feet, reaching for her coat, but Cy held onto it.

"You are talking crazy talk," he said accusingly, in Gitkshan. "You should stay in the village and go to school while you have the chance."

"Who do you think you are? You can't talk to me like that. I don't need your advice." She kept tugging at her coat. "You sound like Miriam's grandfather, that's what you sound like." Purposely, in out-and-out rebellion against the village with all its hampering restrictions, its frustrations, she kept to English. She wanted Mrs. Haney to know exactly how she felt about the village. It was not Mrs. Haney who could hold her.

What she had to fight was Cy, and her affection for him. Even at this moment she felt a compassion for him which might betray her. Cy with his patient, well-meaning protectiveness, his groping for independence; Cy was the one she must at all costs resist.

She snatched her coat and backed away. "Tell Mrs. Haney what Paul Leget said against her at the feast, why don't you?" she demanded of him. "Go on, tell her. Then she'll see what makes me have to get out."

Mrs. Haney started to rise, then sat down again. "June, please! You *must* calm yourself. If only I could make you take the long-term view, then you would understand that Cy is thinking only of your own good."

June looked across the table at this strong, well-intentioned white woman and at her brother, his long arms dangling, bewildered, and deeply hurt. "I'm sorry——" But she could not finish. She felt she was going to cry.

Outside, walking swiftly toward the trading company store, she did cry a little. Why had she been so cruel to him? She need not have been so cruel. But soon she felt freer than in all her life, and as if suddenly her girlhood was all behind her.

20

SNOW CAME LATE THAT YEAR, AND WHILE MEN WHO trapped would have had it otherwise, the open fall suited Cy. Because of his plans to own a truck, good weather for wood cutting was important to him. Everything depended on getting a truck and having the money to pay for it in full by next fall. If he succeeded in this he did not suppose he would ever have time to even go back and visit the trapping grounds again, much less spend a winter there. The grounds had been held by his family for many generations, long before the first whites came, and it was hard to imagine never seeing them again; but more and more the truck was becoming a symbol of liberation in his mind.

The truck and continuing his lessons from the Haneys, these were the really important things. A man with a hauling contract needed to know arithmetic to be able to figure grades of poles and lumber, and all this month he went across to the mission house almost every evening. Mostly Mrs. Haney explained the lessons and Mr. Haney sat beside him while he did the exercises. After lessons they had cocoa or coffee, and the two of them talked of many things and really got to know each other. He would have found it hard to say which helped him more, the lessons or the encouraging, free-and-easy talks with Mr. Haney.

"I cannot explain how he does it," Cy told Miriam as they walked home after visiting Victor and Teresa one Sunday evening, "but he makes you feel we are not much different from them inside."

"Do you know what I think?" Miriam said. "I think that is foolish of him. Anybody knows Indians and whites are different. That is how it should be. We do not have to be the same."

"That is not his meaning," Cy said. He should have foreseen the difficulty of explaining this to her. Difference was not the right word. Behind all of Mr. Haney's talk there was respect.

"But I do not want us to be the same," she insisted. "Grandfather spoke true words to the people. I wish you had heeded him in that and in all else he said at the feast. I know why you could not show yourself at the dance, and I do not like it."

"I made a fool of myself that night. Something got inside of me. It will not happen again."

"If it happened once, it can happen again."

"I promise you it will not. I have reasons for not wanting it to happen," he told her. "And they are reasons I did not have that night." He took her arm and they walked close, their bodies touching. He wished intensely that he dare tell her what those plans were and of her part in them, but this was not the time.

"I do not want to hold you with promises," she told him softly. "All I want is for you to think of yourself highly, in a proper light."

"I am doing that." If only he could say to her that for this he had Mr. Haney to thank! If only he could share with her his feeling of release which his friendship with the Haneys gave him! For of late he had come to think of Mrs. Haney as his friend, too. Before June went to work at the hospital, Mrs. Haney had tried to argue their mother out of it, and while this caused a certain coolness on both sides he thought the more of her for it. She could have helped June in many ways, both in the school and out, but Matt and his mother would not listen. Their hearts were on Stevie and they said she had no right to interfere.

That evening, after saying good-night to Miriam in front of the Leget house, his mind went back to things Mrs. Haney had said in the café that day after June went out.

"I suppose what I said to her at the dance about Bert Silas offended her. But *really!*" Mrs. Haney had told him. "I can't tell you how disappointed in her I am. June was one native girl I did believe would not go flying off like that. I expected great things of June. However, you'll come for lessons, won't you? It's as I always say, who is going to help the native people if they will not learn to help themselves?"

Well, thanks to her and Mr. Haney, he was learning how he could help himself—the truck, with hauling contracts; learning how to save his earnings, and opening up a bank account; and in time having a pole camp or saw mill of his own. "Working for an objective," Mrs. Haney called it. Perhaps, some day, he'd have a crew of native fellows under him, a house in the Junction or in some settlement along the railway line. Some day a car, perhaps, with him and Miriam driving down now and then for a holiday in Rupert, and Old Paul finding out at last that he did not have the say in everything.

On and off during November there were a few light falls of snow. Afterward temperatures dropped sharply, and succeeding snowfalls worked their simplifying transformations. Litter and dead weeds in the village

182

were smoothed over, the weathered totem poles stood
sharply outlined against the steam rising from the river,
and from door-yard woodpiles, by day and often by
lantern light, came the incisive twang of saws.

One day a northerly gale made felling timber danger-
ous, and out of gratitude for his lessons, Cy went across
to the mission house and offered to help Mr. Haney
paint the dispensary. It was good to have fire and a
roof over your head on such a day as this. Cy began
on the ceiling, and from the ladder he saw the young
trees outside the window bending to the gusts, and
snow sifting from the roof.

Mr. Haney hobbled over to the window and stood
looking at the storm. "No day to be travelling the
woods, is it, Cy? How would you like to be back on
your trapline this weather?"

Cy grinned. "All the trappers will be in their cabins
to-day." He thought of Matt's cabin, now in Stevie's
name, drifted to the eaves, the rapids black where they
lipped the edges of the ice, and the jackpines on the
ridges bowed before the wind. He wondered if Mr.
Haney knew the secure feeling which came when you
were far back between the mountains in a snug cabin
with wood and meat ahead and the wind howling outside. Probably white people did not know the feeling
when, however deep the snow, no shadow of hunger
hung over you. There you were, secure and complete,
in a small uncomplicated world entirely your own. The
heavens were nearer to you back there, Matt used to
say.

Cy wondered what would happen to him if his plan
did not work out and in winters to come he had no
choice but to go back to trapping. The life was hard,
but it suited you as long as it was the only life you knew.

He thought of sunny days in March when Matt sent him to spear whitefish through the ice. You lay on boughs with a piece of blanket over your head, the returning sun warm on your back and jays and ravens talking in the trees. You waited for one of the sand-coloured fish and when it came you let the spear drift toward it, struck and pulled up, and one more fat fish was slapping its tail on the ice.

The recollection brought a wistful, far-off feeling. It was strange, and a little sad, to be an Indian and feel all that was behind you. He wondered if Dot ever had that feeling down there in Rupert. Matt used to take her to the grounds when she was little, in the years when her mother was alive. Dot gone, and June gone, and he with his deep, careful plan to get away to something different.

The afternoon was getting on, but Mrs. Haney was still over at the school, practising the children for their Christmas concert. She missed June for that, she said. From something she said the other day, Cy knew she still had not given up hope of persuading June to return to school. But he knew June never would. He wished Mrs. Haney would not worry so much about the people, especially the children. In contrast to his wife's active concern, Mr. Haney seemed to think June's going was something none of them could do anything about. He said he had great confidence in her and that she would make out. It was strange that, in spite of all Mrs. Haney did for the village, in school and out, the people seemed to take to Mr. Haney more than they did to her. When he was needed he helped, and old people said he was the best dispenser the village ever had. He was interested in them, but in an unsuperior way.

Cy had just moved the ladder and was getting up on

it when Jonathan came in. He gave Mr. Haney his mail, answered Mr. Haney's questions about drifts on the road, then waited, cap in hand.

"Something I can do for you?" Mr. Haney asked.

"Got letter from Elora and don't feeling so good," Jonathan said. His English was poor and usually he had Cy interpret, but this time he did not ask. "Spitting lots kinds of blood and want to come home. Crying."

Cy drew the paint brush across the lip of the can and set it down. "His girl at Miller Bay," he explained, as if Mr. Haney could not understand the awful, simple words. "Same age as June."

"Long time at Miller Bay with lung-sick," Jonathan said.

Cy felt a sort of preparatory numbness and he saw Mr. Haney shake his head slowly, stubbornly, in a denial which made no sense.

"Sit down, Jonathan," Mr. Haney said. He brought a chair. "Do sit down."

Lung-sick, Cy was thinking, and by the health books in school, fifteen times as much of it among us as among the whites who brought it. He thought of Stevie's kind of TB and of this other kind, and of the submission and the terrible, terrible patience of this man with the hurt and gentle eyes. He was seeing Elora as she was now, and as she used to be, the lissome, bright-eyed, teasing little girl he could not have because she was of his crest.

"I like it for you writing letter down there for doctor," Jonathan went on. "If all right for bring, we bring. Maybe feeling better if home with own people, own place."

"But you'd have to keep her in the house with your other children, wouldn't you?"

A look passed between Jonathan and Cy, a look and an affirmation. Cy knew the danger, as from the first he knew Stevie's danger, but all the doctors and all the health books could not prevail when the last hope for one of your own was gone. "Do it, Mr. Haney," he pleaded. "It's different with us."

"How long since she went down there?" Mr. Haney asked him.

"I can't remember. Two years I think. The doctor told them they waited too long." Cy spread his hands and gripped the ladder. A stabbing fear, ice and fire together, pierced him. Too long! Had he, knowing, let them keep Stevie too long? Matt and his mother with their blind, tenacious love, Minnie and her murky swamp-root superstition, Paul with his hostility to all things white—and he with his timidity and reluctance to oppose them! If only he could stand aside and let the blame be theirs! But he could not.

Mr. Haney kept shaking his head but at last he said, "Whatever you wish, Jonathan. I'll write your letter. They can't hold her there if you insist you must have her home."

"We want her home." Jonathan started to open the door, then turned back. "We glad you coming here," he said in his deep, slow voice. "You good man for helping our people."

"A fat lot of help I am to you right now," Mr. Haney said. He put his hand on the table, taking the weight off his bad leg. As soon as Jonathan left, he limped into the kitchen.

Cy stayed at the window until he saw Jonathan going up through the trees in swirls of snow. As soon as he reached the house the news would spread from house to house that Elora was coming home to die. The women would be coming to sit in that bleak room, not speaking, but sitting through the failing light and after the lamp was lit and after the children fell asleep on the beds along the wall, the women mute with consolation, remembering other home-comings, other graves.

Mr. Haney was still in the kitchen when Cy turned from the window. He picked up his coat and mitts and went out. He thought with tragic despair of what Matt and his mother would make of this. They would twist it into proof that they had been right all along in refusing to allow Stevie to be sent to Miller Bay. The sting of wind and driven snow made him think of the trapline again. Fifteen to one . . . the heavens once so near . . . and a little girl he used to love was coming home.

21

MARIE HAD JUST RETURNED FROM VISITING STEVIE AT
the hospital and it left her feeling sad.

"I can't help it," she told Nettie. "My heart is
heavy."

"Is the boy unhappy? Is he crying?" They were in
the unheated lean-to off Caleb's front-room store and
Nettie was weighing the frozen herring Marie fancied
for supper.

"No, he is not crying. I could understand it better if
he was. He laughs; he laughs like anything. He is full
of jokes. It is Matt and Melissa my heart is heavy for,
the thing Cy said to them."

"So our young brother is off on that trail again!"
Nettie exclaimed. "Miller Bay indeed! Were the boy
mine I know what I would do. I would bring him home.
That other hospital doctor, and now the new one, have
been much too slow in curing him. It is plain they do
not know their business." Nettie popped her fingers
into her mouth to suck away the icy feel. "Here, your
eyes are better than mine. Read the scales for me."

Back in the warm room, Marie sank into Caleb's
rocker near the heater and set her parcel of fish
beside her on the floor. Nettie tossed a stick of birch on
the fire and slammed the lid. "They will be having a
good time at the hospital for Christmas, I suppose."

187

"I guess so. June sure is having a good time. She bought Stevie his present already. A camera. Poor little fellow wants a camera."

Marie patted her curls into place, rested her hands on her stomach, and sighed. She had put on her corsets for the hospital visit and she wished she had them off so she could slump down in the rocker and have a soft, relieving cry. God should not let people suffer, least of all at Christmas time. Poor Stevie in there, still in his cast, and poor Elora waiting for the end. At the hospital a radio had played "Holy Night". That, and thinking of the girls she had sung it with so long ago at residential school, brought tears to her eyes.

"If Santa brings me a camera I will take your picture," Stevie had told her. He was quick with his words, quick with his hands, and his eyes had the brightness of a bird's. He always did remind me of a bird, she thought, watching the red spot on the side of the heater; he should be out of that cast and free like the birds are free.

"Ho, Marie!" Caleb shouted in English. "I come have little visit with you."

She heard the creak of bed springs, and Nettie scolding him for mislaying his slippers.

Caleb felt his way into the dimly-lighted room. "Good time at hospital, I hope. Good Christian thing you doing there, visiting the sick."

Marie smiled weakly. When Caleb kept to English and brought in the word Christian, it meant that he was leading up to something.

"Village soon full; everybody home for Christmas. Makes good feeling, all the people home, all the people happy. Good for store. We doing all right here; no Jap oranges but doing good. How you doing your store, Marie? Doing good for Christmas time?"

"My candles gone already. Some cards and ladies' things but I should have ordered more." She asked would he sell her a box of apples. "Hand-out for the kids."

Caleb told her the price and she paid him. "Cy coming after supper so I get him take them over. I like see you doing good. Everybody good, so everybody happy. That is how it is; how it got to be, eh?"

Marie agreed, but her uneasiness was growing. With that brew in her cellar, she should have stayed clear of Caleb until after the holidays.

"Everything going to be fine here this Christmas." The break in Caleb's voice made him sound singularly persuasive. "I feel strong in my heart no trouble this Christmas. Not like last Christmas. How you feel about it, Marie? You feel like I feel?"

Marie began rocking. "We sure don't want trouble at Christmas."

Caleb bobbed his head. "Nobody stretched out in the houses?"

Marie made a vaguely affirmative sound. No, indeed. She was sure now of what was coming.

Caleb pushed his face forward. "You kind woman lots of ways, Marie," he said, earnestly. "Apples for children; helping people lots of ways. The same your mudder. She all the time helping people for go the good way, not for turning bad way."

Marie's small eyes filled with tears.

Caleb reached out, making a patting motion and trying to find her hand. "Now, maybe not my business, not for me to say, but you not selling malt those young fellows? You make me happy not doing that this Christmas."

He knows how soft-hearted I am, she thought; he knows I would not hurt a fly. Then, overcome by her pity for Stevie and Elora, and by all the suffering in the world, she rocked harder and began to cry.

A yip from Nettie almost lifted her out of the chair. "Your fish!" Nettie snatched the partly-squashed herring from under the rocker.

Caleb shuffled his moccasin slippers and made consoling sounds.

"It's not your fault if you make me cry." Marie's voice was tremulous and forgiving. "I try my best to be happy; I try all I know; and I want other people to be happy, too. It's all I live for, Caleb, you know it is."

"I sorry for making you cry; I trying for helping you."

"You do help me, Caleb, you do." Marie dabbed her eyes. "It helps to hear such lovely words about my mother. I just loved my mother and I'm going to do it, Caleb. I'm not going to sell one drink for all of Christmas. I say it now and it's a promise."

Walking homeward, Marie marvelled how much better she felt; lighter and freer, like having her corsets off. It was a good thing Caleb got after her, although that was not the way to put it, because if he had scolded she might not have promised.

I know what else I am going to do, she thought, yielding to one of her heady impulses, I'm going to give Elora my herrings. Surrounded by a warm mist of pity, she turned up Jonathan's road. It was darker under the ridge but the light still reflected from the peaks put blue shadows in the ruts and made the snowy trees as pretty as the Christmas cards in her store.

This misty sweetness which she associated with her mother wrapped cosy folds around her. Her mother always helped people to go the right way, like Caleb

said, and how nice of him to tell her so when she was
weighed with so much sadness. Perhaps she had done
things her mother would not like, but that was only
through weakness and she could honestly say that
never in her whole life had she meant harm to anyone.
People just had to do the best they could as they went
along; everybody made mistakes. But she had done
many kind things, too, like adopting Bella and letting
old people have food from the store when they could
not pay, and surely God would not hold her weaknesses
against her. God would be pleased with the promise
she had made, and surely He would see the kind thing
she was doing now.

Jonathan's dogs were tearing at a moose hide in front
of the house, nearly choking themselves with mouth-
fuls of loose hair. She was on the step, rubbing the
snow from her moccasins, when Cy came out.

"How is she?" Marie whispered.

Cy shook his head and walked away.

Lala was in the kitchen and Marie gave her the parcel.
"For Elora, for her supper. All right for me to see her?"

Elora's mother, Lala, took her to the bed, curtained
off from the main room with sheets. Elora looked
beautiful, just beautiful. She was propped up on
pillows and she wore a wool bed jacket. "Cy just
brought it," Lala explained. "June made it herself and
sent it out."

At Miller Bay they had cut Elora's hair a different
way, square all round, with bangs. She looked like a
big Japanese doll, and her skin was smooth and rosy.

"Marie brought you a present," Lala said, doing her
best to make it a big surprise. "Herrings for your
supper." She stood at the head of the bed, fondling
Elora's hand. "Could you eat some?"

Elora's even, white teeth showed as she smiled. "Thank you, Marie. I was all the time fish hungry since I came home." Her English was better since she went to Miller Bay but her voice sounded sleepy and strangely hollow. With her free hand she plucked at a knot in the quilt, her lashes shading her eyes, which were very gentle, like Jonathan's. She did not look up for so long that Marie thought she was shy of her. But it was not that. "Cy says the band is going to play," Elora murmured.

"Nice, eh? Sure be swell." But the knowing behind the words made Marie weak with dread, for she knew that playing in the hall for Christmas was not what Elora meant. They were going to play here in front of the house, the men standing in a circle in the snow and the boys holding gasoline lanterns on their heads so the men could read their music. They were going to play for Elora alone because that was the last they could do for her until they walked behind her from this house, walking so slowly, the big drum measuring the paces from house to church to graveyard, pounding, bruising the silence of the hills around; bruising your heart, too, because a young one of your village had to go before her time—

"Christmas Eve the choir might go around singing carols," Elora said, dreamily, her fingers still at the knot of wool. "I hope they sing for me; I hope I hear."

Out in the room the baby started crying and Lala laid Elora's hand back on the quilt as if it was very precious to her. She went out quickly, dropping the curtain behind her and almost running to the baby, for what she was seeing in her mind was, Marie knew, more than she could bear.

"Miriam came," Elora said. "Will Bella come, do you think?"

Marie could not look at her just then. "Bella would if she was home, only she's staying at the coast for Christmas."

"Maybe she would be afraid to come." Elora moved her legs under the covers. "You know what I mean, Marie. Because of what I have got."

The fat beneath Marie's chin was quivering and her face felt as though it had lumps in it. "She'd come if she was home. Honest."

"She would not have to stand close. That is bad with what I got. I try to keep mother from doing that and from kissing me. But she docs."

"Sure nice Miriam came," Marie said. She was remembering how when they were small Miriam and Bella and Elora and June always went together. She saw them now, braiding one another's hair and coaxing her for ribbons; playing house in the woodshed or sitting on the old sawhorse with their arms around each other, singing.

Marie, her face twitching, leaned over the bed and drew the girl into her arms. "Oh, Elora, little girl Elora," she said in a tight, sobbing whisper. The young body in her arms felt so light that she clung to it lest it be transformed into something too yielding and ephemeral to be grasped.

"You shouldn't," Elora protested weakly. But her body was lonely for caressing and she rested in the fat arms.

Lala went past the curtain to the kitchen. "I'm coming to visit you every day," Marie promised.

Elora did not look up. She was plucking at the quilt again.

When Marie got home she found she was out of kindling. By now it was too dark in the woodshed to split any, so she began scooping chips from around the chopping block with her hands and putting them into a carton. This was the same old shed where the children used to play and she was sniffling and scratching at the chips when she heard steps on the path.

She stayed on her hands and knees. Dick Dawson was making for the kitchen door, and all she could do was hide until he went away. She did not want to hurt Dick's feelings, but after all she had promised Caleb.

Dick knocked; then opened the door. "Hi, Marie!" he shouted. It made her feel mean, keeping him standing in the cold.

"I know you're home." He listened, then went to the corner of the house and whistled. Three fellows came, two of them Junction fellows, and Andy, Dick's partner at the pole camp.

"She must be somewheres around," Andy said. "Take a look in the shed."

Marie got to her feet just in time. "In a minute," she shouted, crossly, as if they had surprised her in the toilet.

"I damn-well knew it," Dick said. His voice showed he'd had a few.

"I just come home," Marie said as all of them came to the shed. "I was getting kindling."

Andy grabbed the axe and began splitting.

"How's that for service, Marie?" Dick asked. "Let's go inside; I'm froze."

Marie could not decide what she should do. Dick knew the door was unlocked; they would come in anyway, so about all she could do was make coffee and joke with them until they went away. No trouble; no hard feelings.

She used the chips to start the heater and Dick pumped the gas lamp for her. "Everybody happy?" he asked thickly.

One of the Junction fellows winked at her and she winked back. "Where'd you get it, Dick?" she asked pleasantly.

"Some house in town."

"Sure, and it set us back six bucks a dozen. No kick in it either," the other Junction fellow said. "Can't beat Marie for the old Christmas spirit, Dick says." He put his hands on her shoulders. "You Dick's friend?"

"Sure I'm his friend. Dick's an old friend of mine, ain't you, Dickie boy?"

"Okay. Then prove it." The fellow put a twenty-dollar bill on the table. "Money on the line."

Marie pretended not to see the money. "What's the rush? All sit down and we have coffee."

"Coffee, coffee, all the time coffee!" Dick shouted. It must be the heat, Marie thought; he wasn't near so bad when he first came in.

Andy had come with the kindling, and Marie ignoring the money struck him as funny. "All for free, eh— a Christmas present?"

"I shouldn't sell any," Marie said irresolutely; but she was relieved that Andy could joke about it.

"Who says you shouldn't sell any?"

"Well, I sort of promised."

"The police, I suppose."

"It's that Haney guy at the mission house," Dick said.

"Gee, boys, I don't want no trouble. I'm your friend."

"Fine friend you are, holding out on us!"

Andy put his arm around Marie's middle and kissed her. "Marie's everybody's friend, eh, Marie?"

"Sure am." She put her head on his shoulder and tried to laugh.

"Aw, cut it out," Dick said.

Andy waved for him to sit down. "She don't like you any more. She's keeping it for her sweetie."

"I don't like it when you talk like that." Marie pulled away from Andy and went to Dick. "I'm your friend, honey. Honest. So to prove it I'll set up a couple of rounds for free, then you boys got to go away."

Nobody can say I didn't try, she told herself as she lifted the trap door and handed up a dozen or so. Soon they would be feeling happy and would go back to the Junction and Caleb would never know. Besides, she was not really breaking her promise; she wasn't selling any. In fact, if she had kept on being mean about it, they might make trouble and spoil Christmas for the whole village.

They were on the first round when the door was kicked open and Sophia Stone and her husband pushed in. Bert Silas was behind them.

The Stones had a bad name at the Junction and at the canneries. Stone's hair was over his eyes and he looked mean. His wife was big and she started yelling, accusing people, something about her three-cell flashlight.

"Nobody pinched your flashlight," Andy told her. He went over to Bert. "What's the idea, driving them up here? We been trying to shake them."

"I know," Bert said. "But if anybody's got it they better hand it over before she busts a gut."

"Nuts to her," Andy said disgustedly. "I bet she lost it the last place we stopped at."

Stone made a grab for Andy but Andy pushed him away and backed into the other room. "Keep your hooks off me," he warned.

"Some guys you are," the woman shouted. "I buy you drinks and you pinch my flashlight. Some guys."

She had herself worked up and the spit was flying from her mouth.

"That bitch," one of the Junction fellows muttered. "I'm getting out of here."

Stone rushed; Andy tripped on the rug, and they went down. Stone hit once before Andy rolled clear and got his back against the wall. The woman snatched a bottle and threw it. It struck Andy's shoulder and he nodded his head in dazed acknowledgement. Stone lunged again. At first Andy was underneath but as soon as he got on top, Stone pulled up his knees and crashed him against the heater. Andy's head struck the damper. Blood began running over the linoleum and Andy did not move.

Marie took one look and ran out screaming.

Dick and Bert dragged Stone to his feet and held him. Stone was as scared as the rest by now and they got busy, propping Andy up and tying a towel around his head to stop the blood.

Andy was sitting up when the Junction fellow came back with the flashlight. "Look at this!" he shouted. "It was in Bert's truck all the time."

"You dumb cluck," Dick told the woman. "I feel like taking it and putting it some place. You started all this."

That made Stone mad, but just then Cy came in, carrying the box of apples. He had seen the truck parked in front and he made straight for Bert. Only last week he had learned that Bert helped himself to the truck, nights, and that June sometimes went for a drive with him. "Where's June?" he demanded.

Bert backed away. "Don't come that big brother stuff with me. She's not here, but what if she was? What's it to you?"

This was their first meeting since the feast and it

made Cy realize how strong his feeling against Bert had become. The story was that Bert acted pretty wild around the Junction sometimes and Cy had tried to warn June, but all she would say was that whenever they went out together Bert behaved himself.

Dick asked if anybody knew where Marie went. "Something fishy around here. How come all of a sudden she got cold feet over selling us? If it's that white guy at the mission house—"

"Forget it," Bert advised. "Haney's okay. It's his wife you got to watch."

One of the Junction fellows was opening more bottles and he said this time they would pay for the round.

"Yes, and you better make it plenty," the one who found the flashlight said. "You guys pretty near wrecked the joint."

Cy was leaving when he saw Mr. Haney pass the kitchen window. Marie was behind him, blubbering. Dick took a quick look through the window and grabbed an empty bottle from the kitchen table. "I should have known she'd squawk to Haney. I'll handle him. Quick, everybody out the other door."

Somebody made for the lamp and turned it off. They were running back and forth, crashing into the furniture and all trying to get out the front door at once. Cy rushed Dick and tried to twist the bottle from his hand.

"Yes, and you, too!" Dick said. "Always sticking around him." He took a swing at Cy with his free hand.

Cy's cheek was cut but he did not lose his grip on the neck of the bottle. Dick slammed him against the door. It banged open and they rolled down the steps, punching at each other. Cy was underneath and struck his head on the bottom step. Blood from the cut was in his eyes as he got to his feet and he saw Mr. Haney on his back and Dick, his legs spread, standing over him.

The bottle lay in the snow. Cy seized it and came at Dick from behind in a crouching rush.

"No, Cy!" Mr. Haney called out sharply. His first-aid bag lay on the path and he reached for it. "That was a stupid thing to do," he told Dick, sternly, but without rancour. He tried to rise but his bad leg gave way. Cy had to help him.

22

ELORA DIED ON NEW YEAR'S DAY. MR. HANEY, WITH Matt on one side and Cy on the other to steady him, came to the funeral service in the church, but he could not make it to the graveyard, and from then on neither Matt or Melissa, his closest neighbours, saw him outside the house again. While school was on, Matt made it a practice to go over and keep the mission-house fires going, and each evening after Cy got home from the wood claim and had his supper, he took the gas lantern and split and carried in kitchen wood and kindling and blocks for the heater.

Cy said that the lessons went on pretty much as before, although Matt did not see how they could, with Mr. Haney having to keep to the cot which his wife had them carry down and set up beside the heater. When Matt got out of bed on the coldest nights to build up their own fires, he saw the lamp still going in the big room of the mission house and knew from this that Mr. Haney was unable to sleep because of the pain. Busy as Mrs. Haney's evenings were, she still gave Cy his lessons, but in early February the pain grew so bad that she persuaded her husband to let Jonathan take him to the hospital.

The following Saturday Matt and Melissa drove in

with the team to visit Stevie and they invited Mrs. Haney to come along. Nothing was said on the drive home which would in any way prepare them, and so it was not until Monday forenoon that they learned what the doctor had advised.

Matt had a pair of snowshoe-frames which he had long meant to fill and this morning, after Melissa swept the front room, he brought in the bucket of rawhide which he had put to soak behind the kitchen stove. The sun was low, but the days had lengthened suffi-ciently for it to clear the ridge and as he settled him-self at the front window, the sunlight gave a good feel even through the frosted glass.

And there was a good feel to filling a pair of shoes again, especially after the turn of winter. Soon the worst of the cold would be over, and the fur would be running on the trapping grounds again. Soon the beaver ponds would be free of ice and the blue grouse would begin to hoot. The strong sun on the snow darkened the faces of the men, and the cheeks of the young women took on that flushed, rosy look which excited you and made you reckless if you were young. You did brave and heedless things, you travelled far and your head was high if you were young, and filling snowshoes here in the sun brought the feel of the old times back and put a kind of wistful singing in your heart.

The memory of Elora's passing still lingered in the village. It was hard to see the young lives fall like leaves when the sap of life goes down, and even yet Melissa's heart was in a steep place because of it. Only this morning, and with nothing said which would bring it to her mind, she recalled the beautiful wreath of red-paper roses Marie made for the burial. And when Cy said that he felt like going down to the hospital to see how

Mr. Haney and Stevie were getting on, Melissa had encouraged him to go. With that doctor gone and a new head nurse at the hospital it was all right for Cy to go. All that nonsense about Miller Bay was safely behind them; the doctor was a stranger, and although Miller Bay was still what Cy wanted, it was unlikely that he would bring that up afresh. Stevie had the life strong in him, they thought, and one of these days there would be snowshoes to make for him, too.

What Cy, and even Melissa, did not understand, Matt mused as he squeezed the water from the first length of hide, was that the ones like Elora had to go. That was the way it was, everywhere you looked. The brightest salmon, heading up from the sea, did not always reach the spawning grounds. Some sickened and grew weak and died, but the run of fish went on and on, sure as the sun and as the time of growing when the snow was gone.

His people were like the run of salmon. They were strong because they stayed together; they did not scatter and die out. Right now, unless his old eyes were tricking him, or he had not heard the woman-talk aright, there were ten or twelve young ones waiting to be born. Ten or more women of this village with babies kicking inside them, and Jonathan's Lala one of them. He had the feeling Elora was not far away. Before you knew it she would be back with them as a new baby, the same Elora hiding behind that baby's face.

Matt's shoulders were hunched over the frame, pulling hard on the second of the six bars of filling he was weaving, when Melissa called out that Caleb was at the back door and was coming in.

"Good, very good. Show him where I am sitting." Matt clamped his thumb to hold the strand while he made a lock hitch. Holding the free end with his teeth, he made a splice and took a turn around his hand, keeping the strand taut until Melissa guided Caleb to a chair beside the window. "Working," he explained.

"Good." Caleb need not inquire what his old friend was doing; the smell of the wet hide and the flick and slap of it as Matt drew it through the over-and-under, three-way pattern, told him. "How many beaver will you take this spring, my friend?" Caleb asked with a wheezy chuckle. "Only twenty for me this spring because I am feeling rich. I will let my ponds make me an increase for next year when prices should be higher."

Matt enjoyed the little joke about the two of them going out to their grounds, eight camps to the north-ward. He would give a great deal to be going, as the Gawas were, but there could be no more of that. No harm in making jokes about it, however.

"The teacher gave good help, Sunday in the church, eh?" Caleb said.

Matt looped the strand around his fingers, levering on the edge of the frame with his wrist until the hide drew tight as wire. It hurt, but it proved the old strength had not left his arms and chest. "She will be lonely with her man away."

"He was a friendly man, friendly to all of us. He did not bring shame on our village by calling the police."

"He has been friendly. May he soon return. Having him with us is good."

"The fault was Marie's," Caleb said, with a show of sternness.

"The fault was Marie's." Matt reached for another length of hide. "My friend, I am on the council. You also. You and I are men of peace, yet if we ourselves went to the police, her house would be searched, the drink destroyed, and another such trouble kept from us."

Caleb waggled his head, considering. "Marie would be severely punished by the law. Would either of us care to go so far as that?"

"If it would end it, I would do it," Matt answered. "But I cannot believe it would end it. The drink has been among us years of years."

"And years of years I have made strong prayers against it. My prayers have not been answered. Our young men, young women, too, are being tempted. What are we to do?"

Matt had no answer.

"On my knees I have prayed the Great Chief Above to turn our sister from her foolishness, but she has not turned. And now, because of her, our good white friend must go on crutches."

They fell silent. Across the street in the school yard the children, out for morning play, were shouting and chasing one another in the snow. At this distance the clear, high voices of boys and girls sounded little different, and who could know which was which? Who could know which boy would go the way Dick Dawson or Bert Silas had gone, which girl would turn out froth? The young eager for life, the old knowing it and afraid for them; the two separated by the mountain of years, and their good intentions going up in talk, mist without avail rising from the river.

Matt heard Melissa set down the two pails she had gone to the school tap to fill, then she came directly from the kitchen and stood before him.

"I have news which is not good. The Haneys must leave us. Two more days and they will be gone."

"Who gave you this?"

"The woman has just now told the children. He must go to see the doctors who fix soldiers from the war. To Vancouver. He must show himself to them there."

Caleb straightened in his chair. He held his stick upright between his knees and rubbed the smooth top of it around and around with the hollow of his hand. "This is dark news you bring."

"Marie is the cause of it."

"Dick Dawson is the cause of it."

"Drink is the cause of it."

Melissa dusted the snow from her moccasins, one against the other.

"I will go now," Caleb said in a flat voice, feeling for his mitts and groundhog skin toque. "All must be told this heavy news."

Matt got Caleb started toward the door. "And on which person will you place the blame?"

Caleb turned his face away. "We were the strong ones once, you and I, but now we are in our age and can no longer hold the people. At whose feet the blame lies, who would dare to say?"

Matt looked across at the mission house many times that day. He wanted to give sympathy, but his understanding was that in times of sickness or trouble it was different with whites. All his life he had noticed that among birds and animals and fishes there was the one kind that stayed together no matter what, drawing closer in danger, and the other kind that went alone; salmon in their mighty schools, hatching, feeding, breeding, dying together, and trout, each keeping to its own eddy; the caribou in herds and the hunting animals who went alone; geese and ducks in flocks, and the solitary eagles, hawks and owls which preyed on them.

Was it the same with people? He had never lived among whites; but natives who had, led him to believe it was. In the big places, or so he had been told, whites might live side by side without a fence between their houses, yet not know each other's names. Some went this way, some that, doing their work in different places, not following the seasons, all together, as native people always had. Here the bad trouble of one was shared by all. But Mr. Haney in his hospital bed, and Mrs. Haney across there, went on alone. The salmon people and the trout people, the geese flying together, feeding together, and the owl in the darkness, free and wise, but so alone.

Cy got back from his wood-claim after dark. He took the news in silence.

That night, from the window of his room off the kitchen, he saw the short, dense shadows hung by the high moon on the sides of buildings and behind the totem poles. Straight ropes of vapour, more heat than smoke, rose tautly from stovepipes, holding shape in the still air to such a height that the village seemed suspended by them. Below, the rapids steamed in the cold. Under the moon the peaks were notches in a remote, unencompassing sky.

Frost clutched the house and it made a sharp, expanding sound. The coldest night this winter, and Mrs. Haney's last one here. She would never come back. Neither of them would come back. An encouragement, immensely fortifying to him, had ended.

And it need not have ended. The utter senselessness of what Dick had done oppressed him and angered him afresh. Cy knew that if he had been quick enough, he could have kept Dick from hurting Mr. Haney. And yet, it was not Mr. Haney as an individual but what, as a white, he represented in Dick's mind which caused the trouble.

"Who will help the Indian people if they will not help themselves?" Mrs. Haney had asked. By his lessons he was trying to help himself. And no white person, but one of his own village, had stopped his lessons. The thought filled Cy with foreboding. But he was not going to be prevented. His way of escape was still open. He would hold to his plan, buy a truck; and when the time came he would get away.

23

IN LATE APRIL CY GOT HIS TRUCK.

It was not as large or as new as the one he had intended to buy, but an order for sixty cords of birch came
from Angus cannery and he and Victor figured that by
delivering the wood to the railway themselves instead of
hiring Jonathan or a Junction trucker, he would earn
enough for his next payment and have a few dollars to
the good. As it turned out, he ended up a few dollars
behind. The roads were in poor shape following the
spring thaw; he broke a spring and damaged the
rear axle and the garage bills for these repairs had to be
met. However, all the wood had been shipped and with
better hauling weather ahead he was confident he could
meet his next payment without much difficulty. If
necessary he could sell his rifle, or accept June's offer
of a loan. This summer he would sign over most of his
cannery cheques to the Junction dealer. By fall the
truck would be his.

Ten days ago, after finishing the Angus order, he had
used the truck in a way which gave him a good deal
of satisfaction. Paul had a canoe cedar near the river,
at the lower end of the wood-claim, that proved to be
too heavy for any of the teams to handle, and after
letting the old man worry for a while, Cy hauled it in

with the truck, easy as anything. Paul, through Miriam, had all along let it be known that he considered a truck a waste of money. Well, already the wind was setting in another direction. In time the old man would discover that the truck was only the first step in the larger plan which would directly challenge his domination of Miriam.

This morning Cy strolled down the path between the wild crabapples to see how the canoe was coming on. On the far side of the big riffle, swelling buds in the crowns of the cottonwoods were a soft green haze against the sky. The robins were back, scores of them on the cropped turf beyond Paul's shed, running, pausing, considering as they searched for worms. A large woodpecker, the kind with the striped neck, was on one of the old totem poles, probing with its beak in the folds of the weathered carving. The short, crisp blows of Paul's adze sounded from the shed.

Paul was on his knees at the far side of the thirty-foot log. He saw Cy's shadow and looked up. "What is wrong?" he asked gruffly. "Why are you not with Jonathan, playing with your new toy this morning?"

Cy shrugged good-naturedly. The time had come when he could afford to be tolerant. "We need a certain part for the engine. Matt will bring it to-night when he comes from the hospital. To-day Jonathan has work on his truck to do."

Paul whetted his adze with his pocket stone, tested its edge with his thumb and continued working. "I found another canoe cedar as good as this," he said after a few careful strokes. "Haul it here and I will teach you to make your own."

The offer took Cy by surprise. He said he would think about it.

"See you do. Soon the last canoe cedars will be gone, and the last of the canoe makers."

"I would like to learn," Cy said, "but we must finish cutting the wood-claim before we go to the cannery."

Paul swept away some chips with his hand. "I could make you into the one young man in our village able to build canoes as they should be built. In the time you waste on that truck of yours—"

"Next fall, when we are home, perhaps." Cy stepped onto the flattened top of the log and as he looked directly down at the figure crouched among the chips, it seemed smaller, in fact shrunken and without authority. For the first time Cy felt a kind of masterful forbearance, not far removed from pity.

"You are not giving me a straight answer," Paul reminded.

"It would be a good thing to know, although I see little use which I, myself, can have for a canoe. I suppose I could get the log down before we leave, then in the fall if I have time—"

"Why not now? You could work on it this summer. The wood does not remain sound so long if cut when the sap is up."

"But you know I am going to the cannery. None of us will be here during summer." Cy was puzzled. Matt's guess was that next winter Paul would raise his pole. The great feast and bestowal of presents which went with a pole raising would cost thousands. Paul would need his cannery earnings this summer, and Miriam's, too, to prepare for it. Of course he is going, Cy thought. Why is he telling me this?

"My meaning is if we did not go." Paul seemed about to say more on that but checked himself. "I will teach you what comes first in the making of a canoe," he said, "If and so you are of a mind to be taught." He pointed to a swamping axe beside his tool chest, then to a line drawn with a charred stick along the log. "Score to that mark, but no deeper."

Cy took off his windbreaker and mounted the flattened top of the log. The shaping was at an early stage, the log was still pretty much a log, and what it was to become was as yet a harmony of lines inside the old man's head. "Until noon," he agreed. "This afternoon some of us are going up the creek to try for steelhead."

As the double-bitted axe scored and slabbed off chunks of sap wood, Cy thought of how, in this and other ways, the tension between them had lessened. No doubt his own attitude had much to do with this because, since he got the truck, he no longer felt cornered and futile before Paul. It was as if the truck and all it signified had become a weapon, and a weapon was a weapon, whether you resorted to it or not. Having the truck made him feel easier in his mind, freer, and ready for whatever came.

He felt easier about June, too, since Bert had been caught helping himself to things from the store and had gone back to Rupert in a hurry. She went to shows and dances with Junction fellows and seemed happy in her job. Mrs. Haney had written her a long, friendly letter and said that if June ever came to Vancouver for a holiday she was to be sure and stay with them. June had not answered the letter yet, but she had sent a twenty-five cent Easter card to Mrs. and Mr. Haney from both of them.

The steelhead net belonged to Clarice, so after dinner Cy went to her house to see if Victor and Teresa were ready to come fishing. Miriam was coming, too, but she had gone up the creek this morning to look along the cut-banks for spruce roots which she would later split and use for baskets. The three of them had arranged to meet her where the trail to the steelhead pool crossed the low end of the ridge.

However, on arriving at Clarice's, Teresa told him that the warm weather had given them a notion. In early summer she would have a baby and she and Victor had decided to cut wood for a living instead of going to the canneries. Too many babies got sick down there. There was a place on the claim where they could camp and have a garden and they wanted to go there this afternoon to brush it out and put up a pole fence. "It will be like old times, living in a tent," she said. "Why don't you ask Matt to go fishing with you? With him and Miriam you will have enough."

Cy bunched the net and carried it home, only to find that Matt had a feeling about Stevie and that he and Melissa were leaving with the team. They would not be home until late.

"Oh, well," he said, "Miriam and I can manage."

He found Miriam at the place, resting against a poplar with her hands behind her head. She had already cached her bundle of roots and as they walked along, single file, they now and then heard squirrels making off over the carpet of last year's leaves. The leaves were so dry that the squirrels sounded like large animals. Miriam smiled back at him and said he should have brought his gun.

Crossing a cleared place, they looked up and saw six swans flying low and strangely large against the clear blue sky. They stirred him, did those great white birds, and he imagined their unlaboured flight over the lakes and beaver ponds and the lonely, familiar places he used to know.

He did not feel like talking much. Nor did she, it seemed. Below them, where the creek dropped down wide steps of rock from the pool, they heard the hollow sound of falling water and he found himself thinking of the falls behind the cannery. The memory stood before him, filling his mind, and he did not try to put it away.

On the ridge the air carried the smell of dry moss and leaves and of the sun on pines but, as they went down, the draft from the creek was cool upon their faces. Here, nearing the creek, the damp moss and hemlock needles were without sound under their feet. The memory rose larger and closer but with a restraining solemnity in this dim, green place.

"Do you feel lucky to-day?" she asked gravely.

But this other was in his mind and he did not know how to answer her. She left him to unfasten the net; then she went to the bank alone, shading her eyes and looking up and down the pool.

Cy came from behind the trees and stood tall beside her. "Many?"

"I see three." She did not point, for he would know where to look.

The water was slightly milky and its flow seemed to run hands along his body, making his flesh seem more alive and giving the sensation of fullness. The first two steelhead he saw lay close to the bottom, three feet down. A third, in front, would be the female and must weigh a good twenty pounds. There was no swept place on the gravel to show she had started ploughing her nest but she must be ready because the two smaller males tailed her closely. It was the swirl of one turning on its rival which first attracted his attention. Along the far bank there would be more but the light made them hard to see.

"Which side will you take?" he asked.

She pressed her palms against her hips, rubbing them down the seams of her denims in a preparatory way. "Whichever you say." He watched her brown, nimble hands make the lines fast to the wings of the net. She coiled her line, laid it on the gravel, then took his axe to cut herself a splashing pole. They looped the net and carried it between them to the head of the pool.

Miriam waded behind him to where the water pulled at her knees. There she stopped and as he crossed she braced herself and paid out the loops. As soon as he was over, they pulled hard against each other to keep the net from dragging until they were ready to lower it into the start of the pool. The float and lead lines tangled at her end and he watched her wade out and clear them.

In daylight it was unlikely the fish would gill of themselves, but they worked the net down cautiously in case the big female struck. A v-shaped ripple ran down the surface, then others. If they took the net closer the fish might stampede out of the pool, so they made the ends fast and waded in, raking their poles along the bottom and stirring up silt to hide the net. Their shirts and denims were tight against their bodies as they came ashore and ran to get between the outlet and the darting fish.

Miriam was waist deep when one of the largest tried to pass her. He saw her fight the current and turn it. "Now!" he shouted.

They wheeled, plunging their poles ahead of them and driving the outwitted fish into the net. As it filled, a reckless, elemental exultation seemed to take hold of her. He knew that their victory over the fish and their need of them were a part of it. Even as children they had been lucky when they fished together, but it was not as children that they fished to-day. We are a couple, a man and a woman fighting for our food, he thought with mastering exultation.

"Good?" she called out. "Have we them all?" Her voice was like clear music against the overhanging trees.

"Enough." He waded to the far shore and was slacking the line when he looked across. Her hair and face were gleaming wet and her shirt was like the skin lifting to her quick breathing. At that moment one of the largest broke from the net and tried to escape between her and the shore, but she cut in front of it and made it ground itself on the sloping gravel. It was writhing back into the water, a twenty-pounder, three feet long, when she threw herself astride of it, squeezing it between her knees to capture it. Its thrashing tail showered her with spray and it was escaping when she plunged both hands deep into its gills, fighting it with the beautiful, intense ferocity of an otter holding to its kill. He kept her in his eyes while she dragged it up the gravel by its throat and clubbed it. As he turned to cast off his line, his hands were trembling.

When he came to her, she was sucking the blood from her thumb, which had been cut by the gill bone of her fish. He saw her shoulders lift, filling her lungs after the struggle, and a completeness, a heart-pounding sensation of culmination swept through him.

They stood a little apart, looking into one another for the soaring moment, the shared thought naked and clean between them. Then, the promise made, they went back to the net and finished their work.

That night it was public knowledge in the village that Cy, son of Melissa, had entered Paul Leget's house to live.

24

MATT AND MELISSA SAT ON BOXES BESIDE THE STOVE IN the yard while the potatoes boiled.

"I do not like it, Paul putting off the feast," she said. "Granted my son is a commoner, but he should not be dealt with as one of no account."

"Paul Leget is a rock. You cannot move him."

"I am thankful that ones of our crest have always done their duty by relatives, but there are limits. If we took the whole cost on ourselves it could cause ill-feeling between the houses. I differ strongly with Paul in this but I would not dare offend his pride."

"He relies on our feeling so. This is why he sees no need to act," Matt said bleakly. A mosquito settled on the back of his hand and he watched it for a moment before he killed it. "How can an ordinary person hold his own with one who keeps his thoughts to himself, who foresees all moves?"

Melissa tested the potatoes with her fork and tossed a handful of chips under the pot. "A pole is a pole, but there are other important things to spend his money on. I feel humbled and because I am humbled I am displeased. But what can we do?"

"Let us admit it. For ourselves, he has us blocked. But Cy is standing up to him more strongly than was to be expected. Do not be surprised if, on their way to the cannery, those two go before the minister in Prince Rupert and have themselves white married."

"That is one way for our young brother to pull the nose of the old one," Melissa exclaimed, her face brightening. "Why yes, it could be properly done in the minister's house. And there is this also. Since June is of a mind to go with Clarice to Angus, earning money while she has her holidays from the hospital, she could stand up with them."

Matt was smiling and nodding his head. "Before that time Stevie will be with us and we can all go down, all of us in the minister's house together."

"If Stevie is home, we will go."

"Ho! Are you again fretting over the little fellow? Of course he will be home. You heard him, our last time in, asking for a cowboy suit."

"And if he is not home?"

"We obey our natures; we stay. But my heart is strong that the little fellow's trouble is as good as ended. Make your mind easy, all of us are going to the cannery. You will see."

Melissa put her apprehensions behind her. This was late May, and from the start of warm weather Stevie's spirits seemed higher each time they visited him. This was often, thanks to Cy and his truck. Seeing that little body so full of life made her wonder with superior satisfaction what that doctor would have to say for himself if he knew. But for the present there was no doctor at all at the hospital, and the new matron knew nothing of that Miller Bay nonsense.

Her desire to have Stevie with her was made even stronger by the need she felt to be out of the village for the summer. It was at this time of year, with *k'Shan* mighty in flood, that the nomadic pull was strongest. The thrusting life in every tree and grass clump, the glazed brilliance of mountain snow, the quickening seen in the flight of birds, spoke of movement and release. Down through all known time, the ebb and flow of village life had harmonized with the seasons, and getting away was a deeper thing than going to the canneries. It had to do with food but it was more than food. The long migrations over the grease trails, families out for roots and early berries, the search for meat and fish on ancestral hunting grounds, had set the pattern. And the pattern, if not the need, persisted.

Already the windows of some houses were boarded up. A few men had gone to try their luck at fishing spring salmon for the canneries, and since there was no teacher, they were free to take their families. Bella had drifted back to Angus after Elora's funeral and had got Marie a job there filleting flat-fish, to Dick Dawson's disgust. People had their potatoes planted and Caleb was giving out passes and travelling money to workers at his cannery. It was when Cy brought home the passes for his house one evening that Miriam astounded him by saying Paul would not be going.

"Why not? What's the matter?" Cy asked anxiously. "Is he feeling sick? I keep telling him he works too hard on that canoe."

Miriam drew his arm around her. "They are doing grandfather a wrong, and it hurts me." Her eyes filled with tears. "Caleb had a letter from the manager. The boss of the boat-shed will not have grandfather back. The only job he can have is in the reduction plant, and he is too old a man for that."

Being rejected by a cannery after working for it for years was a bitter blow to anyone. There was injustice here.

"That boss made the manager believe grandfather does not know his work." Miriam reached up and took his face between her hands. "He wants you in the boat-shed but he will not have grandfather. He says grandfather is lazy and that he makes mistakes. You know that is not right."

"Of course it is not right!" Cy agreed, with indignation. Here it was again, the boss getting him between them and using him against Paul. Of all the native people at the cannery Paul was the only one, himself included, who had not bowed before the whites in one way or another. Paul had fought his fight in the only way left to him, and he had lost.

Or had he lost? This was the boss's revenge for Paul's resistance to him last summer, and how stinging that resistance must have been to make him deprive himself of so skilled a workman! Cy thought that possibly, in the boss's place, he might have done the same. Only he was not in the boss's place, he was not in any white man's place. He thought with reluctant loyalty of the daily, hourly, fight Paul Leget had waged.

Since his union with Miriam, Cy had further cause to realize how unbending the old man was, but thanks to the truck he was also learning how that determination to dominate could be resisted. He had his own fight with Paul, and it was only beginning; but to accuse Paul, of all men, of not knowing his work! To Cy it seemed that the boss's retaliation was working against him also, for it was harder to oppose a man you saw unjustly dealt with.

"Whatever will we do?" Miriam implored. "He says no cannery manager can humble him by sending him to the reduction plant."

"It is not right," Cy said again. Paul Leget, a leading chief of their village, shovelling fish offal!

"Already he has told Caleb he will not go," Miriam went on.

"But I have his pass."

"Yes, and he will tear it up. He is not going, and you know it is not right to leave him."

Cy hardly knew what to say. "My mother would cook for him, if Stevie does not get out in time. Or he can eat with John and Minnie."

Miriam shook her head. "I do not want that."

Cy stroked her hair, letting it flow between his fingers. Now, in spite of all his careful plans, Paul had again pushed him into a narrow place. "You know it is settled that we two are going. I must have good wages this summer or I stand to lose the truck."

"But he needs us here, my sweetheart. We cannot leave him." Her voice was full of pleading.

"We will have to leave him. This time we must do what is best for us—for *us*, you understand."

She started to pull away, then her head was against his chest and she was sobbing.

"You said you wanted to go. We talked it over many times, and you said you wanted to," he reminded. "Already Caleb has spoken for a room for us. I cannot believe you have altogether changed your mind."

"It is only for you I want to go, to get money for the truck."

He pushed back her hair and tried to get her to look at him. "You are my wife; we go together."

The thought was held in silence between them, but then she said. "He is growing old; he is not well, really he is not. Suppose something happened to him while we were gone?"

"I do not think anything will happen to him. He works too hard, as I have often told him."

"Then why does he go to Minnie? Why does he use the swamp root?"

"What makes you think he uses swamp root?"

"I found a piece of it this morning. He hides it under his pillow, but at night I think he hangs it up, because I found a string on it."

"Do not let him frighten you with such superstitions," Cy said severely. "How do we know this is not what he is trying to do, to frighten you into staying? I will get him wood ahead and pay someone to cook his meals." He took away her arms, then softening, kissed her. "You and I are *going*."

Cy went directly down to the shed to have it out with Paul.

"That is an unfair thing the cannery did to you," he began, "but Miriam and I are going. I need the money and we are going."

Paul kept on adzing the forefoot of the canoe. "She told you, I suppose, that she is staying?"

"She does not want to stay."

"She will stay." Paul tested the curve with the heel of his palm and took another careful stroke. "You, also. You cannot find it in yourself to be without your woman."

"Have you no decency?" Cy shouted at him. His feeling of outrage could not have been stronger if he had caught the old man prying on them in their most intimate moments. "You lied to her. That is why she wants to stay. You make her believe you are sick, so she will be afraid to leave."

"Oho! So now you are telling me how I feel. What next? I ask myself."

"If you're sick, why don't you see a doctor?" Cy resorted to English to give it sting.

"Doctor!" Paul spat the word. "I know you. Always you take sides against us with the doctors. Where would that boy of Matt's be now, if your family had heeded you?"

"A doctor knows if a person is sick or not—and no swamp-root either. A doctor would find you out. That's why you are scared to go to one. You say you're sick. All right. Lots of doctors in Rupert. I'll pay for you to go: the train, everything. If you're sick, we want to know about it."

Paul got to his feet. His legs were numb from kneeling and he steadied himself against the upturned canoe. "You young cedar! Daring to tell me what I shall do!" He made swallowing motions, the slack in his cheeks going in and out, but his anger left him breathless, and he put his adze in the canoe and went up the path.

Cy watched him go over the crest; then he sat on the canoe and stared at the river. The flood water was almost to the smoke-houses, and out in the current a large spruce was swept along, turning end for end, its broken branches black against the muddy water. What could you do with a man like that? he asked himself in desperation, what could you do? He was like a massive boulder embedded in the path.

Give them two months away and Old Paul's hold on Miriam could be broken. Here, ready at hand, was his chance to free her. More and more, their union was bringing him a sense of completeness which transcended all his imaginings, the experiences merging into such a whole that separation was unthinkable.

He picked up a cedar chip and broke it into smaller and smaller pieces. If he lost the truck, he could see it going on like this, year after year; the children coming and Paul shaping their lives as he had shaped Miriam's, holding them back as he had her because this was how he wanted it. Taking her to the cannery was vital to his plans, but Cy had said all that could be said, there in the house. He was confronted with the certainty that if he went to the cannery he must go alone.

Go alone and be alone. If Paul was not in his age, if he was able to put up his hands and defend himself, I would have struck him for speaking as though our need for each other is only that, he thought with helpless fury. I can go if I want to badly enough. White workers go without their women and so can I, if it comes to that.

He tried to imagine this was already decided. But the barren weeks, two months of them at the very least, became too real, and he refused to let them reach all this way to torture him.

The refusal helped. He was thinking less emotionally now, and little by little, the suspicion grew that Paul in his deep way was trying to shame him into going without Miriam for the summer. Except when she spoke to Paul, Miriam was using more and more English in the house. This, taken with her admission that the truck might be a good idea, was a sign that Paul's hold on her was weakening. But if Paul could have her to himself all summer, thickening her tongue with native, leading her in a thousand hidden ways to stand with him against her husband, driving a wedge between them . . .

Suddenly he knew he was not going. There was one other way and he would use it.

A dance was to be held at the Junction the evening Cy drove down to take up June's offer of a loan. He had been doing a good deal of figuring, and with June's help this new plan was bound to work. The first plan had been for him to meet his July payment by sending the dealer his first cannery pay check, and he had signed papers promising he would. But if he got June's money now, he would be able to go ahead and do contract hauling for one of the sawmills below the Junction. If you had a truck, the sawmills would hire you, providing you were willing to wait for your money until the carload was sold in Edmonton. But that was all right, because June's loan would let him keep the truck until the sawmill could pay him. In this way he could get ownership of the truck before winter and stay with Miriam into the bargain.

Paul's opposition to borrowing from June showed that all along he had been scheming to have Miriam to himself for the summer, but Cy believed now that going alone to the cannery would have been a big mistake. A fellow who owned a truck had a good chance of steady work around a sawmill, even when there was no hauling. One mill he knew had cabins for the families of men who worked for it, and if all went as planned, before fall he and Miriam would be living in one of them. From then on, things were bound to be easier. He would respect the old man's reasonable wishes, keep him supplied with wood, pay some woman to look after him if he became really sick. He and Miriam would do their duty and more, but it would be of their own free will and not because it was imposed.

Cy got to the hospital after visiting hours and so could not see Stevie, and at the residence one of the native girls told him June had left early for the dance.

It was past eleven, and still light, when he parked across from the hall to wait. The music had started, the saxophones blatantly provocative. The doors were open and he saw only a few couples on the floor. The tune was one Victor played, the one "Five-Foot-Two".

Maybe next winter they would be able to come in from the mill to a dance now and then. Miriam liked dancing, although she was shy out on the floor in front of strangers.

He looked down the street and saw June and four or five others, girls and fellows, come out of the Chinaman's. When they were on the hall steps, he tapped the horn to call her over.

"Don't tell me you're stepping out to-night, big boy," she joked.

"Sit in here a minute," he said, "I want to talk to you." She got in and he told her what he wanted.

"But Cy!" she turned toward him, touching her hair with a quick, agitated lift of her hand.

She was his sister, and she was warm and shapely, and very beautiful. "I only go by what you said. You offered it to me yourself, remember."

"I know. But, gee, Cy, if you'd only told me!"

"Does that mean you haven't got it?"

"Not now, I haven't. If only you'd spoken sooner. You could have had it and welcome, any time, if you had only asked."

"I know. But all that money. You said you had two hundred."

"That's right. Gosh! If you'd only said so at the time. I feel awful."

"It's your money. But what did you need that cost two hundred dollars?"

"Now please don't get sore." She drew her coat closer around her shoulders. "But a certain party you don't rate very high wrote up from Rupert and asked me for the lend of it."

"Bert Silas." There was no need to make it a question.

"Yes, it was Bert Silas if you want to know. I knew you would be sore and that's why I wasn't going to do it, only he and some white fellow got this chance to go partners on a taxi . . . "

She was speaking persuasively, with a defensive urgency, but her words sounded worn to his ears, like a story he had memorized long ago. He should have known. Bert's going had not ended anything; soon she would be leaving for Angus and would be with Bert in Rupert and nothing he could say would stop her.

"Well, your friends are waiting so I better go," he told her.

He had intended to let her know how very important the money was to him but now he was not going to. "Too bad I bothered you."

"Don't be silly. As long as you're not mad. Look at me, Cy. Tell me you're not mad at me."

How could he be, with this tender, unwanted protectiveness heavy on his heart? Warning her against Bert always made her defend him and there must be no argument, because he felt with a peculiar certainty that they would never be so close again.

Before she got out she leaned across and gave him a light, swift kiss. "If Miriam sees the lipstick, tell her it was only me. And don't you worry, everything is going to turn out swell."

He drove slowly going home. He was well across the jackpine flat before he realized he was back on the reserve. Back on the reserve, he thought; that's where you belong, you Indian. He loved Miriam but he could not free her; his sister was in danger but he could not shield her; and if he did not go to the cannery he would lose the truck.

Along the river bottom, mist clogged the lights,

giving him the illusion of travelling a strange road toward a destination he did not know. But he knew all right. He knew he was only one more Indian, hostile and outwitted and insecure, heading back to the reserve.

What was he going to do? Victor could not help him, because Teresa had spent ahead to have the best for their baby, so she could look after it the modern way; what little Matt and his mother had would be needed in case Stevie got out of the hospital in time. Selling his rifle and his few tools would not bring in anything like enough. If the papers had come through in his name for the family trap-line, he could have gone to the extreme of putting it up for sale to whites, or if Bert Silas paid June back her money . . .

Miriam was in bed and sleeping when he got home, so he had until morning before he had to tell her. He would keep his cannery pass and try to find some other way to raise the money. The alternative was very hard to face, with Miriam lying warm beside him. But if he must, he would go to the cannery without her. His and Miriam's future depended on the truck, and without it he saw no hope of ever getting her away.

25

NOW, IN EARLY JULY, THE DAYS WERE STRETCHED SO
long that the end of one overlapped the beginning of
the next like shingles on a roof, and the birds, Matt
thought, hardly went to bed at all. No matter
how late, you could see the points of the mountains
fitted into the skyline and around them some light
stayed on, just waiting, because the nights were so
short it was not worth while to go away. Since the
people packed out, he and Melissa used the house so
seldom that the camp stove in the yard had grown to be
their real home.

It was pleasant, late in the evening like this, to watch
the blue smoke drifting above the trees. Toward mid-
night when the breeze came down the draw of the
creek, it turned cool enough to lie a little distance from
the stove, hearing the kettle singing in its throat and
thinking campfire thoughts while the small, red eye of
the damper hole winked at you.

Matt had been alone around the place all day, just
the two sled dog pups, which Jonathan had given for
Stevie when he came home, keeping him company,
doing this and that, drowsing a little, resting from the
heat. Melissa had gone with Cy to the Junction.
While Cy was away at the cannery, the dealer was

going to look after the truck for him. Cy would be on the train by now, well along on his journey to the coast, and while it was a heavy thing for a young man to have to leave his wife, this was how it had to be.

Right now Melissa would be at the hospital visiting with Stevie. How she would get home to-night Matt did not know, but if need be she could pay a little to some Junction friend to drive her out. On Saturday both of them were going in, because Saturday was Stevie's birthday and they would take him his cowboy suit. It was in its box in the house right now, the hat and the cowboy pants, red shirt and two play-guns in holsters on a belt; four-dollars-eighty in the catalogue. Melissa had ordered it a size too big so it would last him a good while after he got out. The latest was that Stevie wanted a horse to ride, one like Jasper Gawa's.

After he cooked himself a late meal, Matt brought out his special gouging knife and finished carving a block of green alder into a baling scoop for the canoe. The river was dropping and one would soon be needed when they started putting out the net. By all the signs the first of the sockeye salmon were already coming home.

The salmon were born here, the people were born here, and no matter how far they travelled they always came back up river when their natures called them home. They had to; that was the way it was. There were things you counted on which did not turn out, just as, thinking back, things had not turned out as Mr. Lloyd said they would. But all changes were not good changes. And most things did stay the same; the same summer days, the same night breeze as when he was a boy, the day's warmth held in the ground when you stretched out before your fire. These things would never change, and the salmon and the people dying, and the salmon and the people being born.

It was not so childish as it sounded, Stevie asking for a horse. He would need one as soon as this sickness was all behind him. Matt thought that unless his knees failed him completely, he and Stevie were going to travel back to the old family trapping ground some nice fall, two horses to ride and one to pack their grub, and these two dogs of Stevie's trotting behind, each with its load. There he would pass on to Stevie the knowledge of landmarks and hunting secrets which had been told him as a boy. He would tell Stevie more of the old stories their people handed down. When he tried to tell them in the hospital, Stevie would not listen very long.

Miriam and Paul's lamp had just been turned out when Matt heard a car coming up the hill beyond Marie's. That would be Melissa coming home. He opened the damper and set the kettle forward. No doubt she would be serving coffee to her Junction friend. But then Matt knew by the sound that it was not a car. It was a truck, and a good-sized one, like Cy's. What a stroke of luck it would be if Cy had raised his payment money after all, and had turned around and come back to Miriam, instead of getting on the train! By the time Matt got to the gate, the truck lights were shining along the road.

It was not Cy's truck, and it was coming very slowly. It drew up just beyond the gate. Two native men, Junction men, got out, then Cy and then Melissa. Matt opened the gate a little, puzzled and expecting them to speak. But nobody spoke. He saw Cy, walking unnaturally straight, go to the back. Cy passed close to the gate but he did not turn his head or say a word.

Even Melissa, groping past him with strange bundles in her arms, did not speak. All he heard was a thread-like whimper as she went toward the steps. The men went to the back where Cy was and one of them pulled away a canvas.

Matt's hands came up slowly, lifting like separate things, and gripped the top of the gate. It was like the waking from a dream and remembering you had that dream before. There was blackness in the back of the truck but a kind of seeing came to him, which took in all that had been and was to come, and he knew without a word being said that this was how it was meant to be, when the time arrived at last for Stevie to be coming home.

I will read it, Cy was thinking over and over during John Moose's rambling prayer. I will read it and I will make my voice stay steady, if it is the last thing I do.

Melissa and Matt, Miriam and Old Paul, the Mooses, Victor and Teresa, her body heavy with child, sat on chairs around the walls.

A native preacher's book, coverless and old, was trembling in Cy's hands as he stood up to read.

" '*And Jesus called a little child unto him and said* . . . ' " He read it very, very slowly so the older ones could understand. " '*Whosoever therefore shall humble himself as this little child* . . . ' "

He felt alone and exposed and desolate, unsupported by any feeling that they were listening. Melissa had her forehead pressed against the wall at the head of the couch where she was huddled, her hand beneath the sheet which they would presently take away when the body was to be placed in the box with white flannelette tacked around it. To them his voice must carry no

more meaning than the thin crescendo of despair from
the fly trapped in a spider's web above the window, or
the yapping of the two pups rolling in the dust outside
the open door.

But somehow he got through it, and John Moose and
Victor came forward to place the body in the coffin.
After they lifted the coffin to the couch, John brought
the lid from the corner and waited, holding it end up in
front of him, like a long, white shield.

It was a full minute before Matt's boots, slow and
startlingly loud on the floor, made Cy look up. He
could not see Matt's face as Matt stood, his shoulders
squared, before the couch; then at last, and with a kind
of formality, Matt bent forward and took up the thin
little hand and held it.

He seemed to grow taller as he stood there, an
angular, primitive-looking man with a dignity in his
submission which sheared through all creeds and forms
to the heart of the meaning of life for all humans here
on earth.

"Goodbye. Goodbye, my little brother," he said in a
strong voice. But, as he returned to his place, tears
were running down his seamed, brown face.

Minnie whispered to her husband and the two of
them tried to raise one of the laments which were
from the beginning among the up-river people. But
their cracked voices wavered, and even with Paul's
growling monotone, the song-at-parting died, Melissa
and Matt being unable to join in, and the rest too young
or disinterested to have learned the words.

When the lid was on, Victor brought Teresa's paper
flowers, the cowboy suit, the belt with pistols, the
camera and, lastly, a small, adult's felt hat with tissue
paper still in its crown, just as Melissa had bought it

last evening when she selected the shoes and the suit for the burying. Cy helped arrange these on the lid; then, as his mother threw herself across the box, he rammed the book in his pocket and strode outside.

He walked back and forth at the side of the house, trying to control himself and muttering "Jesus! Jesus!" in a sort of outraged prayer.

I am to blame for this; I killed him, he thought, striding back and forth, swinging his shoulders and beating his fist into his palm. His diffidence, his vacillation, his softening the blow for Matt and his mother when he should have, at whatever cost, defied them— all this seemed to be accusing him.

He should have known better, and the agony was that he *did* know better. He believed what the doctor said, and what the health book said, and yet he saw now, too late, that he had acted as if he did not completely believe. For had he really believed, he would have got Stevie to Miller Bay, no matter what. In himself, in all of them, unrealized and far deeper than they knew, was something which caused them to suspect the doctor's motives, a resistance based on outworn beliefs and superstitions which made them resort to deception— even self-deception—to shield them from facts their emotions would not accept.

And it was not primarily because he was a doctor, but because he was a strange white, that they distrusted him. Had the doctor been Mr. Haney, as they knew him toward the last, Stevie might have lived, because there was one white man most of the people trusted. But the doctors were strangers; they came and went; they understood your bodies, but they did not seem to know those inner things which made you what you were.

How or when this instinctive distrust had been

created he did not know. But whether by the government, with its impersonal, authoritative handling of the Indians, or by the Indian's failure to understand the need for regulations, and wanting to hide his ignorance even from himself in order to preserve his remaining self-respect, it made no difference now. Stevie was dead. Perhaps he, Cy Pitt, had killed him, or perhaps the killer was this deep distrust of one race for another.

Chair legs scraping on the floor warned him it was time to go back in and help carry the box to the graveyard; and to-morrow he must go to the Agency office to have that form filled, the one they called *Death of an Indian*.

26

FOR A WHILE, THE WEIGHT OF SADNESS ON THE HOUSE,
and Cy's feeling of failure and guilt, sapped his resolve.
Leaving Miriam had called for all his resolution, without this being piled on top of it. Then came a letter
from the cannery manager to say that all jobs had been
filled and would he please return his pass. He knew
then that the truck was lost. He went alone to the
Junction the day the dealer took it back. By the time
he walked home that night, Teresa had had her baby.

Helping with that made his mother live again.
"Melissa is a good one to get me started," Teresa told
him, one afternoon shortly before she and Victor closed
the house and went back to camp. "The only thing is,
she bundles the baby up too much. My people are the
same but the Sisters taught us better." She was nursing
the baby and she looked down into its face with linger-
ing, sweet severity. "Do you know what Melissa says?"
she asked with an indulgent laugh. "She says these
women who do not want to nurse their babies should
have been born in the shape of insects or fish, if they
care for their young no more than that."

Cy was pleased that his mother had taken such good
care of Teresa, because Teresa had been of great help to
them in their time of trouble. She had written the

letters to June at Angus and to the others, trying to get word to Dot of what had happened, and when nothing came of it, she sent a notice to the Prince Rupert paper. Within a week Dot wrote to her father explaining she had come north again and she thanked them for making her boy's last year on earth a happy one. She gave her address and said to drop around the first time any of them went to Rupert.

Watching Miriam with Teresa's baby in her arms touched Cy in a mysterious way. Miriam was not sure of it yet, but she asked Melissa's advice and the signs were that their own baby had been started.

In August, when Miriam became certain of it, the prospect of fatherhood gave a solemn, final sense of completion to their union. Alone in the night, their bodily intimacy came between him and his failure over the truck. But now he knew that before another fishing season the little fellow would be here. What was he going to do?

"I don't want you to tell Paul," he said to Miriam one night. "My mother is the only one who knows and I asked her to-day to keep it to herself."

"You sound like some frothy person who does not like to be a father," Miriam teased. "The little one is growing all the time and we cannot fool grandfather for long even if we wanted to."

"All right, but let him find out for himself."

She worked herself more snugly into his arms. "If that is what you want. But I did not think you would be one of those who is shy for people knowing."

Long after she sank into sleep, he lay with his arm around her, thinking. And whenever his thoughts wandered—principally to his mother's mounting anxiety over June's not returning to the hospital on

time, and as they habitually did, to losing the truck—
the feeling of Miriam relaxed in his arms invariably
forced him back to the need for escape from this house
and all it stood for. As soon as Paul found out that
Miriam was with child, he would stop at nothing to
increase his hold on her. Paul had repeated his offer
to teach him canoe making, and slighting the offer was
making matters worse between them. To one so proud
of his craftsmanship, this was an affront. Where they
would go, or what pretext he would use to get her away,
he did not know. But it must be done. This time he
must succeed.

Paul was cutting spreaders for the five-fathom canoe
when he saw Cy coming down the path. To help Matt
with their net, no doubt, Paul thought. He turned his
back on the path and continued working.

The canoe was almost ready for steaming and this
was always an anxious time. If it turned out he had
selected a tree whose wood was too brash to take the
steam, the canoe would split and the work be lost, to
say nothing of the shame of it.

He felt tense, for this was indeed the time when a man
put himself on trial for what he knew. As with all of his
many canoes his anxiety mounted as the time for steaming drew near. Only with this one there was the added
hazard of the breathlessness which had been hampering
him of late, and if a man were to allow his mind to
dwell on that, it could unnerve him. But he was not
going to fail. Matt, who had an eye for a good canoe,
frequently told him he had not seen a better.

Well, be that as it might, it was a work he need never
feel ashamed of. Most builders would call it finished
now, but there remained those certain touches, the
blending of those final indiscernible curves, the careful

testing for thickness before the steaming, and he was not going to hurry it. Many pails of water must be carried from the river and many stones, of the sort which do not crumble in fire and which hold the heat. And wood, a cord or more, was needed.

Paul had marked the length of the midship spreader, but before cutting it, he went to the stern for a final look, studying it from under his wrinkled lids, seeing it as it was and as it would be when all its harmony of line was brought out by the steaming. Then he moved to the other end and sat on his heels, visualizing how the lines would conform at the water level. His eyes dwelt on the proud bow with its hollows melting into the wood. A mistake there would have been a mistake indeed, for the knife edge of the short fore-keel must bite and hold in the swift water until the rounded stern swung into the eye of the current. He was about to get up, when Cy spoke.

"I have time to-day; I will cut your wood for you," Cy said. "A cord, two cords, whatever you need."

Paul shifted a few inches, squinting along the opposite gunwale and not turning from his work.

"There is a big spruce over by the riffle. It has two cords easy in it. Will it do? Do you want it?"

"That is the firing wood I plan to use," Paul answered curtly.

Cy reached for the crosscut saw hanging on the corner post of the shed.

Paul thought he was going, then heard him pause at the end of the shed where he could get a full view of the canoe. "It looks good; I like it," Cy said.

As he walked off, the flanges of Paul's nostrils rose and fell like the gill covers of a stranded fish. He felt his arms and neck quiver and his heart thumping

against his ribs. The young cedar! What did ones like
that know, what were they capable of knowing, of the
discipline and brooding which went into the shaping of
a good canoe? No patterns or white man's measure-
ments as at the cannery boat shed, only your eye and
the feel of the wood under your hand, while the tender
strength came out of the log and lay before you. For
weeks you worked on your knees, inside and out, chipping to thickness, not quite a thumb's breadth along the
midship gunwale and slightly thicker toward the bilge
and across the flattened bottom, chipping and feeling
and chipping again, making the wood give itself to you,
coldly watching yet loving too, as you gauged the force
and direction of every blow, the life going out from you
and into the thing you fashioned, the old life drained
away and spent for ever, but nothing careless and
nothing, no part of you, withheld.

So it was good! So he liked it! To speak so, like a
person choosing some cheap thing across a counter!
And the maddening part was that, if the young man
had yielded to instruction, he could have learned,
because he had the hands and the head for the work.
But see what had happened! Those two at the mission
house turning his head and making him into an imita-
tion white man, who admired that race's kind of knowledge and was neglectful of his own.

Slowly Paul lifted his hands and stared at them with
grim veneration. These hands; these very hands! They
were shaking, outworn things now and their work was
almost finished, but in them was the skill of the generations of the master builders, and from them the young
man could have taken it and passed it to the hands now
forming in his daughter's daughter's womb. It was his
for the taking, all of it, and he spurned it. Now his

chance was gone for ever. This was the last canoe, the very last canoe. The breathlessness and the trembling told him there would be no other.

It was past noon when Cy put away the saw and went up to the house.

"Melissa was here just now," Miriam said. "She had a dream last night about June, and she is afraid. She wants you to go down and ask is there a letter." She poured his tea and looked anxiously at him across the table. "Her tears were almost coming."

"You did not tell her about the two hundred?" He had withheld that bad news from his mother.

"No, but I thought of it all the while she was talking. Do you suppose he continues to take June's money and this is the reason she is unable to come home?"

Cy drained his cup and set it down. This possibility had not occurred to him, but it would be like Bert Silas to do it. "I'll hitch the team as soon as I eat. Will you come?"

Miriam said she would. "I will run and tell Melissa we are going. She will give grandfather his supper."

The post office was in the trading company store. He left Miriam in the wagon and went between the counters to the wicket. There was a letter from June but it was very short. "I have the chance of a better job and I am going to take it," he read. "Tell Mama I have money and will be O.K. I already wrote them at the hospital to send my trunk." The address he did not understand. It said "General Delivery" in Prince Rupert and this, the postmaster explained, was only where she got her mail; it did not tell where she was living.

There was a rack of axes to one side and he began hefting one and then another, looking at the prices and testing the grain with his thumbnail as if he were going to buy one. When he went out, he took the reins from

Miriam without speaking and drove to where the street ended in a grove of big cottonwoods beside the river. He stopped the horses in the shade and looked at his watch. He had two hours until train time.

"You can be home by dark if you start pretty soon," he said. "I am going to the station. I am going to get her home." He read the note aloud. He remembered Dot's address and she would be able to tell him where to look for June. "You are right; Bert Silas is behind this."

"I am afraid so. But you cannot make her come if she does not want to," Miriam said. "Melissa will say you are right to try, but you cannot make June come. How many days will you be gone?"

"You know June. It may take a little time."

"Will you have more than one talk with her?"

Cy nodded thoughtfully. "I might look for a job down there."

"Why do you tease me? This is no time for teasing."

"I am not teasing." The possibility had lain in the back of his mind for weeks, since soon after he lost the truck. He had turned it this way and that. It was what his father had done, and going to Rupert now gave it immediacy. He knew of native men from other villages who had moved to Rupert. They went out to the canneries in summer, but between fishing seasons Rupert was their home. Those men made good money all the year round, they did all right. They got themselves enfranchised, as the boat-shed boss had advised him to do, and they sent their children to white schools. If he got a job down there, he could rent a house and send for Miriam. If June would not come home, she could live with them and in this way he could keep an eye on what Bert was up to.

"If you are not teasing, then you are talking foolish talk," Miriam told him. "You speak so because you know grandfather was mad at you to-day."

"You know what he will make of the little fellow, if we do not get away."

"Let us not talk so far into the future."

"If I can get work in Rupert, I am going to keep after you until you come," he said aggressively.

Her lips trembled. "Don't you like me any more? We belong to the village."

Belong to it! You can say that again, Cy thought in English.

"Look." He yearned to put his arms around her but dare not trust himself. "It's for both of us."

"You know I love you. I am your wife for ever. Can we help it if we are Indian? If you stay down there, what will people think?"

There it was again—the people, always the people, wanting to hold you and all you hoped for in their mold of blind conformity to a past no longer adequate. "I don't care about the people," he told her. "All I care about is you—you and the little fellow. If I can get a job down there, you have got to come."

She clung to him like a terrified child. "Oh, my sweetheart!"

"Miriam! Miriam, please! Don't be scared. One day you will see and you will be glad." Their arms were around each other, but she no longer felt close to him. Only her entreating voice seemed close and real.

He knew with piercing certainty that if he yielded to her, Old Paul would win. Miriam, shaken by sobs, lay limp and unresponsive in his arms. But this was his chance, his supreme and final test. She kept sobbing and pressing herself against him.

"It will be hard for me, too," he whispered brokenly; "it will be worse for me. But if only you will promise me to come—"

"But he needs me. You know that he needs me."

Cy held her off a little and searched her face. "If he did not need you, would you come, would you leave the village?"

She looked up, reaching out to him, holding him with her eyes. Then she nodded, a frightened little nod, and threw herself into his arms. "I am a part of you, my sweetheart. When he no longer needs me, I will come."

It was dark and rain drops, a myriad of tiny, impotent fists, beat against the window of the day coach. When he boarded the train he had a feeling of purpose, but now the feeling was deserting him.

Sprawled on the seat, he thought of last year at the start of the cannery season, going down to where Miriam was, and of his coming home and expecting everything to be the same. It might have stayed the same if he had never left the village. Jasper Gawa was happy there, but even if he could recover that kind of happiness it could not satisfy him now. Last summer he believed Jasper was the one for June, and how long ago that seemed!

He tried to fortify himself with Miriam's parting promise. She would come when Paul no longer needed her, but who could tell how long that would be? His bold talk of getting a job in Rupert had become no more substantial to him than his breath of a winter morning, or these rain drops shattering themselves against the glass. To-night he felt that without her he was no longer complete and a part of something.

Was this awful feeling of separateness what his father had to endure, when the village got too much for him and he struck out alone? It is hard for Miriam now, Cy told himself, she does not see that some day she will be glad. But the words seemed like someone else's words; he was saying them but he could not make them real.

27

CY WENT TWICE TO THE ROOMING HOUSE DOT HAD NAMED
as her address, but he failed to find her. Just now,
before coming back up town, a woman sweeping the
hall told him it was the right place but that Dot had
not showed up for several days. "She comes and she
goes," the woman said. "You know how it is with
them." She took him upstairs and pointed out the room.

Walking the wet streets, he wondered what he should
do if he did not find Dot to-night. He must have walked
miles since morning on the chance of meeting June, all
the while watching the taxis in case Bert was driving
one of them. Many taxis met the train in the early
hours, but the driver who took him to rooms near
Cow Bay said he had never heard of Bert Silas.

The street he was on now was mostly stores. The
rain was coming harder. Before he went to his room to
dry out, he looked in the windows for the present he
wanted to send to Miriam. One store had women's
things in its window. He saw a nightdress, black, with
lace, but when he went in the woman asked him did he
mind telling her whom it was for? Then she brought
out others, ones she said his wife might like. He chose
a rather plain one made of a soft, blue kind of silk.

"A nice choice," she said. "And now, about the size?"

"Your size, I guess," he told her, "only younger."

The woman laughed pleasantly. "I should think so." She put it in a box and wrapped it in special paper for a present, and over that, put strong paper to keep it from the wet.

Her friendliness, and having a present for Miriam, made him feel better. On his way out to the room, he decided he would go to the train to-night and look for some native person returning to the Junction from the canneries who would send it out to Miriam.

His room was on the right at the head of the stairs, above a pool hall. While he was getting out his key, he heard men's voices in the opposite room, then a woman's laugh. Early this morning while he was trying to sleep there was a party in there, the door banging and people coming and going.

He turned on the light. The room had a wash basin and taps and it cost one-fifty a night, money down. He stood at the window for a moment. The heavy rain made night come early and over the roof of what he took to be the cold storage plant he saw moving lights in the harbour. To the right were the floats at Cow Bay where coast natives tied up while living on their boats.

He took off his windbreaker and placed it over the back of the chair, then sat on the bed, leaning on his elbows. What would it be like, living down here, eating in cafés and going to a different show every night? If he had found Dot home, right now he and June might be at a show, or in some café having it out about Bert.

He heard the woman singing. "Buttons and Bows", it was. A push of wind shook the window and sent rain sluicing down the glass. The reflection of the lights magnified the film of water so that it resembled ripples in the sun, crisping across the white sand of a shallow in the river.

He looked at his watch. Not quite six o'clock. If the rain kept on like this, he would get soaked going to the station with the parcel, so why not go and post it now? He knew where the post office was because he had gone to it a number of times during the day, on the chance June was calling for her mail. That was what he would do, post it. He pulled on his windbreaker and got the parcel from the table by the window.

The girl came out of the opposite room while he was locking his door. She wore a yellow dress with fur around the neck and she pulled on a cigarette and stood watching him.

"Brother! What a stinker of a night!" she said to him, with no trace of an Indian accent. "Taking in a show?"

"Who you talking to?" a man's voice demanded.

The girl winked at Cy. "This guy out here."

"Bring him in. Let's have a look at him." Then loudly: "You coming or ain't you?"

"He means you," the girl whispered.

Cy shook his head and was turning to go down the stairs when a thickset, middle-aged native came out and got in front of him. He pushed the girl away and took Cy by the shoulders. "I said, come in, and you're coming in, see?"

"Sure," the girl said. "What the hell, we don't want no trouble."

Cy was afraid that if he pulled away the man would fight him.

"Only for a minute," the girl said. "He's got to talk to somebody. Look at me, I been hours listening to his bull." She leaned toward Cy. "Gee, kid, come on. Nobody's going to hurt you."

"Only for a minute," Cy said.

A second man, tall and very thin, sat on the far side of the un-made bed with a bottle in his hand. The ceiling light filled his temples and cheek hollows with shadow, like the picture of a skull. He reached down and handed the other man a bottle to open, then he held it out to Cy. "Here."

Cy took it and set it behind him on the washstand.

"It's all right, kid. We got permits," the girl said.

"You damn right we got permits." The thin man scowled and spoke to the other in an Indian language Cy did not understand. "Fresh off the reservation, eh?"

Cy did not answer him.

"Well, we got the franchise, see? We're as good as whites, see? Buy all we want."

The first man was keeping his eyes on Cy and at the same time feeling behind him for the window sill. He was going to sit on it when the other pulled him away. "You dope," he said angrily, "you want to fall out and bust your neck?" The two began arguing.

"He's right, Charlie," the girl said. "Stay away from the window." She sat on the bed and motioned Cy to sit beside her. "Boy, has he ever got a load on!"

"What's eating that stick Indian?" the one called Charlie demanded. "Ain't he going to drink his drink or ain't he?"

"Aw, leave the kid alone," the girl said over her shoulder. "You're all right, ain't you, kid?" She got up, took the bottle from the washstand and slipped her arm around Cy's neck, trying to pull his head down against her breast. "Come on, kid, come to momma."

Cy pushed her away but she did not seem to mind. "Okay by me, you don't have to if you don't want to." Under the light, her hair was frizzed and dead-looking. "What's in the parcel? Come on, show me. Don't be shy. I bet it's something you don't like for me to see."

He started to push Miriam's present under his wind-breaker but she snatched it away and darted behind the bed, laughing at him.

"Give me that." His face was burning and a sicken-ing sort of anger came over him.

The girl backed closer to the men, holding the parcel against her and watching him with both defiance and invitation in her eyes. The men stopped wrangling and watched him too.

"You guys keep out of this," the girl said sharply. She held the parcel behind her. "We're friends, eh, kid?" She pursed her lips and took a step nearer. "Got a kiss for momma? One kiss and you can have it back."

The revulsion on Cy's face turned her teasing to vicious anger. "Why, you dirty stick flat-head you!" she screeched. "That's what I get for being friendly." She clawed at the parcel with her nails and held the nightdress against her body. "Take a look, fellas. Wouldn't I look sweet getting into bed in that? Here." She flapped it across the bed at him, then threw it in his face. It fell to the floor and Cy kicked it from him.

"Why don't you pick it up?" the girl taunted. "Your stick dame won't know the difference."

Cy's eyes narrowed. It was as if Miriam herself had been defiled.

The tall man was coming at him, an empty bottle in his hand. "Sure," the girl said. "He asked for it."

Both men were making for him but Cy knew, if he wanted to, he could get out the door. Instead he waited. He felt abased, choked with disgust for him-self. Then suddenly he jumped forward and struck. It was a looping, inexpert blow, but it had all of him behind it. It took the tall man on the side of his head and dropped him on the bed.

Cy felt a queer, consuming oblivion. He rushed the other man, took him by the throat, the span of his big lean hand enclosing half the neck, and pounded his other fist again and again into the man's face. They fell but Cy's fist kept smashing. The only feeling he had was an overpowering one of assertion, the explosive triumph of emotions bursting through layer upon layer of frustrations that had shamed his very manhood.

The man was as limp under his hands as a fresh-killed rabbit but he kept on battering him, lifting him by the throat and knocking his head back against the floor. Everything was narrowed down to a red glow in his mind. Deliberate thinking was gone and he felt only release. For all he knew he was killing the man, but what did that matter, compared to the exhilaration he felt?

It was the girl's screams for the police which brought him to his senses. He found the door and raced down the stairs. Still running, he splashed through oily puddles in the pavement, past the street light at the corner, and toward the shadowed slope behind Cow Bay. When he came to a scattering of houses with overgrown lots between, he stopped running. The next street-light was a block away but he must keep clear of that, because by now the police would be looking for him.

Just ahead was a small bridge. It spanned a gully with high bushes on both sides and he heard a creek. His hands were bloody. If he went down he could wash them, then hide under the bridge. But down there they could corner him. He had better keep moving. He hid in the bushes and wiped off the worst of the blood with wet leaves. There was an overgrown path and he took it, angling down toward Cow Bay.

Could he, Cy Pitt, have done this thing? There he was, wanting only to get out of that room to avoid trouble and suddenly, like a light snapped on, an over-whelming reversal of desire made him want nothing so much as to smash the face of the man who in some unguessed way stood for all his defeats and humiliations. The feeling of impact was still in his fist, its wild plung-ing up and down like a machine gone crazy.

The path brought him to a lower street where he stayed in the bushes, sucking his knuckles and spitting out the blood, watching both ways for the police. If they caught him it would all be in the paper—"Drink Crazed Native Jailed," or "Indian Charged with Murder". At the end of the street he saw the string of lights along the Cow Bay floats, with many fishing boats tied there. If he were a coast native, he might know somebody in one of those boats who would help him get away. Or if he even had a canoe, paddling close inshore, he might work his way up river, travelling at night, losing himself among the mountains of his trap-ping ground for years until the police forgot about him.

A taxi came unexpectedly and splashed to a stop a few yards from where he was hiding. A well-dressed native man got out, paid the white driver, then reached inside and took a woman by the arm. As they crossed in front of the headlights, Cy noticed the mud on her face. The man kept walking her, and when she staggered, he got his arm around her and held her up.

"Can you make it?" the driver called after him. "Want me to give you a hand?"

The man did not answer. They passed under the lights leading down to the floats. The man had her arm now, pretending there was nothing wrong with her. Cy felt his shame and wished he had not seen.

As the taxi backed and turned, its headlights showed the path continuing across the street in the direction of the tracks. Dot was the only one who could tell him what to do. Perhaps she would hide him; she knew the town and might tell him how to get away. He ran across, keeping low, and came out at the bottom of a steep bank behind a long line of box cars. Some of the sidings were empty, but there were no lights and when he was pretty well back into town, he went up steps to the end of a street. It was not the right one, but he knew where he was and soon he was at Dot's house. He kept his head down as he hurried through the lighted doorway. Dot's door was locked. He knocked as loudly as he dared, then went away.

His chest felt tight and he wanted to run, only that would draw attention to himself. What if Dot did not come back to-night? What if she never came back? Walking the main streets watching for June was his only chance. But there were police up there, and because of what he had done, he must keep away from her. I must keep away from her and Miriam and from everyone I know, he thought. And if the police catch me I will not tell my name.

Someone was coming and he dodged into the doorway of an empty store. It was a white man and a native girl and they were walking arm in arm. Before they came opposite, they crossed the street to a house with a lighted sign, ROOMS. The man looked old enough to be her father.

This doorway was as safe a place as any. He would stay here for a while and try to think things out. He felt wet and cold and hungry. Imagine being able to feel your hunger at a time like this!

Another native girl passed, a girl no older than June, and she, too, had a white man with her. But why should he care? Why should he keep noticing? That shamed man and his drunken wife, the Indians he had seen to-day loafing along the streets, tittering girls pointing at gaudy stuff in store windows which no white girl would fall for, why should he always think of them? Why did he not think of the well-dressed native men and women; of his father, clean and respectable, going along these streets to his well-paid shipyard job; or of those others of his race he had read about who had made themselves doctors and lawyers, nurses, teachers?

On the top of the hill, above the business streets, was the white part of town, self-contained, successful, knowing what it wanted and how to get it. Out there, beyond the misty darkness of the harbour, were the strong old villages and the good clean sea, and in between were the native people he wanted to forget—the human drift, the rootless ones cast up on this sordid tide flat of the in-between, unable as now he was unable to return to the proven old they had deserted, yet failing to strike roots in that other world which only the most gifted and resolute of his race could make their own.

If only he had not come; if only he could go back! But now it was too late. He was a no-good Indian, and the police were after him.

He rested his head against the doorway and tried to pray. But very soon he found he was not praying for himself at all; he was praying for June, for Dot, for those two young girls, for the many people of his race with their hidden sorrows. His heart went out to those poor rootless ones and it gave him a stilled, mysterious comfort to know that from to-night he stood among them, one of the many seeking fulfilment outside their villages, standing before a door which would not open.

He walked on, no longer avoiding the lights, not greatly caring if they caught him. If they caught him, he would tell them nothing, not even his name, for this was a trouble which must end with him. He was thinking of Miriam and remembering that he had prayed for ones he did not know, yet felt no need to pray for her. He hoped she would forgive him, leaving her with the little fellow coming; but all he could do for her was keep the shadow of his wrong from touching her.

Not knowing how he got to it, he found himself in the little park above the station. There was the rocky hill with the three totem poles he and June had stopped to look at. He went to a bench beside a rock-walled pool and sat, leaning forward with his elbows resting on his knees.

Would June, too, end up as human drift? She might be in some house, some room quite close, and he could not find her. Slowly he got to his feet and stood without moving, a lanky figure in the misty drizzle, his mind wearied and beaten down by thought.

He lifted his face to the white town beyond the hill. *Oh, you white race! What have you to do with us and what have we to do with you?* The words were not his, they were wrung from all the sorrows and perplexities, the yearnings and undefined hostilities of his great company of the rootless ones. *Our strongest you accept and our weak ones you belittle. You are so positive you are right and we are wrong. You teach us your ways, but you teach us also to scorn our past which alone can lift our heads and keep us whole. We imitate and resist you, depend on you and suspect you. You shield us, like children, but deal with us as lesser men you cannot trust. You are the builders and the breakers down. You think you understand us, but you will never know what it is to be an Indian in our land which you have taken for your own.*

Below, at the station, he heard the train bell ringing, the train for home. Only now he was not going home. He had no home. He looked at his watch, then went blindly up the path past the three totem poles standing like crosses on that dark hill.

DOT WAS STANDING IN THE DOORWAY OF HER ROOM.
She gave him a disregardful glance as he came along the
hall, then she straightened and stared. "Cy!"

"I tried all day to find you."

"Look at your face; your hands, too! Don't tell me
you've been drinking, that you've started that. Get
in here and clean up." She drew him into the room.
"You look like you've been through the wringer."

"The police are after me. I got in a fight. I think I
killed a man."

Dot shut the door quickly and bolted it. "Cy,
you didn't! Whereabouts was this?"

"Out near Cow Bay, where I took a room. There's
a pool hall."

Dot started the water in the corner basin and got out
a towel. "Hurry up, get that blood off yourself. Who
were you fighting with?"

"Some native fellow, some Charlie."

"What's he look like, this Charlie?"

Cy described him. "He didn't do anything to me,
nothing much, anyhow, but all of a sudden I was out to
kill him. I must have been crazy."

Dot hung a cigarette between her lips without light-
ing it. "You get that shirt off you. You can't go out

on the street like that. All that blood, they'd spot you in a minute. I know where I can dig you up a clean one. You get yourself cleaned up, and if anybody comes, don't open. I know the place you mean and I'm going to phone. If it's the lug I think it is, anything you did he had it coming."

Cy was drying his hands when he heard a quick knock and Dot's voice, telling him to let her in. "Relax," she said, giving him her slightly mocking but sincere smile. "You had me petrified there for a minute, but you're all right. You can forget about the police. He'll never report it. The last people that character wants to talk to are the police."

Cy groped behind him for a chair. All of a sudden he needed to sit down. "I was sure he was dead. He felt like it. You—I mean he's all right?"

"I hope to tell you he's not all right. My friend up there says Charlie got his for once." Dot's smile broadened. "By all reports you gave him one wonderful going over. What in the world did you hit him with?"

"Only my fists."

"Well, you must have made a job of it." She unfolded the clean shirt and gave it to him, then she picked up his bloody one and the towel and tossed them into the closet. "I'm expecting company, but we've got a few minutes." He put on the shirt and after she handed him a comb, she asked when he had come down. "It's been a long time, Cy, and we've lots to talk about. How are dad and the rest? Tell me about them."

Cy said what little there was to say.

"I sure did appreciate all you folks did for Stevie. Not much a person can say, but I guess you got the general idea from what I wrote . . . after."

"They miss him, Matt and my mother." Cy gave

her the comb. She put it on the table beside her bed, then stood facing him with her back to the wall and her hands slid in behind her. It struck him that she looked older and thinner, there under the light; on her forehead he saw a mark that could be a bruise.

"I felt good, him being up there with the family," she said, her eyelids drooping against the smoke of her cigarette. "What brought you down to Rupert this time of year, Cy?" she inquired off-handedly.

"I came about June."

"June's all right, Cy. She's doing fine. Just fine."

"I want to see her."

"If it's over Bert Silas, I wouldn't worry too much if I were you. Bert's out of circulation for a while."

"How do you mean?"

"He got sent down last week. It was all there in the paper. Rolling drunks is nice work if you can get away with it, but it seems Bert couldn't, poor devil. But I suppose you could say he had it coming."

"Too bad for him," Cy said. Bert was no fit person for June, but what had happened to-night, or almost happened, made Cy feel sorry for him. "Where did they send him?"

"Down south, to Oakalla prison farm. He's in for eight months, so he should be out of the picture for a while." Dot crossed to the ash tray and put out her cigarette. "Now, tell me straight. What you want June for?"

"We want her home."

A curiously tired, pitying smile passed over Dot's face. "Where have I heard that before? I hate to say this to you, Cy, but what in God's sweet name have you got back there for a girl with June's class?"

"Rupert is no place for her."

"Back in the sticks is no place for her, that's for sure.
Use your head, Cy. Why do you suppose she keeps from
giving you people her address?"

"You know where she lives, I bet," he told her. "She
could be right in this house, for all I know."

Dot looked down at him for a moment without speaking. "I know what they take me for back there, but I
didn't know it had come down to that. You're green,
Cy, but you're not *that* green. You must know what
kind of a house this is."

"I didn't mean it that way," he protested.

Dot's eyes were sombre with resentment. "I'm only
taking it like it sounded. June's not in this house, and
she's a long way from any house like this. But you
folks keep hounding her and you'll put her into one,
first thing you know. Can't you get it through your
head you've got to leave her alone?"

"Did she tell you that? Did she say she wants us to
leave her alone?" he asked, fearfully.

"She didn't have to. All I'm saying is you folks
better stop acting like June was headed straight for hell.
If you don't, she could end up where a cousin of hers by
the name of Dot has ended up. June knows what she
wants, and she has the brains to get it—which is more
than can be said for me. You can't tell ahead how it
will all work out; nobody can. But give the kid her
chance, why don't you?"

Cy got up and stood beside his chair. "She's all
right? You're sure of that?"

"So far as I know she's all right. But get this straight,
Cy. June will never go back to the village, any more
than I would. She's more like her father was, and of
all the kids from home she's the one should make the
grade. So lay off, see? I'll call her up, if you like, and if

she wants to, she can meet you uptown and have a talk. But if she doesn't want to see you, don't ask me her address because I wouldn't give it to you. Is that a bargain?"

They went along the hall and down the stairs. Dot went into a room and phoned; when she came out she gave him the name of an uptown café and told him how to get to it. "The kid was in bed but she'll be with you as fast as she can make it."

Dot walked with him to the front door. "Maybe I'll see you again some time," she said. Cy thought this was good-bye, but she changed her mind and came outside with him. The wind from the sea was blowing the drip onto the soiled tiles of the entrance. "Gosh, it's cold out here," she said. She folded her arms tightly, with her shoulders raised and her hands out of sight under her arms. "Well," she said finally, "I better be getting in."

Now, at the very last, he was reluctant to leave her. There was a solitary honesty about her; a hard, open-eyed acceptance of life and of what it had done to her, but a part of her seemed to preserve itself intact from what she did and from what she was. Cy wet his lips and made a swallowing motion. "Too bad I made you so much trouble," he managed to say.

"Forget it. I like you, Cy. Some ways you remind me of my father. You'll be like him; you'll have a life that suits you back there, you and Miriam. Tell dad I'm fine. And one more thing. Don't you ever so much as hint to the kid that because she's Indian she can't make the grade. That's the very worst thing you could do. Take it from me; I know. Good-bye now." She gave his arm a pat and went quickly in.

After Cy crossed the street, he looked back and saw

her head and shoulders against the glass of the door.
She was watching the street and he almost went back
to tell her his other reason for coming down. She would
be surprised that he was down here looking for a job,
and perhaps she could advise him where to ask.

It was drizzling and he stood on the curb in the dark
for several minutes, his eyes on the shape of her inside
the glass. All of a sudden he wanted to cry. His arms
hung at his sides, yet the feel of them was the same as
though he held them out to her. "Come home, Dot,"
he whispered. "Come on home."

A man—not Johnny—was coming along the opposite
side of the street. Dot opened the door for him and he
went in.

The café June named had tables along both walls,
but no booths. The people in it were mostly white
people, but there were some well-dressed native people,
too. Thanks to Dot, he need not care who saw him, but
that hunted feeling was not easy to forget. He thought
of her, and of Bert. How long did Bert hide from the
police before they arrested him? And when an Indian
was put in jail, did they put him with only Indians or
among the whites? It hurt to see Bert end up this way.
What would he be like when they let him out?

He had not eaten since noon and he was bent over
his second bowl of clam chowder when June entered.
She wore a long, dark blue coat and had a plain white
kerchief over her hair. She did not see him at first and
stood, trim and self-assured, just inside the door, taking
off her gloves and looking for him among the people at
the tables.

Her face broke into a smile at sight of him. "Sorry if
I kept you waiting," she said. Rain beaded the fringes
of her hair and as she sat opposite him the scent of it
was fresh and pleasant.

A waitress came and June ordered a milk-shake for herself and a second one for him. "Is anything wrong at home?" she asked. "There was this telegram to-day." She opened her bag and passed the telegram across to him. "It came to me, care of General Delivery. I got it just before six."

The telegram was signed by Teresa. It read:

PLEASE TELL CY MIRIAM SAYS COME HOME

"Whatever happened?" June asked with concern. "I can't believe you two would quarrel."

"Who says we quarrelled?" He crumpled the telegram. "It's Paul again. He must have found out from Miriam that I'm after a job down here. I'm going to rent a house; bring her down. This is a trick of his to stop me."

June clasped her hands on the table in front of her, looking at him thoughtfully. "Do you think it will work out?"

"It's got to."

Slowly she shook her head. "I'm afraid it won't."

"You'll see. I'll get her away."

"You're only trying to fool yourself, Cy," she said. "You know you can't get Miriam away."

"Don't keep telling me that," he protested. "If I get a job I'd be crazy to go back."

"You'll go back, Cy," she said gently. "What else is there for you to do?"

For an hour they had been walking the empty street. For most of that time she was trying to make him understand her side of it. "You think I'm taking awful chances living down here, don't you? But even if Mother got the Agent after me for being under age, they couldn't keep me in the village. First chance I got, I'd run away."

"Then why get after me for running away? You said that, don't forget. You said I was running away."

"I mean it differently for you. I don't belong there any more and you do, if only on account of Miriam."

Cy refused to accept this. Because he wanted her to approve his plan, he had told of the baby that was coming and now she was using that fact against him. "I could make things easier for Miriam down here."

"No, you couldn't. She'd always feel strange and people would notice. You've got to be fair to her, Cy. One thing I learned this summer, and it's what Mrs. Haney used to tell me, only I hadn't the sense to see it; and that is you've got to believe you're as good as anybody else before you can prove to them you are."

"Miriam's as good as anybody."

"Of course she is. Miriam's one swell girl, but that isn't how I mean. I watch natives, here and around the cannery. Lots of them really do believe they're not as good as whites. It makes them act dumb or else they turn out the don't-care kind. The rough element. Like Bella."

"Bert thought he was as good as a white," he argued, "and see what happened."

"You're wrong there, Cy. Actually he didn't."

"Don't tell me that!"

"Bert fooled you and he fooled me for quite a while; and worst of all he fooled himself. At least he tried to, and I guess that was his trouble."

"Do you think he'll be different when he gets out?" he asked.

She wished she could tell him she did not expect to be living here when Bert got out. She wished she could tell him that the two hundred for a taxi was a made-up story, and that Bert would have ended up in jail that time, if she had not sent it. What the money really went for was to pay back what Bert had taken from some drunken logger.

Bert confessed all this, weeks before his latest trouble. Until then she had trusted him in most things and he could have kept it from her. Instead he owned up and at the finish he was crying. Poor Bert, he was all mixed up inside, and soon after she came to Angus she realized the two of them were going different ways. She pitied him, and at the same time she would always be grateful to him. It seemed strange that a person who had no real confidence in himself should have been the one to give her confidence. When he first took her out, she thought he was wonderful. She depended on him at a time when she was uncertain of herself, but at the last it was Bert who needed her.

By now she and Cy were on a tree-lined street which mounted in a long curve toward houses behind the hill. "If I show you where I'm staying will you keep it to yourself?" she asked. "Even Mother mustn't know, because Marie might get it out of her and I don't want Bella hanging round. The family I'm staying with know about you and I'd like you to come in. I've got something to show you."

The house was one of a row built for workers during the war. June had a small housekeeping room in the basement, which they entered by an outside door. It was neatly painted, though somewhat bare and smelling of damp plaster. She turned on the electric heater before taking off her coat and overshoes.

"How do you like it?" She drew the one chair closer to the heater for him and sat on the bed. "Warm yourself, Cy. You look cold." Her hands were flat on her hips, her legs straight out and with the toe of one shoe she traced a pattern in the rug, studying it and feeling slightly breathless because of what she had decided to reveal. "Well, hold your hat. I'm not telling anyone but you. Two weeks from now I expect to be working in Vancouver." She reached for a photograph on a shelf at the head of the bed which was piled with catalogues and fashion magazines, and handed it across to him. "I'll be working for her."

Cy looked hard at the picture. "She's Indian." His voice had a note of disparagement.

"And is she ever tops with me! She's opening a little dress shop down there." June got up quickly and sat on the arm of his chair, looking down at the picture he was holding in both his hands. "She was forewoman at Angus this summer. Her husband's skipper of a big seiner. He owns it, and they're the swellest people."

Cy kept staring at the picture with a challenging expression on his face. She wasn't a young woman, but she wasn't old, either. Her eyes had a clear, questioning directness which was increased by her arched brows. Her jaw was firm and a little pointed. It would have been severe except for a certain latent playfulness at the corners of her mouth. He had to admit she had the look of an honest person.

"What kind of work has she for you?" he wanted to know.

"In her shop. There will be only the two of us."

He closed the folder and held it out until she took it. "You don't know about store work." Vancouver was too vast, too distant. The world he knew began at the coast and ended in wilderness at the limit of their trapping grounds. She was only his sister, younger than he was, and her audacity alarmed him.

"I can learn. She believes I can, if you don't." She

ran her fingers through his hair. "Aw, Cy, don't be like that." This was by far the biggest chance that had come to her. "Do you know what she said to me?" She clasped her hands over one knee and leaned forward to look into his face. "She said she had been watching me all summer, how I did my work and behaved myself, and my choice in clothes. Near the last she took me out, here in Rupert, and one weekend when her husband was in port they talked it over and decided I was the type they wanted."

"She looks all right. I got nothing against her." He rose and stood drying the backs of his legs at the heater. He wanted it to be clear it was not the woman he objected to. "All I mean is, you don't belong down there. You know you don't. Like with Mrs. Haney. You could have stayed friends with her and I guess you could have gone to Vancouver with her, only you turned against her. But I bet anything you would never go with her, no matter what."

"I know, but this is altogether different. This lady is a native."

"It will be the same if you work for her. You'll have to do everything like she says."

"But Cy, don't you see? That's what I want to do."

How could she explain to him the inspiration this woman gave her, not so much by her spoken encouragement as by being what she was—a person of their race who had freed herself and who had moved out into the world of whites with unassertive confidence in her ability? This woman was the verification of her own groping hopes.

Since leaving school she had known times when the dream became so tenuous that she had almost ceased to care. Had it not been for a saving fastidiousness she might have become like Bella and sought good times wherever they were offered. Most of the gratifications she craved seemed to come to white girls as a right. She was not permitted to forget, for long, the limitations of being an Indian, so what was the use of trying. Then, at the very time she was losing her trust in Bert, this woman had opened the door on a whole new area of experience.

"I got nothing against her," Cy said again. "You must think she's pretty good."

"She is good. At Angus they said she was the best they ever had. The work she has for me down there is exactly what I want. I want to know just everything about dresses and materials. I can work in a store. I'm not afraid of meeting people. I like new people." She moved to the bed, then came and stood before him. "It's no use trying to stop me. I'm going."

He weighed his fears for her against his pride in her. In her speech and bearing she was little like the June he used to know. The trusting readiness was there, but now it was more a trust in herself, a welcoming, calm-eyed composure. People would be attracted to her as always, and she to them, but there had come to be a controlling self-reliance, a steadfast determination, friendly, and at the same time objective and appraising.

"I guess you are." The opposition was gone from his voice and he was no more than acknowledging a fact.

"I wish you sounded more—well, glad," she said with a low laugh. "It's a wonderful chance for me. I'll make good, you'll see. And next summer, when I get my holidays, maybe I'll come back to the village and visit you. I'll want to see that baby."

"What makes you so sure I'll be in the village?"

"Because I can't think of you living any place else, I guess."

"We may be living down here by then."

He was hunched down awkwardly in the chair, holding his hands, one and then the other, to the heater. Something made her rest her arm across his shoulders, as if to shield him; something compassionate, and very deep. Over the phone, Dot had told her more of what had happened to him to-night than she would ever repeat. How much more dare she say to him? After to-night it might be years before they were together and she shrank from hurting him. But now is the time, she thought. He has got to know.

"Look at it this way, Cy," she began, very quietly. "If the Haneys had stayed, or if you had got farther in school, it might be different. But supposing you did move down here, what would you do? You know the kind of jobs you would have to take, and the element you and Miriam would have to live beside. All you could afford is a couple of rooms and it would be even worse for Miriam after the baby comes. No place to play or anything. Like with Stevie when he was little." Her arm tightened across his shoulders. "I hate to tell you this, but I can see as clear as anything that it will be better for you in the village."

She felt his shoulders harden in angry withdrawal, and when he raised his head his eyes had the hurt, bewildered look of a little boy's.

29

THE SMOKE-HOUSES ON THE RIVER FLAT WERE CLOSED,
the hay and potatoes in, wild berries gathered, cured
salmon stored for winter use. The fattening snow was
on the mountains and when the last families returned
from fall fishing, the cycle scribed by thousands of
years of communal living would be rounded out.

It was now, more than at other seasons, that Melissa
felt the full, strong pulse of the village deep within her.
There was food for all, and a woman who was a woman
wanted her children near at this time of year. June
had written Cy a letter from Vancouver and what was
in it told what her heart already knew, that her girl had
gone from her and was never coming back. Visits, yes.
But what were visits when the words, all English,
minced like flighty women on her lips, and her tongue
and throat had lost facility for native speech; when the
too-emphasized delight in native food implied con-
descension, and the young heart could not take shelter
in the old heart because of what had come between?

As many smoked fish put away, as many berries, as
many potatoes in the pit, but no longer the lives to be
nourished by them. June gone, and Stevie gone, and
Cy cared for by another woman. Families with children
were waiting for the new teacher, believing education

was the thing, but was it not education which took her girl from her and made Cy rebel against what had satisfied him before? The life here had not changed, only her children had changed. The content remained, the strong, sure discipline of seasons, the authorities worn smooth by long obedience, the regulated comings and goings, but her children's heads were filled with all new things. They saw restrictions where she saw protection; they resisted where she complied, and felt the safer for it. Yet this was spoken of as education! It held up enticements beyond their grasp, offering them the moon but at the price of the authenticities which were before schools were.

She knew that Matt's heart, like hers, was heavy with the burden; his daughter taken from him by white allurements, his daughter's son by the white man's sickness. He rarely spoke of Stevie any more, but since the death his old, lean zest was gone and a mood of negation had come upon him. He was not bitter nor weakened by repining—he walked, an empty, upright man, into the ancient darkness, grateful for, but not accepting, the consolation which Caleb offered. Their sorrow was the old, old sorrow, known before Caleb's words of Christian comfort were spoken among their people.

Was she, after a life of wanting and being wanted, so soon to face the empty years? It was not enough. She would not permit them to be empty, not as long as *k'Shan* salmon ran, and berries grew on the familiar hills, and enough of strength remained for her to fill the mouths of others. She had carried sorrow before and found it bearable through being needed, and so she would again.

Melissa was seldom in the Leget house. You could

not say she avoided it, it was merely that she did not go. Miriam came to see her sometimes with Cy, but when Old Paul was at home there was a rigidity, an undercurrent of strain, which hampered talk. Paul had his will, and Cy had his, and for one so young there was little of yielding in his nature.

But this afternoon, as she went to the school tap with her water pails, she realized, quite unexpectedly, that she was of a mind to go. To-morrow was Paul's big day, and he and Matt were down at the canoe getting ready for the steaming. Cy had only just returned from Dick Dawson's pole camp with a wagon-load of wide strips of cedar bark for covering the canoe while the heat was in it. She saw the team tied at the gate and heard Cy's axe blows from the shed where he would be splitting wood for the supper fire. She set down her pails and went.

Miriam was on the front steps, knitting.

"Having the sun while it has its warmth," Melissa said placidly. "The air grows cool. Not many more days to sit outside."

Miriam's lips were silently counting stitches but she looked up and nodded.

Melissa wondered if she kept to the native counting, in tens and forties, as did older women, or if she had gone over to reckoning in hundreds. The girl was of a good colour and was eating well, by all accounts. It was then Melissa remembered her decision to go to the mountain-side for moss before cold weather. Spring would not be soon enough; the soft, absorbent moss for the newly-born was now at its prime, and the girl should be made a present of it well before the birth.

She heard Cy drop an armful of wood into the box, then he came and stood in the doorway with a letter in his hand.

"It is not from June," he said, to prepare her. "It comes from Marie. Jasper brought it this noon but the thing she asks is so foolish, I did not care to tell you."

"Read it out," Miriam said. She had folded her knitting and laid it in her lap and was watching Melissa's face with odd expectancy.

Cy began to read. The letter was addressed to Miriam.

> Just a few lines to let you know am doing fine. Made good this summer so staying to end of fall fishing.
>
> I guess Teresa looking for somebody to set her hair. Maybe the same you, ha-ha. I be home in few weeks and give you a good one. I got some new ways a woman down here show me.
>
> We sure sorry for Melissa and Matt, bad trouble. Too bad for them.
>
> I guess you know poor Bert throw in the can. Good kid lots of ways but that how it is. June big city girl I hear. She got lots on the ball that kid. We sorry to see her go but glad for her.
>
> I sorry to tell you Bella into mitchief, some coast fellow. Sorry to tell you this but everybody down here wise by now so all right for you. Four month to go. A man and wife here want to adopt it but Melissa got first chance, she got it coming to her poor woman. She sorry for Stevie and we like to help her all we can. So ask her if she like to put in for it or not.
>
> Well friends, that all I got to say. All well here and doing fine. Keep smiling from Friend Marie.

Melissa folded her arms. Her gaze was straight before her as if she were studying the horses as they stood with lowered heads, their tails switching method-ically at the flies. "She does not say she is bringing the girl with her."

"I think Bella will come at the last," Miriam said. "It is natural to want your baby born in your own village."

"No need to wait until Marie gets home," Cy said. "I will answer for you and take it out."

"How soon will you write?" Melissa inquired.

"After the steaming. In good time for Saturday."

She turned her body and looked up at him. "To think you had this news hours ago and did not bring it!" Then to Miriam: "Two new ones before next spring!" Now there was indeed strong reason to look ahead. "No, Saturday is not soon enough. I will repay Jasper in dried fish and have him take the answer in the morning."

"But I will be going down myself on Saturday. Saturday is soon enough," Cy said.

"And have some coast woman get ahead of me? You must write to thank Marie to-night."

"You see?" Miriam said, smiling at Cy. "I had a feeling she would want it."

"Well, naturally, I want it."

"You are too old," Cy objected.

"I am first of all a woman. Better still, I am a native woman. Do you take me for some kind of white?"

"What have the whites to do with this?"

"Never mind." But she could have told him a thing a coast woman at the cannery read out to her from a big city paper—a white baby abandoned by its mother, left on a bench in a park, then locked away from loving arms in a building with other unwanted white babies, like animals on a farm. He went too much by whites, but she could tell him that some of their customs were beyond human understanding.

She rose and stood at the bottom of the steps, her hands on her hips, her feet solid on the ground. The emptiness had been lifted from her and again she saw meaning in the work she had to do.

Cy remained on the porch after Miriam went inside. He saw his mother pick up her pails and cross the road, her back thick and straight, her shoulders broader against their weight. Her figure appeared squat against the slanting sunlight. She closed the gate behind her, testing the latch as she always did, then moved on and passed from his sight behind the house.

He knew she was not taking Bella's baby through pity; that sort of pity she associated with weakness and it had no place in her mind. She always knew what she wanted and her motives had an elemental directness, as if she stood a little back from life and refused to be jostled by it. She knew better than to expend herself striving for the unattainable, but for what was within her grasp she exerted great strength of purpose. Her world was limited but she moved in it with a confidence he did not have.

Time and again since his return from Prince Rupert he thought that if only he could content himself with his mother's world his old, lost peace would return. This was what June appeared to believe, but he still was not going to accept it. He admitted that Miriam had done wisely in asking June to send him home, because on the evening he went to Rupert, Paul had a bad spell. The pain, he told Miriam, was like a mountain sitting on his chest. Yet next morning he was back at his canoe, driving himself to finish it.

Cy heard the rattle of stove lids and went in. "I had better write that letter for her now," he told Miriam. "She will have her way, but I cannot agree that she is wise. She thinks it will help her to forget Stevie, but I believe it will only make it worse."

"She is a woman," Miriam said.

The writing materials were on the clock shelf beside the door to Paul's room, on top of the arithmetic book Mrs. Haney had left for him. He was getting them down when he chanced to see a piece of swamp root hanging from the door frame. He pulled it from its string and took it to the kitchen. "When did he put this fool thing up?"

"Why, it has been there for days," Miriam said pleasantly. "It is only that you did not notice."

Cy turned the wizened, hairy thing over in his hand. "Of all the superstitions!"

"Don't be cross with him, Cy. Please." Miriam turned away to get something from their own room off the kitchen. "You are funny sometimes. All this fuss over a little piece of swamp root. I do not see why."

I know you do not, Cy thought. What chance has he ever given you to see? "Don't tell me you believe in it!"

"I did not say I believe in it. But where is the harm? It cannot hurt him—and you never know."

"I know, all right." He was thinking of that other piece of swamp root that his mother had hung at the head of Stevie's little bed. She had left it there for weeks after Stevie went to hospital and he suspected she believed it had the power to heal Stevie even though he was not within miles of it. Several times he had started to take it down, but something—he could not have said what—had stopped him. He supposed it was because finding it gone would upset his mother.

Miriam asked him to put more wood on the fire. He opened the stove, and without her seeing, tossed the piece of root in with the wood. It crackled spitefully, and seeing it burn brought a relieving sense of audacity and independence. But when it was too late he realized that Paul would find out the root was missing and he wished he had left it where it was.

The steaming began early next morning. The faces on the totem poles along the bank looked strangely knowing through the mist, as if aware that what their sunken eyes were to behold to-day had been done in this place countless times by a long succession of people who now were dead.

As Cy led one of the team, harnessed to the stone-boat, down the path, Paul and Matt were bedding the canoe in chips and sand. The big fire for the stones was beginning to crackle, its heavy smoke billowing into the shed and merging with the morning mist over the river. Neither of the old men spoke while Cy lashed the water barrel in place. With their heads low against the smoke they were like a pair performing some dark ritual that was very old.

Cy hauled water until the canoe was half full. By this time the big, square fire was blazing and he helped insert more stones in openings between the criss-crossed lengths of spruce. The sun had eaten the night mist before the first stones were hot enough to shovel into the canoe. When steam began rising, cedar bark and poles were brought to cover it. Victor and his father were the first to appear. Before noon the canoe was almost surrounded by men, some taking out stones for reheating and dropping in hot ones, others looking on, not talking or joking because Paul's anxiety was felt by all.

The water was close to boiling before Paul inserted the first spreader amidships, not forcing it, but bearing down cautiously with his hands. From time to time shorter spreading bars were placed, some at bow and stern and others at water level along the bilge. Each

time a section of bark-covering was lifted the old man
examined the wood for indications of splitting, running
his fingers across the grain and staring at it command-
ingly and with beseeching grimness. The hot, wet
smell of the cedar filled the shed. While this was a good
sign, the older men knew that a split usually came
during the period of cooling.

It was late afternoon. All but the watching was over;
old Paul had every spreader precisely where he wanted
it, and still he had not touched the sandwiches Miriam
sent down.

"Say what they like, the old boy knows his stuff,"
Victor said to Cy as they watched from the far side of
the dying fire.

Cy nodded. Did the thing or the person exist that the
old man could not bend to his will? he thought. For
Miriam's sake, since coming home from Rupert he had
let Paul have his way about most things, but this
swamp-root stuff was just too much. Darkening her
mind with superstition was one thing he did not mean
to tolerate.

For there were superstitions and superstitions. There
were the harmless ones, like icicles being the north
wind's teeth and if you broke them the north wind
blew the harder; the story that people's teeth were
ivory long ago and now they were only bone; the
bad luck which followed if you mistreated the blind and
helpless. But this was vastly different. This was like
the stories told around camping fires which sent a
tingle of dread through you when the wind sobbed in
the pines and wolves howled in the darkness: of the evil
heart which would not burn when a body was cremated,
and of misfortune in the touch of a girl who was changing into her womanhood. Teaching Miriam that

swamp-root could charm away sickness was wrong, and the first chance he got, he would tell the old man so.

The sun was down and the yellow glow fading from the frosted poplars on the ridge when Paul and Matt gathered up the tools. The rest had gone and as the two left the shed they turned as one man and took a last look at the canoe.

"Good," Matt said. "Very good."

Paul accepted the praise in silence. When he reached the house he went directly to his room and lay down, for he was very tired.

Cy was splitting wood and when he came to get the kindling box Miriam said they would have supper as soon as her grandfather changed into moccasins and came from his room. "It is nearly ready," she said. "I am hurrying up the potatoes."

He went back to his splitting. Some minutes later while he was filling the kindling box he happened to look up in time to see Miriam hurrying down the path to the street.

"Something you need from Caleb's?" he called.

"I will be right back," she answered over her shoulder. "Pump up the gas lamp. I will only be a minute."

He ran and caught up with her. "What is it? What do you need?" Then, because of the evasion in her eyes, he held her by the shoulders, and made her face him. "Miriam, look at me."

She tried to pull away. "Make fun if you like, but he needs it. Minnie has some more and I said I would go for it. It was helping him and you took it away. What did you do with it?"

"But swamp-root is all foolishness."

"*You* said that; I did not say it." Her voice rose with disavowal and she struggled to break his hold on her.

"No," he said. "No."

"You hear me? Let me go."

The struggle of her shoulders under his hands roused him to deep anger—not at her, nor solely against the old man, but against the imposed superstition and all the hampering ignorance. "No, Miriam, no. I tell you no." This time he was the one who must be listened to. "You are not going. I will not let you go."

She pressed her hand over her mouth and her eyes widened with reproach. "If anything bad happens to him, it will be you who are to blame," she accused. "I am warning you." She was struggling again but he held her with all his strength; then she began to cry. "Let me, Cy. Let me. You never know."

"I know all right." He began walking her toward the house. She hung back but he put his arm around her and took her up the kitchen steps.

The door was open and they heard a low, choked, inhaling sound coming from inside. Miriam broke from him and as he ran after her, he saw Old Paul on all fours in the middle of the room. His head hung almost to the floor. Then he flung it backward, straining his neck and raising his distorted face toward the ceiling.

Cy lifted him to the couch. With vague, dilated eyes Paul stared at them. Or was it past them? Cy could not be sure.

"Look at my tongue, gone dead." Paul's words came in a bubbling gasp. He rocked forward and as he threw himself back hard against the cushions, it was like an animal fighting a trap. He let his tongue loll for them to see.

Miriam broke into wild sobbing.

Presently, as the torture of his air hunger lessened, Paul sat straight, cocking his head as if straining to hear some distant sound. "Hoi!" he shouted. The strength in his voice was startling.

"Grandfather!" Miriam dropped to her knees and clung to him, but he seemed not to hear or feel her.

In his day Paul had been a famous hunter of the mountain goat and it was as though he were again on the mountain, lost in fog and straining to catch the echo of his own voice among the crags to give him his direction. Time after time he shouted, and his frowning concentration made it so real that Cy, too, listened for the echo. Then the old man shook his head in a dazed way and fell back.

He lay still, staring upward with a perplexed, attentive look on his face. The wrinkles in his forehead deepened and he gazed in Miriam's direction. "Minnie?" His voice was only a whisper now.

"I did not get there." She started to rise but Cy stopped her.

"Stay with him," he said. "He's dying." He bent over Paul. "Miriam should stay with you." He spoke loudly as if Paul were at a distance.

"No," she protested. "I want to go. All along I wanted to go. I want him to have it. I will go now." She tried to withdraw her hand but Paul kept hold of it. He looked searchingly toward Cy, and their wills met in final struggle.

He's almost gone, Cy thought, but he won't give in to me, ever.

"You know what he wants," Miriam screamed. "Get Minnie." She flung herself at him, pounding her fists against his chest. "You hear me—Minnie!" Her voice was shrill with terror.

Cy stood, his arms down, letting her and wanting her to strike him, only shaking his head and watching Paul.

She tried to push him aside and reach the door, but he caught her by the wrist and drew her back to the couch. Paul's gaze did not shift but he seemed to be withdrawing behind his eyes, the command in them blurring and fading.

He held her close, trying to calm her and knowing it was almost over. "Stay with him," he whispered. "I will get it for you." Either way, it could make no difference now.

But couldn't it? As he ran from the house he saw shapes of women along the street at the school tap and he shouted to them to come, that Paul was dying.

No difference? No difference when Miriam was being swept away by ancient, shapeless fears; no difference, in the days to come, to have her pass them on to the little fellow, and always to know that by his refusal now he might have been able to conquer them for ever? It was sheer coincidence that this was happening to Paul so soon after he threw the swamp root in the fire. Of course it was. And yet . . . and yet . . .

As he plunged down the short-cut toward Minnie's house, the ghosts came slinking back—the sinister implications of tribal myth, the lore which for centuries the old had imposed upon the young, the retribution, the dark revenge and the looming, nameless dread. Was Miriam right? Was it true you never could be sure?

What had got into him?. Why did he keep running instead of turning back? Ahead, half seen and brooding in the river mist, he saw the two spruces flanking Minnie's gate. In the turmoil of his mind the thought came that surely he was doing this for Miriam alone and that he had not yielded. He seized upon that thought and tried to hold it, but he could not.

Somewhere on the ridge behind the houses a dog began

to howl. Then, thread-thin at first, he heard the ululating, primitive distress of women's voices. They soared and fell, swirling like a flock of storm-tossed birds. More dogs in other parts of the village lifted their muzzles to the dark sky and swelled the off-key lament of the wailing women. He could go back to the house now. Old Paul was dead.

But something within him prevented and he could not go back, not yet. His hand was on the latch of Minnie's gate but then he saw a moving light, and John Moose holding a lantern and helping Minnie down the steps. Here and there in the village other lanterns appeared, converging. He took his hand off the latch and went along outside the fence to the start of the boat shed path.

The moist, strong smell of cooling cedar came up to him. To the left of the shed he could make out the remains of the steaming fire, the charred ends of the wood down there like huddled shapes, their dull red eyes staring up at him. Their smoke sagged across the ground and was lost in the heavier layer of mist spreading from the river.

Why was he here? Why had he come at all? His consenting had not helped, and he was haunted by the knowledge that by refusing to come he could have changed things. By yielding to Miriam's frantic appeal he had not helped her, but had harmed her. He had given vitality and continuance to the dark thing which was in her mind. Was the dark thing in his mind and had he yielded, not to her, but to it? He felt he would never know.

He stood at the top of the path, tall and high-shouldered and awkward, a primitive and curiously inept figure in the gathering darkness. He felt that he had always been here and that, in spite of Miriam's promise, he would never get away. Perhaps June was right. Perhaps this yielding was the final, unanswerable proof that he was not fit to get away.

At the back of the house, Miriam was waiting for him.

"They want you," she said. "Come now. You must go in."

"No," he said stubbornly. "I know what they are thinking." He could not get the swamp-root out of his mind and feared they would be blaming him. Still so much to be free of; still so far to go!

She touched him with her hand. "They do not know of that," she said. "I have not told them, and I never will."

The words were life to him. "Then you yourself do not believe—?"

"I cannot be certain of what I really do believe."

With new and tender understanding, and humbled by the realization that even within himself the long fight was far from over, he drew her to him. Now, for the first time, the whole of him grasped the fact that Paul was dead. With infinite gentleness he put her from him and went in. Around the walls of the big room all the chairs were filled. But one chair at the head of the room had been left empty and he went to it and sat down, taking his rightful place among his people.

THE NEW CANADIAN LIBRARY

POETS OF CANADA:

o 1. vol. I: POETS OF THE CONFEDERATION / edited by Malcolm Ross
o 4. vol. III: POETRY OF MIDCENTURY / edited by Milton Wilson
o 5. vol. II: POETS BETWEEN THE WARS / edited by Milton Wilson
o 6. THE POEMS OF EARLE BIRNEY
o 7. vol. IV: POETS OF CONTEMPORARY CANADA / edited by Eli Mandel
o 8. vol. V: NINETEENTH-CENTURY NARRATIVE POEMS / edited by David Sinclair

CANADIAN WRITERS

w 1. MARSHALL MCLUHAN / Dennis Duffy
w 2. E. J. PRATT / Milton Wilson
w 3. MARGARET LAURENCE / Clara Thomas
w 4. FREDERICK PHILIP GROVE / Ronald Sutherland
w 5. LEONARD COHEN / Michael Ondaatje
w 6. MORDECAI RICHLER / George Woodcock
w 7. STEPHEN LEACOCK / Robertson Davies
w 8. HUGH MACLENNAN / Alec Lucas
w 9. EARLE BIRNEY / Richard Robillard
w 10. NORTHROP FRYE / Ronald Bates
w 11. MALCOLM LOWRY / William H. New
w 12. JAMES REANEY / Ross G. Woodman